Inheritance

OTHER BOOKS AND AUDIO BOOKS
TOM ROULSTONE:

Elisabeth

Inheritance

❧ PASSAGE OF PROMISE ❧

A Novel

TOM ROULSTONE

Covenant

Covenant Communications, Inc.

Cover image © Casey Nelson

Cover design copyrighted 2006 by Covenant Communications, Inc.

Published by Covenant Communications, Inc.
American Fork, Utah

Printed in the United States of America
First Printing: July 2006

11 10 09 08 07 06   10 9 8 7 6 5 4 3 2 1

ISBN 1-59811-110-8

To Serenity . . . life begins again.

⚜ACKNOWLEDGEMENTS⚜

I appreciate the help of Ron Warren and Maria Szijj, who read the first draft of the manuscript and offered helpful suggestions. My thanks also go to my wife Serenity for her editing assistance. As ever, Angela Eschler of Covenant has been a constant source of help in all aspects of preparing the manuscript for publication.

❧ CHAPTER 1 ❧

Sir Gerald Langton knew he was dying. "Jenkins!" he breathed through dry, scaly lips.

John Jenkins, the Langton butler for forty years, shuffled into the room and took a servile position beside his master's bed. "Aye, sir," he said, barely concealing the disgust he felt at his master's face, ravished now by age and improvident living. *He deserves what he got,* Jenkins thought.

"Get me Twiddy and look sharp about it."

"The bishop?"

"Do you know any other Twiddys?" he hissed snidely.

"No, sir."

"Then be off with you." Sir Gerald emphasized his words with a weak wave of his blue-veined hand.

The butler muttered under his breath as he shuffled out. He would be glad when his master was dead. Unfortunately, young Master Stephen was no better. If there were only some way he could get his hands on a little more money, he'd retire and be shut of the Langtons for good. He sighed as he pulled a cloak around his thin shoulders and went out into the foggy London night.

A half hour later, Jenkins ushered the Right Reverend Horace Twiddy into the master bedchamber of Sir Gerald's ancient townhouse near Bloomsbury Square.

"It pains me to see you in such a state," the bishop said self-importantly. "But we must all run our mortal race with fortitude, and—"

"Enough, Twiddy," Sir Gerald groaned. "I didn't call you here to listen to your sanctimonious drivel. You know I'm not religious. But a gambler likes to hedge his bets. Will it do me any good on the other side if I confess something I did thirty years ago, and if I donate a priceless object to the church?"

The bishop took a seat beside the bed, placed both hands together in the attitude of prayer, rested the point of his chin on his fingertips, and closed his eyes in thought. After a moment's meditation he opened his eyes and gazed on the dying man. "It is never too late, Sir Gerald, to confess one's sins, and any gifts to the church of a pecuniary nature will undoubtedly redound to the patron's spiritual welfare."

Sir Gerald grunted. "Jenkins, leave us. And shut the door behind you."

Jenkins sorely wanted to stay, but he obeyed. Closing the door, he knelt in the hallway and placed his ear to the keyhole.

"Thirty years ago," Sir Gerald was saying, "I was in a card game in Soho and lost all my ready cash. I'd been drinking heavily and . . ."

Jenkins's eyes went wide at his master's next words.

* * *

Timothy Smollett sat behind a desk piled with papers. He glanced up as his assistant opened the office door. "A Mister John Jenkins to see you, sir," the assistant said.

Smollett waved the butler in. "I'm a busy man, Jenkins," the newspaperman rasped. "Out with it. What've you got?"

"You'll have time for this, Mr. Smollett," the butler said. "Aye, indeed. You'll have time for this." Uninvited, he moved a stack of paper from the chair in front of the desk and slowly lowered himself onto it. "Do you recollect the murder of Lord Eustas Claverley some years back?"

Smollett's eyes lit up, and he sat forward in his chair. "Claverley?" he queried, going back in his mind. "Shot to death in Soho about thirty years ago?"

"The very same." Jenkins leaned forward and placed his hands on the desk. There was less than a yard separating the two men. He dropped his voice an octave. "I have the whole story from the horse's mouth." He smiled with satisfaction to see the interest in the newspaperman's face, sat back in the chair, and was silent.

"Well, out with it," Smollett demanded.

With a wave of his hand Jenkins indicated he was not ready to reveal his scoop. "First, let's talk brass," he said. "How much will you pay to know who did away with his lordship? Say . . . two hundred quid?"

Smollett jumped to his feet. "Two hundred pounds? You're daft, man. Maybe twenty, if your story pans out."

Jenkins slowly rose from his chair and turned toward the door. "Thank you for your time, sir," he said over his shoulder. "Perhaps the *Chronicle* or *Gazette* will be more interested."

The newspaperman's attitude instantly changed. He laughed and sat back down. "Sit down, sit down, man. Don't let a little horse trading scare you off. All right. I think I can come up with fifty. How does that sound?"

Jenkins stood with his hands on the back of the chair and pursed his lips. "A hundred. Not a penny less. You know the story will sell papers. Besides Claverley's murder, it has to do with a priceless ring that once belonged to a Muhammadan king called Saladin."

Smollett's heart started pumping faster but he tried not to show it. "Saladin, eh? I've heard of him." He sighed as if defeated. "All right, Jenkins. You win. It'll probably cost me my job, but you have a deal. Now out with it."

"Not so fast. I don't open my mouth till the brass's in my pocket."

The newspaperman heaved another sigh. "You're like a ferret with a rabbit in its teeth. All right, Jenkins, sit down. I'll be right back."

Soon Jenkins had the pound notes in his hands. Smollett impatiently tapped his fingers on the desk while Jenkins slowly counted the bills, meticulously folded them, and placed them in an inside pocket of his black coat jacket. He looked up and smiled. "One more thing, Mr. Smollett. I want your word you won't publish what I'm going to tell you until after the guilty party's gone. Agreed?"

Exasperation showed in the newspaperman's florid face. "Gone? Gone where?"

"Deceased."

"How long will that take?"

"Not long. A day or two at the most. He's on his deathbed."

"How can you be sure?"

Jenkins's lips formed what could pass for a smile. "I'm sure. Believe me. I'm no stranger to death. In my many years of service—"

"All right. All right," Smollett interrupted. "The story stays in my hands till he passes. Now, can I have it?"

"One other thing," Jenkins said. "I must remain anonymous. I'm still serving in the Lang . . . in the household of the murderer."

Smollett noted the slip and for a moment considered making use of it. But he had already paid out the money and decided to let it slide. "You have my word. Newspapermen don't reveal their sources. Out with it."

To Smollett's consternation Jenkins rose, opened the office door, and made sure no one was listening at the keyhole. After firmly closing the door, he resumed his seat. Only then did he lean forward and relate all that he had heard through the keyhole in his master's house.

The more Jenkins said, the more the newspaperman knew that he'd gotten a bargain for his hundred pounds. With the fall of Khartoum a year earlier and the butchering of the English hero Chinese Gordon and his Anglo-Egyptian troops by the followers of the fanatical Mahdi, the English public could not get enough of things Moslem. Knowing who killed Claverley was sensational enough. The Saladin connection would be a lucrative bonus. *Yes*, Smollett thought, *this isn't just a front-page story; it'll make a series of articles.* Even more satisfying to the newspaperman was the knowledge that the *Times* would scoop the other papers. *I hope Langton croaks soon*, was his thought, as he ushered Sir Gerald's manservant out of his office.

↭ CHAPTER 2 ↭

"Mother, are you home?" called Kenny Sanderson excitedly as he entered his parents' large house in Salt Lake City, Utah Territory.

"Yes, Ken, I'm in here," Elisabeth Ashcroft Sanderson said from the elegant parlor. "What's all the excitement?"

He entered the room brandishing a copy of the *Deseret Evening News.* "You're in the paper. It's a reprint of an English article."

Elisabeth smiled at her grown son's boyish enthusiasm. "Do tell," she said, laying aside the medical book she had been reading. "Just the gist of it. I'll read it with your father when he gets home from his meeting."

Ken pushed a lock of light brown hair from his eyes, dropped his slim, five-foot, ten-inch frame onto the sofa across from his mother, and let the words tumble out of him: "It's about your late husband's murder thirty-odd years ago. A man called Langton has confessed to it. The article says Lord Claverley and Langton were in a card game, and Langton ran out of money. He had a winning hand, he thought, so in order to stay in the game he pulled a ring off his finger and put it in the pot. But Claverley won the hand and the ring. Langton, who had been drinking, sobered up pretty fast when he realized what he'd done. Apparently the ring had been in the family for over six hundred years and is considered priceless."

Elisabeth's eyebrows came together quizzically. "I wonder what could make the ring so valuable? Anyway, go on, son."

"After the loss of the ring, Langton was out of the game and left the room. But he didn't go home. He waited for Claverley in the alley. When Claverley came out of the building, Langton accused him of cheating and demanded the ring back. Claverley refused and pulled out a pistol. The two men struggled and the gun went off, killing Claverley. Langton absconded with the ring and kept the secret for all these years."

Elisabeth's stomach tightened. She was silent for a moment as her mind went back to the great mistake of her life: marrying Lord Eustas Claverley. It had taken her only days to discover he had married her only for her inheritance. "How has all this come to light?" she asked.

"Langton confessed to a minister before his death, and somehow the papers got hold of it."

"And how do I figure in all this? Does the article mention me by name?"

Ken shook his head. "No. Only as Claverley's estranged wife and widow. Apparently the resurfacing of the ring's created a firestorm of controversy in England and a scramble to own it. The Church of England, a Miss Karen Gage, Stephen Langton—who's Sir Gerald's heir—and even the British Crown are all after it. The article says, and I quote, 'Claverley's widow, who lives somewhere in America, has as strong a claim as anyone, as she was Claverley's only heir.' It goes on to say that you also have a moral right to it because it is well known that Claverley squandered your fortune on drinking and gambling. So what do you think, Mother?"

"About what? You've overwhelmed me with information."

"About your claim, of course. Are you going to throw your hat into the ring, so to speak?" His brown eyes sparkled at this inadvertent witticism.

Elisabeth smiled wryly and shook her head. "Of course not. Lord Claverley is a distant, unpleasant memory. I have no intention of claiming anything of his, especially something he obtained through gambling."

"But, Mother . . ."

"No buts, Ken. I will not change my mind, and I know your father will agree with me."

Gren Sanderson did agree with his wife, and as far as they were concerned the subject was closed. But the subject remained very much open in Ken's mind. He could not shake off the feeling that it was his destiny to right the wrong done to his mother. As he lay abed that night he coveted Saladin's ring, not for himself, of course, but for his mother. He could see no reason why she should not claim it. After all, it was only fair. Lord Claverley had squandered the fortune Ken's great-grandfather had left his mother. In his mind Ken pictured himself returning home from England as rich as Midas, a hero who had righted a great wrong. The only obstacle blocking his path to glory was his mother. He knew it would be almost impossible to change her mind. Nevertheless, his brain churned long into the night, searching for an answer. Light was creeping into his bedroom when a plan finally took shape in his mind.

"Mother, Father," Ken said as he joined his parents for breakfast. He was second from the youngest of four children and the only one still living at home. "I have a proposition for you. I would like to go to England—"

"If this is about that ring," his father said, "we don't want to hear it. You know how your mother feels about it, and I wholly agree with her."

Ken put out his hand, palm out. "I know, I know, but please hear me out."

Gren shook his head. "Not now, Ken. We don't have time. If you're free this evening after supper, we'll discuss it. All right?"

Ken sighed and nodded.

Later, as he and his father walked to the *Deseret Evening News* office, where Ken was a reporter and his father a senior editor, Ken again tried to broach the subject, but his father refused to discuss it.

"What I would like to talk about is your future," Gren said. "You're doing well at the paper, and your mother and I feel that it is time—"

"I know," Ken interjected, "time to find a wife and settle down."

"You're almost twenty-five, son, and your sisters are all married, even Sarah."

"What's the rush to marry me off? You and mother were both over thirty when you married."

"True," Gren said, "but as you well know that was due to extraordinary circumstances."

Their conversation ended there. Throughout the day Ken had a hard time concentrating on his job. He liked being a reporter, and people told him that he looked like one: intelligent face, slight build for his average height, ordinary brown hair. Certainly not an overpowering physical presence, but pleasant enough. This day, however, he found little satisfaction in interviewing two wrangling neighbors about an upcoming court case resulting from the one neighbor's horse constantly breaking through the other neighbor's fence and despoiling his garden. Saladin's ring was so much on Ken's mind that he could hardly wait until the day was through and supper over. Although he loved his parents very much, when the time finally came to discuss the ring, he was ready to do battle with them.

"Well, Ken," Gren said as he and his wife sat with their son in the parlor, "let's get this over with. Your mother and I have discussed it again and we haven't changed our minds. We do think, though, that we owe you an explanation. Primarily, we feel that going after this ring smacks of the 'spirit of speculation' which our leaders have warned us against."

"What's wrong with speculation?" Ken asked. "America was built on it."

"That may be," Gren said, "but there's often a fine line between legitimate speculation, or investment, and the 'spirit of speculation.' Some people can't seem to tell the difference.

Let me try to explain. Do you recall from Church history a man called Sam Brannan?"

"Of course," Ken said. "He was a member of the Church and California's first millionaire."

"Yes, at least one of the first," Gren said. "I knew him personally when I served as a gold missionary in California. He was a man of exceptional abilities, a leader of men. He presided over the Eastern Saints who sailed from New York to California in 1846, the same year as the exodus from Nauvoo. When President Young chose the Great Basin as the new home of the Saints, Brother Brannan was outraged. Convinced that the Saints should settle in California, he tried in vain to talk President Young into removing there. When unsuccessful, he became so disaffected that he wouldn't turn over to the Church the tithing money he'd collected in California. President Young wrote to him with a promise and a warning. He promised that if Brother Brannan did his duty as a Church leader, the Lord would continue to bless him, but if he did not repent, he would lose all he had and die in poverty. Unfortunately, Brother Brannan was so obsessed with the spirit of speculation that he chose to defy the Lord and eventually lost his family, his health, and his fortune."

Ken knew Brannan's story, but he was respectful enough to hear his father out. When Gren had finished, Ken said, "I don't actually see the parallel. How would our contending for this ring put us at odds with the Church?"

"I think what your father is saying," Elisabeth said, "is that there's a right way and a wrong way of acquiring riches. As Latter-day Saints we believe in enterprise and even speculation. But we must have the right motives. As the Savior said, 'Seek ye first the kingdom of God'—"

"I know that, Mother," Ken said impatiently. "I've been taught that all my life. But how would we be amiss in seeking to win this ring, which should have been yours in the first place? It seems to me that it would only be justice for you to get it, since Claverley got your fortune and squandered it."

"Ken," Gren said, a little perturbed, "can't you understand that your mother doesn't want the ring and doesn't want you running off to England in search of it? Have you considered why you are so set on acquiring it? Is it a righteous desire? Or would going to court for it be chasing after filthy lucre? As your mother started to say, the scriptures admonish us to be careful about seeking after riches. For instance, Jacob warns us about pursuing wealth without the proper motivation. Please pass me the Book of Mormon." Ken sighed and reluctantly passed the book to his father, who thumbed through the pages, found the passage, and read, "'But before ye seek for riches, seek ye for the kingdom of God. And after ye have obtained a hope in Christ ye shall obtain riches, if ye seek them; and ye will seek them for the intent to do good'—"

"But I already have a 'hope in Christ,'" Ken said.

"We know you do, son," Elisabeth said patiently. "But do you seek these riches to do good, or just to right a supposed wrong? Perhaps losing my fortune was a blessing in disguise. Who knows if I would have accepted the gospel if all had been well at Claverley Hall? No, son, I have no regrets about losing that fortune. As you well know, the Lord blessed me with another fortune, my inheritance from Mrs. Kenny. But much more than that, He has blessed me with the riches of eternity."

Ken heaved a sigh. His mother's heartfelt words caused him to reflect and pause to regroup his arguments, giving his father the opening to press the advantage his wife had won.

"Part of having a 'hope in Christ,' Ken," his father said, "is pursuing a path in life that will lead us back to God. Your mother and I feel that rather than your going to England on this ill-advised adventure you should concentrate on your vocation and, as we talked about this morning, find a wife and settle down. Furthermore, President Young was always telling us to stay out of gentile courts—right up to his death he preached on it. And finally, it would undoubtedly cost a lot of money to pursue this court case, and your mother and I adamantly refuse to use our money in that way. So there it is, son. Please accept our counsel and put the idea of getting this ring out of your mind."

Ken didn't want to be argumentative, but something wouldn't let him give up so easily. "But you haven't given me a chance to give my proposal," he said.

"That's true, sweetheart," Elisabeth said to her husband.

Gren drew in a mighty breath and slowly exhaled. "All right, Ken," he said, "let's hear what you have to say."

Ken also took a deep breath before saying, "With the Church disincorporated by the federal government, you know we're in a precarious position. President Taylor and others are on the underground, and things are falling apart. In fact, if my information is correct, the Church is facing complete financial ruin. An infusion of cash right now would be a godsend. I propose to go to England and claim the ring. If I'm successful, we can sell it and give the money to the Church. So you see, I do have an 'intent to do good' with the money. Furthermore, now that temple work for the dead has started up again, if I go to England I can get the genealogical records at the vicarage where you grew up, Mother. You know you've been wanting to get them."

At the mention of the Ashcroft genealogical records, a spark of interest showed in Elisabeth's eyes. Upon fleeing her brutal husband and immigrating to America thirty-five years earlier, she had brought only her personal belongings. If her son could retrieve the Ashcroft family's genealogical records, it would lead to great personal satisfaction and help her fulfill her religious duties to her ancestors.

Sensing that he'd piqued his mother's interest, Ken continued with greater fervor. "Furthermore, there might be a way of getting the services of a lawyer free. If Mother has a valid claim, as the newspaper reporter says she has, perhaps a lawyer would take the case on contingency. Are you still corresponding with that lady in England—the one you met on the steamboat?"

"Lady Brideswell?" Elisabeth asked.

"That's the one. You could have her check with her lawyer about whether your claim has merit. If it does, he or a colleague might be interested in taking the case on a contingency basis. If he loses, it wouldn't cost us a penny, but if he wins we could pay his fees from the sale of the ring and donate the rest to the Church."

Admiration for her son's calculating and clever mind made Elisabeth smile. She turned to her husband to see if he was as impressed as she.

Gren shrugged. "I hate to admit it, but he is making sense," he said.

Elisabeth smiled at her son. "Have you been spending every waking minute hatching this scheme?" she asked.

"Just about," Ken said with an exaggerated yawn.

Elisabeth glanced at her husband, and he indicated with another shrug and a tilt of his head that it was up to her to decide. "It would be wonderful to get my family records," she said. Turning back to Ken she sighed and smiled. "I'll tell you what, dear. I'll write Lady Brideswell as you suggest. If her lawyer feels that I do have a legitimate claim to this ring and is willing to take the case on a contingency basis, your father and I will discuss your proposition further. However, if we receive a negative reply from England, we want to hear no more of Saladin's ring. Agreed?"

Ken's confidence rose. "Agreed," he said with a broad smile.

❧ CHAPTER 3 ❧

Over the next month the subject of Saladin's ring was not discussed in the Sanderson home, but it was never far from Ken's mind. He immersed himself in research about the twelfth-century Kurdish Moslem military leader, learning that from his base as sultan of Egypt, Saladin drove the Crusaders out of Jerusalem and united a good part of the Moslem world. Eventually, to stop the bloodshed between his forces and those of the Europeans, he agreed to the Peace of Ramla, which permitted the Crusaders to retain possession of part of the coast of the Holy Land. According to Ken's research, to seal the peace Saladin took a ruby ring off his finger and gave it to the chief crusader, King Richard the Lionhearted of England. At Richard's death the ring passed to his brother, King John. Later, King John awarded it to Stephen Langton, the Archbishop of Canterbury, and it had been in the Langton family for six hundred years.

Over the centuries the name Saladin became a symbol of Moslem power and prestige. Even Western historians wrote of him in glowing terms. The more Ken read about Saladin, the more he coveted the ring. He found it almost impossible to perform his duties at the newspaper. *If I have to write one more story about the relentless pursuit of co-habs by federal marshals,* he thought one day, *I'll go mad.* By the time a reply finally came from England, Saladin's ring had become Ken's obsession.

"What does it say?" Ken said as he burst through the door of his home, "—the letter from England? Don't keep me in the dark."

Elisabeth pursed her lips and shook her head. "Your impetuosity is going to get you into trouble someday, Ken," she said. "Please calm yourself, sit down, and I'll tell you." Ken did so and his mother continued, "Lady Brideswell's barrister, Sir Jeffrey Lyttle, feels that I have a very good claim. In fact, so confident is he, that he's willing to take the case on a twenty percent contingency basis."

"Fantastic!" Ken exclaimed. "Since it won't cost you a penny, win or lose, there's no reason for me not to go to England and claim it."

"Not so. There's a very good reason: President Young's injunction for us to stay out of gentile courts. Besides, what about your position at the paper? Would Brother Penrose give you leave to go abroad?"

Ken gave a satisfied nod. "He already has. He's all for my going and will appoint me a 'reporter at large.' All I have to do is send back articles on a regular basis and my position's secure."

Elisabeth nodded thoughtfully. "It appears you've covered all angles. Actually, I think it would be wonderful for you to visit England. But pursuing the ring through the courts is another matter. Let me think about it some more."

That night as Ken lay in bed his thoughts were full of England. He somehow knew he'd be going there whether or not his parents agreed to the court battle. The only cloud on his horizon was a vague feeling of guilt about leaving Utah at such a trying time for the Church. He felt as if he were deserting a sinking ship. Getting out of bed, he prayed for guidance. While still on his knees, the thought occurred to him that the Church had weathered worse storms and would endure this one as well. He tried to recall the Prophet Joseph Smith's stirring words about the Church surviving every challenge and spreading throughout the world. *Where is it found?*

Now I remember. It's in the letter to the editor of the Chicago Democrat. He quietly padded downstairs to the library. After some time, he found the copy of the *Times and Seasons* containing the letter and read the part he'd tried to recall: "No unhallowed hand can stop the work from progressing; persecutions may rage, mobs may combine, armies may assemble, calumny may defame, but the truth of God will go forth boldly, nobly, and independent, till it has penetrated every continent, visited every clime, swept every country, and sounded in every ear, till the purposes of God shall be accomplished and the Great Jehovah shall say the work is done."

With all his heart Ken believed these words, and reading them now gave him comfort, assuaging his guilty feeling. Sitting there alone in the silence of the library, he felt something. It began in the pit of his stomach and slowly worked its way up toward the region of his heart, where the feeling began to acquire form and substance. Without warning the feeling became an overpowering conviction. Ken somehow knew it was his destiny to go to England. Even more importantly, he understood that awaiting him across the ocean was something of far greater value than a piece of jewelry or even genealogical records. With this newfound assurance he returned to his bedroom and was soon sleeping peacefully.

Elisabeth smiled at the anticipation in the face of her son as he sat at the breakfast table the next morning. She took her husband's hand and said, "Your father and I talked and prayed long into the night, son. He has something to tell you."

Gren nodded. "First, Ken, you do not need our permission to go to England or anywhere else. You're old enough to make your own decisions. And despite our initial reaction, we think your going to England will do you a world of good. It's time you got out into the world and gained some more experience, and in bringing home the Ashcroft records you'll be doing the family a great service." Gren paused to give emphasis to his next words. "We have *not*, however, changed our minds about the so-called Saladin's ring. Court cases can, and often do, turn into sordid, bitter affairs and we don't want you mixed up in this one. Go to England with our blessing, enjoy your mother's homeland, get the records, and return to us; but stay clear of this court case."

Ken was elated at the partial victory, but it was not enough. He was silent for a moment before saying, "How about this—"

Elisabeth smiled at her husband and shook her head. "I told you he'd come up with a counter offer," she said.

Determination in his voice, Ken said, "What if we engage Lady Brideswell's lawyer to act for us anonymously—keep the Sanderson name completely out of it. I'll go over there only as an observer. As far as anyone's concerned, I'm just another American searching out my roots. Except for the lawyer and Lady Brideswell, no one will know that there's any connection between the court case and me. I won't discuss it with a soul. If the lawyer's not successful, it will cost us nothing. But if he does win the ring, the money could really help the Church. I would, of course, like to attend the actual trial, but only as a spectator."

Ken's parents looked at each other and by tacit agreement conceded defeat.

"All right, Ken," his father said with a sigh. "As long as you stay completely out of it. But remember, this court case is your idea, not ours." Turning to his wife, he asked, "Would you like to add anything, dear?"

She looked thoughtful and said, "Perhaps you should take Maggie Stowell into your confidence as well, Ken. She works for Miss Gage, whose late parents bought Claverley Hall. As you know from the newspaper article, Miss Gage is also contending for the ring. I wouldn't want Maggie to get caught in the middle."

"Okay," Ken said, "the lawyer, Lady Brideswell, and Maggie Stowell. No one else, I promise."

"One last thing," Elisabeth added. "After prayers last night your father and I both felt a strong impression that there is some other reason—a very important one—for you to go to England. We don't know what that reason might be, but we do know—in fact, we can assure you—that if you live close to the Spirit you will be led to it. We have no doubt this journey will be for you a passage of promise."

Ken's heart beat faster. "That is truly amazing! Last night after praying for guidance, I too received the very same impression. It was overpowering. I've never felt like that before."

Elisabeth smiled. "Even though we've pestered you about finding a wife and settling down, we do love you and appreciate your strong testimony of the restored gospel. I'll write to Maggie tonight and let her know you're coming. When you're over there, if you need someone to talk to about anything, Maggie's the one. She's pretty rough and ready, but she is the soul of practicality. When you're in England, of course, you should stop in and see Jonathan. When I saw Aunt Becky last, she said he was serving at the mission home in London. Finally, we've set aside some money for you so that you can enjoy England." Elisabeth paused and her eyes took on a thoughtful look.

"What are you thinking, dear?" Gren asked.

Elisabeth gazed at her husband and smiled. "I was just thinking of Somerset at this time of the year, and it brought the words of one of Browning's poems to mind. The poem captures my feelings as I, too, sometimes ache to see England, especially Somerset, once more."

"Recite it for us, dear," Gren said, always interested in the poems and snippets of prose his wife put to memory.

Elisabeth smiled. "I'm not sure if I can remember it all," she said. "Perhaps if . . ."

Gren anticipated his wife and soon Elisabeth had a book of poetry in her hands. She leafed through it. "Here it is," she said. "'Home Thoughts, From Abroad' by Mr. Robert Browning." She looked up and smiled at her husband and son, and then in a voice tinged with nostalgia, she read:

Oh, to be in England
Now that April's there,
And whoever wakes in England
Sees, some morning, unaware,
That the lowest boughs and the brushwood sheaf
Round the elm tree bole are in tiny leaf,
While the chaffinch sings on the orchard bow
In England—Now!

She paused and her eyes were moist when she said, "You'll miss April, Ken, but you could get there by May:

And after April, when May follows,
And the whitethroat builds, and all the swallows!
Hark, where my blossomed pear tree in the hedge
Leans to the field and scatters on the clover
Blossoms and dewdrops—at the bent spray's edge—
That's the wise thrush! He sings each song twice over,
Lest you should think he never could recapture
The first fine careless rapture!
And though the fields look rough with hoary dew,
All will be gay when noontide wakes anew
The buttercups, the little children's dower
—Far brighter than this gaudy melon flower!

Through teary eyes she smiled at her son. "Take the time to see everything you can, son, and come back and share it with us. Since I'm not going there myself, I must be content to experience it vicariously."

Ken's eyes lit up. "What's to stop you from coming with me, Mother?" he asked.

"Yes," Gren said. "What's to stop you, sweetheart?"

For an instant Elisabeth's lips formed a small smile as she contemplated the offer. Then she shook her head and said with finality, "No. I feel strongly that this is your adventure, Ken. Go with our love and blessing."

Ken's next words caught in his throat. "Thank you, Mother. Thank you both for your blessing and for being the best parents in the world." The three of them embraced. Afterward, Ken said, "Father, will you give me a blessing before I leave?"

Gren nodded. "I'd be honored, son."

The next evening after supper, Ken received his father's blessing. Then his father left for a meeting and Ken and his mother sat together in the living room.

"There's something I wanted to say, Mother," Ken said. "Yesterday you said I have a strong testimony. It kind of bothered me, because I don't think my testimony's very strong. It's true I've tried hard to live the commandments and have some kind of testimony, but it isn't strong, not like Jonathan's. As you know, I've always looked up to Jonathan. I've always envied him for his certainty about what he believes and for his knowledge of the scriptures."

Elisabeth listened patiently as her son went on to say that it was true that if anyone derogated the Church in any way, he was the first to defend it. But he felt that his testimony had developed in the protected hothouse of Zion and had never really been tested in the gentile world.

Elisabeth pondered her son's words for a moment before saying, "Perhaps your trip to England will be the test you need. When you're over there, please promise me that you'll stay close to the Church and away from gentile girls."

Despite his confession of a weak testimony, Ken had never strayed from the Church and had no intentions of doing so now. As for pursuing gentile girls, the thought hadn't entered his head. He gave his mother an assuring smile. "I'll stay close to the Church, Mother, and I promise that when I marry it'll be to a member. Satisfied?"

She smiled. "All right, then, son. Be assured that I'll hold you to your promise."

❧ CHAPTER 4 ❧

A month later Ken was in London standing on Gray Street in the legal district. It was Monday, May 10, 1886. He had just come from visiting his cousin, Jonathan Kimball, at the mission home of The Church of Jesus Christ of Latter-day Saints. A pavement artist's work had caught Ken's attention. In various hues of colored chalk, the artist had produced an exquisite rendering of the *H.M.S. Beagle.* Beneath the ship in bordered boxes were finely wrought images of iguanas, turtles, penguins, and other creatures Charles Darwin had found on the Galapagos Islands.

"Excellent work," Ken said to the one-legged artist. "Were you with Mr. Darwin on his famous voyage?"

The man looked up from his kneeling position and laughed. "To you, lad, I prob'ly look like Mr. Coleridge's Ancient Mariner. But I'm not that old. Mr. Darwin sailed to the islands way back in '31. Meself visited 'em years later aboard the *H.M.S. Albatross.*"

"So you were a seaman?"

"That I was." He slapped his thigh. "Lost the leg in the Crimea when a cannon exploded, and I've been wearin' this peg here ever since. Jack Tolley's the name. Call me Jack."

Ken took the outstretched hand and introduced himself. He continued to study the drawings. "You really are a talented artist, Jack. If you don't mind my saying it, I'm surprised you don't put your talents to better use."

The man didn't take offense. "There's not much call for a one-legged sailor what's given up the sea, lad. I does what I can to make ends meet." Ken nodded, removed a pound note from his wallet, and put it in the artist's upturned cap. "Ta," the artist said. "It'll be cakes and ale t'night."

Ken surveyed the drawings once more, nodded, and went up a set of stone steps. His eyes scanned the name on a brass plaque attached to the wall: "Sir Jeffrey Lyttle, Q.C." *Queen's Counsel.* He smiled, pleased that a barrister of distinction would be representing his mother. He entered the law chambers and introduced himself to a young man sitting atop a high stool in the outer office. The clerk, Nathaniel Nuttall, reciprocated, then showed Ken into Sir Jeffrey's office and introduced him.

"Ah, Mr. Sanderson," Sir Jeffrey said, rising from his meticulously clean desk, "you've come at last." The barrister was a big man with a rounded stomach and full beard. "I assume you came by way of New York. How is the French statue coming along?"

"Slowly, sir. The pedestal is up and they are beginning to work on Lady Liberty. The newspapers say it should be ready by the fall."

"Good. Do you have the document authorizing me to act for your mother?"

"Yes, sir." Ken withdrew a sealed envelope from the inside pocket of his coat and handed it to the barrister.

"Please take a seat," Sir Jeffrey said. He opened the envelope, withdrew three items, studied them, and nodded approvingly. "All seems to be in order. There is one snag, though. The docket's full. It will be at least a month before the trial begins. It will, of course, give us extra time to prepare. I imagine you'll stay in England until it's over. Will you have enough to keep you occupied?"

"Yes, sir. Tomorrow I'm going down to Somerset to visit my mother's former home and arrange to get her family records."

"A lovely place, Somerset. I visited there in my youth." A faint smile played on the barrister's lips as he mentally revisited the southwest. Then his visage resumed its customary mask of gruffness, and he asked, "Would you happen to have a picture of your mother when she was a young woman?"

Ken shook his head. "No, sir. But I'll be visiting my mother's former maid, Maggie Stowell. I'm sure she has one."

"Good. See what you can do. I also need one of Claverley. There must be a portrait of the old scoundrel around Claverley Hall—or Gage Hall as it's now called. I can send an artist down there. Perhaps you could have this Maggie Stowell find a portrait of Claverley and arrange for the artist to sketch it and one of your mother."

Ken hesitated. "I promised my parents that I'd not get involved in the trial, but perhaps this one thing wouldn't hurt. Do you have an artist in mind?"

The lawyer shook his head. "No. But there are enough starving ones around. It won't be hard to find one."

"How about the pavement artist outside?"

Sir Jeffrey screwed up his nose. "That scruffy lot? Out of the question. We'll find someone respectable."

Ken refused to give up. "I'll admit he is rather scruffy, but he seems like a good person, and there's no denying his talent."

Sir Jeffrey shook his head and sighed. "You egalitarian Americans. Hopeless optimists, all of you." Opening a desk drawer, he withdrew several bills. "Here, take this. Get your artist cleaned up and buy him a suit of clothes."

Ken smiled. "Fifty pounds! Very generous of you, Sir Jeffrey."

The lawyer glowered at the young American. "Generous of your mother, Mr. Sanderson. It will be added to her fees when I win the ring."

"Not *if* you win it?"

Unsmiling, Sir Jeffrey looked over his wire-rimmed spectacles and sternly said, "I don't take on cases I don't intend winning.

Now, before you go, tell me all you know about why your mother fled to America and why she didn't try to inherit when Claverley died."

"Actually, she doesn't like to talk about it. All I know is that Claverley was a brutal man and blocked her getting an annulment. Maggie Stowell's the one you should talk to, but she's in a tricky position, being Miss Gage's maid now."

The barrister grunted. "I'd like to put the maid in the witness box, but I see what you mean. Well, I'll have Nuttall scour the archives for dirt on Claverley. Enjoy Somerset. It truly is a lovely place."

The lawyer dismissed Ken with a wave of his hand.

Outside on the street, Ken approached the pavement artist. "Let's go, Mr. Tolley . . . Jack. I have a commission for you."

The artist looked up, his eyebrows raised, his head cocked to one side. But without a word, he picked up his chalk box, slung it over his shoulder, and, much to Ken's surprise, followed him down the street.

That evening Ken found his way to Lady Brideswell's London townhouse. It was set back from the street in fashionable Bloomsbury Square. The center of the square held a pretty park with trees and shrubs and a well-manicured lawn surrounding a fountain.

Ken was pleased that his luggage, which he had sent on from the boat, had arrived. The servants treated him as if he were royalty, evidence of the high esteem Lady Brideswell held for Ken's mother and father. The lady of the house, well into her seventies, had the deportment and carriage of a younger woman. And, although she exhibited the innate elegance common to many born into wealth, she also evidenced kindness as she greeted Ken. His initial appraisal was soon verified as Lady Brideswell, who was preparing to leave for her country estate when Ken arrived, took the time to visit with him in the drawing room.

"I'm so pleased that you are safely arrived," she said. "I can see both your mother and father in your countenance. It seems a lifetime ago when Sir Anthony and I met them on that steamboat in America. They were still unwed then and so much in love, but they couldn't show it because your mother was still married to that awful Claverley. I was so pleased when he . . . when circumstances allowed your parents to finally marry."

"I'm happy to say that they're still very much in love," Ken said. "They asked me to convey their condolences on Sir Anthony's passing."

The old woman looked back in her mind and a fond smile touched her thin lips. "Thank you. I miss him every day. I appreciated the nice letter of condolence from your mother." After a pause she asked, "Have you been to see Sir Jeffrey yet?"

"I have. Rather a gruff gentleman."

Lady Brideswell acknowledged Ken's comment with a tilt of her head and a smile. "On the surface, yes. But his bark's worse than his bite. He likes to give the impression that his only goals in life are winning court cases and amassing money, both of which he does extremely well. What few people know is that he is the main source of financial support for St. Swithins Foundling Home. I understand that at present he's helping St. Swithins raise funds to buy a country estate so when the foundlings grow they will have a place to go outside the dirty city." With a slight wave of her delicate hand, she quickly added, "But don't tell him I told you any of this, or he'll be very cross with me."

The butler entered the room. "Your carriage is waiting, your ladyship," he said.

"Thank you, Bramley. I'll be along directly." Turning to Ken she said, "Well, Mr. Sanderson, I must be on my way to the country. Please make yourself at home here. Come and go as you please. The servants will see to your needs. I will no doubt see you again before you return to America."

❧ C H A P T E R 5 ❧

"This be it, young fella, Gage Hall, long known as Claverley Hall," the pony trap driver said. "A gloomy place in such weather. The local folks say it's cursed."

Ken agreed. "A gloomy place indeed. It could be the setting for Dickens's 'Bleak House.' Cursed, you say?"

"Aye. The story goes tha' long since, old Lord Claverley drove a poor squatter woman and her brood from the estate, and she cursed it, sayin' the hall would go into ruin and never flourish again till the laughter of children rings down the corridors. Well, the curse seems to be workin'. The late Lord Claverley was an only child with no heir, and so's Miss Gage. Every year the old place gets more tumbled down."

Ken paid the driver and surveyed the dilapidated manor house, sulking in the morning mist and mizzling rain. Had Ken been of a superstitious mind, he might have agreed that the stained stone, cracked concrete, and peeling paint evidenced that the building truly was cursed. The grounds were equally in need of work. *It would take a small fortune to put this place back in shape,* he mused as he started up the stone steps leading to the huge front door. *Obviously, Miss Gage doesn't have the money. I wonder why she doesn't get rid of it?* Suddenly, his heart skipped a beat as a dark, caped figure rounded the corner of the house and, seeing Ken, retreated back into the shadows. Ken swallowed hard and sprinted up the remaining steps. He worked the sturdy, dolphin-shaped brass knocker, and after a nervous wait was ushered into the somber old house by an equally somber old butler.

"Mr. Sanderson!" a plump, apple-cheeked, middle-aged woman exclaimed from behind the butler. She executed an abbreviated curtsy. "I'd know you anywhere. You favor your father for looks. Come in, come in. I've been expecting you." She turned to the butler, who had been glancing from one to the other. "Thank you, Mr. Bennett. I'll see to Mr. Sanderson." The butler nodded and retreated into the cavernous house. Turning back to Ken, she said, "Your mother's letter came only days ago. How was your journey?"

"Very good, Miss Stowell, but very long."

"Maggie," she said as she helped him off with his coat. "Everyone calls me Maggie."

"Thank you, Maggie. You may call me Ken, short for Kenny."

Maggie nodded. "Aye. Your mother said she named you after Mrs. Kenny. But 'twouldn't be right me callin' you by your Christian name. I'll call you Mr. Ken. How *is* your mother?"

"Just fine. She sends you her fondest greetings."

Maggie heaved a sigh. "Oh, how I missed her when she removed to America. Even after all these years, I can see her pretty face as if it was yesterday."

Maggie led him down to the kitchen, where the enticing aroma of fresh baking greeted him. "Sit down and have some scones with butter and jam. Tea?"

"Milk, if you have it."

"Milk it is."

Maggie excused herself while Ken ate at the kitchen table. She quickly returned carrying a small picture. "Do you know this?" she asked.

Ken nodded and when he had finished a mouthful said, "Yes. Yes, I do. It's the same one my folks have on their dresser.

I believe it was taken in Philadelphia before they were married. So that's how you knew I looked like my father."

Maggie nodded and placed the tintype on the table. "Aye. I've treasured it over the years. When I first saw it, I says to myself, 'Miss Elisabeth's found herself a good man.' It made my heart happy, so it did, after all the trouble she went through with Claverley. She wrote me that you was here to get your *gemmeology* records from the vicarage."

Ken smiled. His mother had warned him about Maggie's tendency toward mispronunciations and malapropisms. "Yes. I'll go down and meet the vicar from here. I'll be here a few days before going back to London. Can you recommend a lodging in the village?"

"I can, and it won't cost you a penny. My cottage. It's been empty since my folks passed on years ago. I lodge here at the hall, but now and then I go down to the old place and keep it clean. You're welcome to it as long—"

"Oh, I'm sorry, Maggie," said a pretty young woman at the kitchen door. "I wasn't aware you had company."

Ken leapt to his feet, feeling guilty for being there without permission from the lady of the house.

The young woman seemed equally embarrassed as she pushed a lock of red-blond hair from her forehead.

Maggie was unperturbed. "This is my friend Mr. Kenny Sanderson from America, Miss Gage. I knew his mother when I was just a girl. He's here doing gemmeology."

Ken smiled. "Genealogy," he said, bowing his head by way of introduction. Miss Gage acknowledged his bow with a gesture of her delicate hand and a welcoming smile that to Ken's eyes lit up the room.

"Welcome to Gage Hall, Mr. Sanderson," she said. "I'm sorry to greet you like this." She indicated with her open hand the silk dressing gown she was wearing and the fact that her hair was free on her shoulders. "Will you join me for tea upstairs when I'm properly attired?"

"Thank you," he said. "It will be my pleasure."

"She's a sweet girl is Miss Karen," Maggie said after her mistress had gone, "But she's sometimes too hard on herself and a little *nave.*"

"A little knave?" Ken said, smiling. "She's dishonest?"

Maggie's eyebrows came together in puzzlement. "Oh, no. She's honest as the day's long, a very proper girl what reads the Bible and goes to church every Sunday."

"Ah—a little naïve."

Maggie tossed her head impatiently. "What I mean is she's led a sheltered life and is kind of innocent. Ever since both her folks died of cholera in the same year, I've kind of looked out for her. They left her with money troubles, and this big house's a *milestone* around her neck. Lately, a mad idea's took hold of her. She's all for getting her hands on some foreigner's ring—it's been in all the papers—and paying off her debts. If you ask me, she's lowering her bucket into a dry well. She'd be better off to sell this place and get out from under the debt." Maggie paused before adding, "I must say, I was surprised to read in her letter that your mum's also after this ring. It's not like her. She did say she wanted you to stay out of it and that's smart. The whole thing's good money after bad if you ask me."

Ken waited for Maggie to finish. Then, glancing toward the kitchen door and back at Maggie, he leaned forward and in a conspiratorial tone said, "I'd like to talk to you about that, Maggie."

"I'm all ears," she said, hunching her shoulders and staring at him across the table.

Ken nodded. "To be fair to my mother, she refused to have anything to do with Saladin's ring. It was I who talked her into engaging the lawyer, Sir Jeffrey Lyttle, and claiming it. I think it's only fair after Lord Claverley stole her inheritance."

Maggie thought on this. "That's true enough. But won't the barrister's fees cost an arm and a leg?"

"No. It's on a contingency basis, which means if he doesn't win the case he doesn't get paid."

"A body can do that? I think Miss Gage has to pay, win or lose."

"Most likely. I'm sure her lawyer doesn't have Sir Jeffrey Lyttle's confidence. Speaking of Sir Jeffrey, he's asked for your help."

"My help?"

Ken nodded. "He's sending down an artist from London and he'd like you to let him into the hall so that he can sketch portraits of my mother and Lord Claverley. He also wants to call you as a witness to testify of Claverley's brutality. But I told him that that would not be possible since your employer is also after the ring. It would put you in an impossible situation, caught in the middle. I wouldn't want you to do anything you don't feel right about."

Maggie's brow creased. "I don't know what to do. I love both your mother and Miss Gage."

"I'm sorry to put you in this predicament, Maggie."

Maggie thought for a moment before saying, "Could the barrister call me to testify whether I liked it or not?"

"I think so. This won't be a regular trial, so I don't know what the rules will be."

"I suppose I could help him with the pictures."

"It's up to you." Ken picked up the tintype of his mother and father. "It would take more time, but my mother could mail her copy of this image to Sir Jeffrey, and I'm sure he could find a picture of Claverley in the newspaper archives. So don't feel obligated to help."

Maggie pursed her lips. "There's a picture of Claverley on the wall upstairs. We was going to take it down, but the wallpaper is faded all around it and the mistress didn't have another to take its place." She was silent for a moment while she considered the dilemma. Then she said, "What's best for Miss Gage is the thing. Actually, I wish she'd give up on this daft scheme. It'll only burden her with barrister's fees and plunge her deeper in debt."

"If you don't mind my asking, Maggie, why is she in debt in the first place? This large estate must produce a fair income."

Maggie nodded. "Managed proper, I suppose it would. Miss Karen's a darling girl, but she's too softhearted to run this place at a profit. After Mr. Gage passed on, Miss Karen tried to run it but it was no use. She ended up renting the land. In a good harvest year, the money she gets from the farmers covers the mortgage and our living expenses. In a bad year, she falls behind. If the bank manager wasn't a friend of her late father, the bank would've taken the place long since. She was threatened with foreclosure a while back. That's when she heard about the ring and got the idea it would save her. But I have m'doubts. Even if she does win the ring and gets bags of money, she'd only pour it into this awful place and that would be foolish. If she loses the case and has to sell, she'd be free to get on to other things. Her only relative's her father's sister, a maiden lady up in London. She—the aunt, I mean—never approved of her brother wasting his money on this place. She'd be happy to see Miss Karen sell it and get out from under the debt." Again she was silent. Then a possible solution enlightened her face. "Let's say Sir Jeffrey wins for your mother. With all that money could you see your way to doing right by Miss Gage? Would you help her with her money problems, at least with her legal fees?"

Ken gulped. "Uh . . . I'd like to, but any money coming from the ring will belong to my parents and is already spoken for." He paused, wondering if he should mention that it was going to the Church. He decided not to. "I'd really like to help Miss Gage, but . . . I'll tell you what. I'll speak to my mother on Miss Gage's behalf. When I explain the circumstances, I'm sure she'll help."

Maggie nodded. "Fair enough. Then I will help Sir Jeffrey."

"Good. He's sending an artist down from London to make the sketches—a Mr. Jack Tolley. Be assured that I will not fail Miss Gage. She seems like a very nice person—and very pretty."

Maggie looked warily at Ken. "I can see you're taken with her, lad. But be careful. Her heart's as delicate as a robin's egg. 'Tis not two years since a man broke it to pieces. They was betrothed. But when he found out the hall was mortgaged and her only income was from renting her fields, he decamped." She locked eyes with Ken and added, "She kind of reminds me of your mother at that age. Don't trifle with her *affectations* unless you're in earnest, or you'll have me to answer to." With that warning, Maggie changed the subject. "I'd better go up and see if she needs me. Will you be all right down here? Have another scone."

"Thanks. Take your time. Oh, one last thing. Did you mention to Miss Gage that my mother was once married to Claverley and is also contending for the ring?"

Maggie shook her head. "No. Like I said, the letter's only just come."

"Good. Please don't mention it. It would only muddy the waters."

When Maggie had gone, Ken thought about what she had said. His mother's words came into his mind: *Stay away from gentile girls.* He sighed as he picked up the picture of his mother and father and gazed fondly at it. He had always enjoyed the story of his parents' adventures in Philadelphia and New York, and of their unconventional courtship, requiring them to wait for years before they could be married.

"Is that Claverley?" Ken asked later, nodding at a portrait on the wall, as he and Maggie went up the main stairs.

"That's him, all right," Maggie said, "looking like butter wouldn't melt in his mouth. We should've took him down and put him in the cellar where he belongs."

Maggie ushered Ken into a parlor and left to get refreshments. A shiver of pleasure coursed through Ken as he gazed on the mistress of Gage Hall. She was dressed in a pretty, black-and-white-checked frock, her luxuriant hair piled on top of her head.

"So, Mr. Sanderson, your family are from here?" she asked.

Ken wondered how much he could say and still keep his promise not to reveal his connection with his mother's bid for the ring.

"Yes," he said, "my mother, though it's been several decades since any of her people were here. A lot of Americans are coming over to Great Britain to search out their roots."

Miss Gage nodded. "So I understand. My roots go back to Newcastle, up near Scotland, but I was born here. You probably think it an ugly house, but it has been my home all my life. When I get the money, I will restore it to its former splendor."

"You . . . you have expectations?"

"I do," she said, ignoring his hesitation. "Have you heard of Saladin's ring?"

"I have. It's in all the newspapers."

She nodded. "After Lord Claverley's death, my parents bought this estate, and it is my barrister's belief that the ring should have been part of it. Unfortunately, others also claim it. A court case at the Old Bailey will determine its ownership. It begins in a month or so. I'll be going up to London to attend. I want to be there in person when I am awarded the prize."

She is *a little naïve,* Ken thought. But this didn't lessen his admiration for her confidence, her appearance, and her delightful accent. "I wish you all the best," he said, feeling a little hypocritical in saying so.

After a while, Maggie brought tea and scones—and another glass of milk for Ken. For a few minutes after Maggie had left, the two young people ate in silence. Miss Gage's dainty way of holding her teacup, drinking her tea, and eating her scone all added to Ken's fascination with her.

"Will you be in Somerset long, Mr. Sanderson?" she asked.

"A few days. Maggie—Miss Stowell—has generously offered me her cottage in the village."

Miss Gage smiled. "'Maggie' is fine. No one would know to whom you were referring if you say 'Miss Stowell.'"

When they had finished eating, Ken felt that he should go, but he had no desire to do so, and it appeared his hostess was equally reluctant to end their conversation.

"America is a large place," she said. "Where is your home?"

"Salt Lake City in Utah Territory." He waited to see her reaction. It was typical.

Her face clouded over. "Are you . . . are you a Mormon?"

"I am," he said with conviction. "I see by your expression that you've heard of us and that what you've heard is not favorable."

She blushed and lowered her pretty green eyes. When she looked up, she smiled sheepishly. "I'm sorry, Mr. Sanderson. I'm not a bigot. Really, I'm not. It's just that . . ." She left the sentence unfinished.

Ken gave her a reassuring smile. "I'm sure you're not. Considering how we're represented in the press, I can understand your reaction. The current battle between the Church and the U.S. federal government over our right to practice polygamy is grist for newspapers all over the world. But all newspaper reports and other writings aren't negative. I'm sure you're familiar with Mr. Charles Dickens's writings."

"Of course. I've read most all of his novels."

"About twenty years ago Mr. Dickens went aboard the Latter-day Saint emigrant ship *Amazon* to write an article on the Mormons. You can read about it in the *Uncommercial Traveller,* but I jotted down Mr. Dickens's assessment of the Latter-day Saints he found there. May I share it with you?"

"Please do."

Ken withdrew his wallet from an inside pocket of his jacket and removed a well-worn sheet of paper. "First, Mr. Dickens says that he went aboard the ship to 'bear testimony against' the Mormons 'if they deserved it,' and he freely admits that he 'fully believed they would.' But after thoroughly inspecting the ship and its occupants, he wrote that to his 'great astonishment they did not' deserve it. Then he concludes with these words: 'I went over the *Amazon*'s side, feeling it impossible to deny that, so far, some remarkable influence had produced a remarkable result, which better known influences have often missed.'"

"I think there's a copy of the *Uncommercial Traveller* in the library," Miss Gage said. "I shall read it." She smiled impishly. "Of course, Mr. Dickens is known for fiction. Are you sure he can be trusted with fact?"

Ken answered with a smile. As she asked him questions about his life in America, it touched him that she seemed genuinely interested in his answers. All the time they were talking, a persistent thought kept coming into his mind. *Since she's not a member of the Church, would I be trifling with her affections if I asked to walk out with her? I can't see anything wrong with it. It's not as if I'm asking her to marry me. On the other hand, those we court, we marry.*

He wondered if he'd be in trouble with Maggie and his mother if he did see Karen Gage socially. With some pangs of guilt, he finally cast aside his misgivings and during a pause in their conversation asked, "Miss Gage, while I'm in the area would it be permissible for me to call on you?"

She blushed fetchingly and nodded. "I would like that, Mr. Sanderson."

"My mother mentioned boating on the River Barle. Is that still done?"

"I believe so—up above the Tarr Steps."

"The what?"

She smiled. "It's an ancient clapper bridge from medieval times."

Ken had no idea what a clapper bridge was but didn't want to show his ignorance. "I see. Would tomorrow afternoon be suitable?"

"The morning would be better. The Barle is quite a jaunt from here, so we should leave early. We can ride in my trap to Withypool, where we can hire a boat and go downriver to the Tarr Steps. You say you're staying at Maggie's old place in the village?"

"Yes."

"Would you like Maggie and me to collect you in the morning?"

Ken looked at her quizzically. "Maggie will be going with us?"

"I'm afraid so. Although things are changing rapidly as we approach the twentieth century, a chaperone for young unmarried people is still *de rigueur* in some circles, although I am not rigid on that score. In the old days propriety did not allow an unmarried woman under thirty to go out of the house by herself. But I often go about the parish alone." With an impish smile she added, "Of course, finding excuses to get away from under the eyes of a chaperone is all part of the game. I happen to know that Maggie doesn't like boats, so we should be alone on the river. Now, should we collect you in the morning?"

Ken smiled inwardly. *Perhaps she isn't as innocent as Maggie thinks.*

In answer to her question, he said, "No thanks. I'll walk over. I'm a reporter-at-large for a newspaper back home, and since I plan to write an article about the area, I'd like to get the feel of it. Perhaps I should go now and see the vicar about my genealogy."

"Of course," she said. "Maggie will show you the footpath through the wood and across the fields. It's not far."

They shook hands in parting, and Ken was intoxicated by her delicate floral fragrance.

The rain had stopped and the sun was shining by the time Maggie led Ken to the footpath. She told him about the horrible time she and his mother had fled from the brutal Lord Claverley along that same path on a cold, rainy night.

"On a day like today," Maggie said as they parted, "it's a pleasant twenty-minute jaunt to the vicarage and only five minutes from there to my cottage."

As he walked along the footpath and breathed in the blossom-scented air, he suddenly became aware of a warm feeling somewhere in the vicinity of his heart, filling him with an enormous sense of well-being.

❧ CHAPTER 6 ❧

Ken observed that the fields were "rough with hoary dew" early the next morning as, full of anticipation, he ambled toward Gage Hall. The path led along the edge of a field of still green wheat, or corn as they called wheat in England. At the edge of the field he climbed over a stile and up ahead saw a red fox trotting toward him. Ken started along the path wondering when the fox would give way. When they were less than thirty yards apart, the fox sat down on the path. Ken stopped, and man and beast studied each other. When it appeared that the fox had no intention of moving voluntarily, Ken continued along the path. When they were about ten yards apart, the fox got to its feet and nonchalantly relinquished the pathway, loping through a hedge and stopping in the adjoining field to look back. "Thank you, sir," Ken said, tipping his hat to the curious animal.

As Ken continued on his way, he contrasted the lush English countryside, domesticated by centuries of permanent habitation, with arid Utah, still very rough around the edges.

When the towers of Gage Hall came in sight, a surge of warmth coursed through him in anticipation of seeing Miss Gage again. A pang of guilt soon accompanied it. He brushed it away with the rationalization that if he and Miss Gage did become romantically involved he could teach her the gospel. This thought was quickly followed by the truth that he didn't know a great deal about the gospel, not like his cousin Jonathan. He sighed and with an act of will thrust all negative thoughts from his mind, determining to enjoy the day in the company of the mistress of Gage Hall.

That afternoon, Ken and Miss Gage found themselves floating down the beautiful River Barle between green hills and tree-bordered meadows. The sun smiled down on them as birds filled the air with nature's music from leaf-laden thickets. From his seat in the middle of the boat, Ken awkwardly manned the oars.

Dressed in a yellow frock with a pale green sash and matching bonnet, Miss Gage sat in the stern slowly twirling a parasol in her gloved hands. She smiled at his attempt to keep the boat mid-channel. "I perceive that this is the first time you've sculled, Mr. Sanderson?" she said.

Ken smiled. "I know things are a little more formal over here, but would you please call me Ken?"

She considered the request. "Perhaps when we're alone. And you may call me Karen. Our names both begin with *K*." She laughed and the enchanting sound became one with the rippling of the water under the bow.

"Karen's a lovely name. And, yes, this is my first time in a rowboat. You'll have to be the navigator. I can't operate the oars and see behind me at the same time."

"You are doing brilliantly," she said. "This is heavenly. I haven't been on the river since I was a child. Thank you for inviting me."

"It's my pleasure." He smiled and, looking straight at her, added, "The view is marvelous."

She blushed. "Keep your eyes on the riverbanks. We don't want to have an upset."

"I was trying to figure out the color of your hair. It's not really red and it's not really blond. I've never seen such a color."

She twirled a strand in her fingers. "I guess it's what they call strawberry blond. I'm glad you find it fascinating. But I think you should be paying more attention to the boat. We're getting pretty close to the bank." She grasped the gunwale with her free hand as the boat brushed the bank. Ken made the necessary corrections, and once the boat was in the center of the river, he gave up rowing and let the current propel them downstream.

"Tell me," he said, "what does a lady of leisure do with her time?"

She raised her eyebrows and gazed at him. "I'm hardly a lady of leisure," she said. "Much is expected of me as the lady of Gage Hall. I visit the sick, preside at the annual fete, and judge a variety of contests—flowers, pies, pickles, and the like. Also, I help the vicar in organizing social events like whist drives and so forth, sing in the church choir—I lead a very busy life."

"And for pleasure?"

"Oh, various things. I love to view and sketch birds. Do you know that there are over three hundred kinds in this area?"

Ken cocked his head, put his hand up to his ear and listened to nature's cacophony from the trees bordering the river. "I think I hear all three hundred," he said with a smile. "Listen, what's that one?"

Karen strained to hear the one bird above the others. "I do believe it's a Dunford Warbler," she said.

Ken again listened. "I do believe you're right!" he said facetiously and they both laughed.

As they drifted with the current, he again became aware of an immense feeling of well-being enveloping him. He tried to observe the scenery and not stare at Karen, but his eyes kept drifting back to her and she invariably smiled back, causing his heart to race.

"I also cultivate a small area of the original garden at the hall," she said. "It's my special place. Perhaps I'll show it to you sometime." She paused before adding, "Here on the river it seems that all my cares have evaporated."

"What cares could you possibly have?"

She sighed. "As much as I love the hall, it is a millstone around my neck, or a 'milestone,' as Maggie says. You may think that I'm a wealthy woman because of the estate, but actually I'm in debt and I despise the feeling. As I mentioned, I'll be glad when I have the money to pay off the mortgage and restore the estate to its former glory."

"Have you ever thought of selling it and getting out from under the debt?"

"Yes, I have thought of it, and of removing to London to live with my aunt. But it's my home. And who'd want to buy such a place? It's in such poor repair it would probably not bring enough to satisfy my creditors. I would be destitute. No. My only hope is to win Saladin's ring."

A pang of guilt went through Ken. He wanted to tell her of his mother's claim, but he had promised not to, and he felt that it would ruin the idyllic day. Instead, he said, "I understand St. Swithins Foundling Home Association is looking for a country estate. I know one of the board members, so if you ever do decide to sell, I could put you in touch with him."

"Thank you. If I don't win Saladin's ring, I might consider your offer."

They proceeded in silence for several minutes.

"Obstruction ahead," Karen suddenly sang out.

Ken turned to see a low bridge of stone piers overlaid with huge rectangular flat stones. "The Tarr Steps?"

"Yes," she said, placing her parasol in the bottom of the boat. "Since it's too low to go under, you'll have to find a place to land."

Ken had already seen this. Frantically working the oars, he managed to run the prow up onto the gravel beneath a low bank. The boat stopped with a jerk and Karen, both hands firmly clasped on the gunwales, cried out excitedly, "Well done!"

Ken exhaled. "Rowing is not as easy as it looks."

He climbed out of the boat, pulled it farther onto the beach, and held out his hand to her. Picking up her parasol from the bottom of the boat, she rose and took his hand. A thrill of pleasure went through him at her touch. When they were both safely ashore, he surveyed the Tarr Steps and said, "Now I know what a clapper bridge is."

Soon they were sitting on the grassy bank gazing down on the bridge. "Do you know the origin of the words *clapper* and *Tarr?*" Ken asked, taking out his notepad and pencil. "I plan to write an article about boating on the Barle."

"I believe *clapper* comes from an Anglo-Saxon word meaning 'bridging the stepping stones,'" she said. "And if I'm not mistaken, *Tarr* means 'causeway'." Ken jotted down this information. "Like most ancient things in England, the bridge has a legend. I'll tell it to you if you'd like to include it in your notes."

"Thank you. I'd love to hear it."

"Well, the story goes that the devil built the bridge and wouldn't let anyone else use it. If anyone tried, he or she would disappear in a puff of smoke. But the local people so needed the bridge, they appealed to the parson to make it safe. The parson first sent a cat across, and puff, it was gone."

"Puff, just like that," Ken said, imitating her mannerism.

She frowned and shook a finger at him. "No teasing, or you won't hear the rest of the story."

"Sorry," he said, bowing his head in mock contrition.

Satisfied, she went on. "Next, in spite of what happened to the cat, the parson bravely ventured onto the bridge himself. The devil suddenly appeared and began furiously swearing at him. The parson reciprocated in kind—"

"Naughty parson," Ken interjected, grinning.

Karen placed a finger on her lips, indicating for him to be quiet. She continued, "When the devil realized he had met his match, he reluctantly agreed to let people use the bridge, but only when the day was very cool or very hot. On pleasant days the devil reserved the right of taking the sun in comfort on *his* bridge."

"An interesting legend," Ken said, standing up. "Today is not too hot nor too cold, so I'm going to test it." With head held high, he marched across the bridge singing at the top of his voice a nursery rhyme his mother had taught him:

The grand old Duke of York,
He had ten thousand men,
He marched them up to the top of the hill
And he marched them down again.
And when they were up they were up,
And when they were down they were down,

And when they were only halfway up
They were neither up nor down!

Karen clapped her hands. "Bravo!" she exclaimed when he had marched across the bridge and back again. "You have defied the devil." Glancing around, she spied a clump of primroses and plucked one. When he returned to her, she said, "Please accept this flower as a token of your bravery."

"Thank you, milady," he said doffing his hat and bowing at the waist. He was putting the flower in his hatband when he said, "Speaking of the devil and such things, when I first arrived at your house the driver said it was cursed—"

"An old wives' tale," she interjected, shaking her head with derision.

"—And then I saw a caped figure lurking in the shadows," he continued. "He disappeared when he saw me."

She took this statement more seriously. "You've seen him too? I told Maggie that I'd seen such a figure near the front hedge, but she dismissed it as my imagination."

Ken suddenly regretted bringing up the subject and ruining the jocular mood. "I'm sorry I mentioned it," he said as lightly as possible.

"You're forgiven," she said. "Let's talk about more pleasant things."

"Of course—what was that?" he said, staring past her.

Jumping to her feet, she turned to look, but saw nothing out of the ordinary. She shook her head. "Mr. Sanderson, what am I to make of you? First you talk about my house being cursed, then about a mysterious stranger, and now you startle me."

"I'm sorry, I truly am; but I did see the grass move beneath that bush."

They both went over to the bush, and he gingerly moved the blades of grass aside to reveal what appeared to be a ball.

Karen laughed out loud, breaking the tension. "It's a hedgehog," she said, picking up the small animal with her gloved hands.

"Shall we have a game of croquet?" Ken asked. "All we need are two flamingoes to use as mallets."

"All right," she said, grinning. "I'll be Alice and you can be the Mad Hatter! Would grey herons do? We have them hereabouts but no flamingoes. They're not as colorful but perhaps they'd serve." They both laughed and Karen added, "Let me put this little fellow back to bed. They're nocturnal creatures, and I fear we've interrupted his slumber."

Ken was touched by the way she gently placed the little animal in the grass where they had found it. Again the contrast between England and America came into his mind. "The closest things we have to hedgehogs in America are porcupines, and I don't think you would want to pick one of them up."

"I don't think I would," she agreed. "Actually, even though both hedgehogs and porcupines are prickly, they are not related. Porcupines are rodents and hedgehogs are insectivores."

He stared at her with admiration and, looking over her right shoulder, saw the pony and trap—carrying Maggie and the boatman's boy—coming down the road. "Ah, here's Maggie with the food," he said, "and not a moment too soon. This omnivore is famished."

Karen laughed and he loved the music of it.

While Maggie and Karen laid out the meal, Ken helped the boy portage the boat around the low bridge. Once the boat was again in the water, the boy got in and picked up the oars.

"Don't go yet," Karen called as she went to him with a napkin filled with food.

"Thank ye kindly, mum," the boy said, placing the bundle on the seat beside him.

"How will you get home?" she asked.

"Me da's meetin' me at Dulverton wi' a cart, mum." So saying, he nodded and expertly maneuvered the boat into the middle of the stream.

Karen's kind act touched Ken's heart.

After they had eaten, Ken and Karen wandered down to the bridge while Maggie repacked the basket.

"Were you successful at the vicarage?" Karen asked as they dangled their feet over the edge of the bridge.

"Yes. My mother had written to the vicar and he was kind enough to go through the records and set aside those pertaining to my family. However, he won't let me take the originals. I'll have to do a lot of copying. It will be tedious work, but it's one of the main reasons I've come from America."

"Would you like me to help you?"

He looked at her with amazement. "You would do that for a perfect stranger?"

Karen smiled impishly. "Come now, Ken. No one's perfect," she said.

They laughed, and Ken said, "Yes, I would very much like your help. I confess I'm not a very neat amanuensis."

"Then we're a *perfect* match. I'm a very neat copyist, myself." She smiled, then asked, "And when will you be returning to America?"

"Not for a while. As I mentioned yesterday, I work for a newspaper in Utah Territory. While in England, I plan to visit famous sites and send back reports—I just had a wonderful thought. Would you like to be my guide to this area?"

Karen's face lit up. "I'd like that very much. There are so many wonderful places to see in the southwest. We can use my pony and trap for the close ones."

The sun was sinking in the west when they arrived at Maggie's cottage in Ainsley Village where Ken would be staying. Maggie went inside on some pretended errand, leaving Ken and Karen to say good-bye.

"I can't remember when I've had a more lovely day," she said. "Are you sure you won't come up to the hall for a bite of supper?"

Ken shook his head. "Thanks just the same, but I have to finish an article I started on the steamship and get it in the post. I should also send off a letter to my parents letting them know I arrived here safely."

Karen nodded. "There's a post office in the dry-goods shop here in the village. Perhaps I should use this evening to go through Papa's papers for documents relating to the purchase of Gage Hall. My barrister may need them for the court case." Her eyes fell on the picnic basket. "Please take this food. There are enough leftovers for your tea and breakfast. Perhaps you can have supper at the hall tomorrow night. I'll ask Maggie to make us a nice meal. Would you like that?"

"I'd love that. Thanks for the marvelous time today. Where will we go tomorrow?"

"We'll start with Glastonbury Abbey and then on to Wells Cathedral. Would you like to go to the seaside while you're here?"

"Very much."

"Good. Later in the week, we can take the train from Glastonbury to Weston-super-Mare."

Ken's eyebrows came together. "Weston-super-Mare? That's a strange name."

Karen smiled. "It used to be just plain Weston, but as it became popular as a seaside resort they gave it a fancier name, which simply means Weston-on-the-Sea. It has a beautiful, sandy beach and views across the Bristol Channel to Wales. Eventually, I'd like to take you to a strange place called Stonehenge, but that's quite a bit farther. The abbey and the cathedral are the closest, so we'll start there."

"I'm in your hands. Until tomorrow," he said as Maggie rejoined them and climbed aboard the trap.

"Until tomorrow, then," Karen said to Ken, and to the patient pony, she added, "Walk on."

Knowing he would be with her again the next day caused his heart to swell within him. His eyes didn't leave her until she was out of sight. His spirits brimming, he opened the gate to his temporary home, waltzed up the flagstone path, and entered the thatched cottage through a Dutch door framed by climbing red roses.

That night as Ken lay in bed he couldn't sleep. It was not just the musty smell in the ancient cottage or the scampering of little feet—of what he hoped were only mice—that banished sleep. Two concerns had eroded his earlier elation, and they both involved Karen. Quickly dismissing the mice and the must as annoyances rather than threats, Ken turned his thoughts to the first of his concerns.

Recalling the events of the day, he smiled in the darkness as he pictured Karen sitting across from him in the rowboat. When she had pushed the boat away from the bank as they drifted too close, she had knocked her bonnet askew. Her delicate features, framed by the twisted bonnet, had looked impish as shade and sunlight alternately highlighted her fair complexion. Other images from the day's outing floated through his mind, causing the upturned corners of his mouth to pull down into a worrisome frown. He realized with a nagging feeling that he could easily fall in love with Karen, and then where would he be? He promised his mother that he'd only marry a member of the Church. *Perhaps a miracle will happen and Karen will become a member.*

His second worry was whether or not to tell Karen that his mother was also a claimant of the ring. He had promised his parents not to tell anyone other than Maggie, but that promise had been extracted from him almost five thousand miles away and long before he had met Karen, who had turned out to be not the middle-aged spinster he had originally visualized, but a delightful and intelligent young woman whose company he enjoyed and in whose good graces he wished to remain. It now seemed all wrong not to tell Karen. What if she found out some other way? Would it destroy their budding friendship? Would she feel he was deceiving her, exploiting her good nature, attempting to construct a relationship built upon subterfuge and designed for ulterior motives? *But how would it benefit her if I did tell her?* he asked himself. *Not in the least! So why tell her? It would only make things awkward between us. On the other hand, I feel so guilty keeping it from her. Maybe I will tell her.* This half promise to himself eased his conscience and he eventually fell asleep.

⊰ CHAPTER 7 ⊱

The next morning, Ken, Karen, and Maggie visited Glastonbury Abbey, the reputed burial place of the legendary King Arthur. That afternoon found them in the trap approaching the town of Wells. "Magnificent!" Ken exclaimed upon seeing the huge cathedral dominating the cluster of dwellings and shops at its base.

"It's probably the best example of twelfth-century Gothic architecture in England," Karen said proudly.

Ken stared in awe. "This is probably a silly question, but what qualifies a church building to be designated a cathedral?"

Karen smiled. "It's not a silly question. In Church of England parlance, a building is designated a cathedral when it is the headquarters of a bishop, or in other words, the center of a diocese. In this case, the bishop's palace is that building over there, the one with the moat around it."

Ken jotted down this information in his notebook. "The top of the cathedral's main spire looks like a miniature of our temple under construction in Salt Lake City," he said as he gazed on the huge, square, castellated tower. "I wonder if the architect, Truman Angel, was influenced by this cathedral. He spent some time in England studying the architecture before designing the temple. I'll have to ask him when I get home."

"How interesting," Karen said. "It certainly is a magnificent structure. Someone once said that rather than Wells being a town with a cathedral it was more like a cathedral with a town."

When they got within the actual precincts of the cathedral, Ken and Karen got down from the trap, which Maggie borrowed to visit a friend in town, leaving Ken and Karen to explore the verdant grounds together.

"Oh, no!" Karen exclaimed as they approached the cathedral's main door. Heedless of her lovely frock, she knelt on the grass and gently picked up a small bird. "Its wing's broken."

Ken knelt down beside her. "It is," he said, inspecting the sparrow.

"Perhaps we can nurse it back to health," she said.

Karen's compassion filled Ken with admiration. Although he could see no hope for the bird, he didn't say so. Rather, he found himself rooting around in a flower garden to find a worm. Meanwhile, Karen had taken the almost-lifeless bird over to a small fountain. By the time he rejoined her, the sparrow had expired. He took the small creature out of her hands, returned to the flower garden, and buried it. Her eyes were still moist when they silently entered the cathedral.

Later, seated in the building's main hall, Ken was overawed as he gazed on the famous scissored-arch supporting the roof of the nave. "Considering that it was built seven hundred years ago," he said, "the engineering is breathtaking."

Karen nodded in agreement. "It is," she said. "However, the scissored-arch was built about a century and a half afterward to support the roof, which was collapsing." For a moment she was silent and then said reflectively, "Whenever I'm in such a building as this, I'm filled with awe, and yet . . . somehow this grandeur seems far removed from the simple, beautiful teachings of the Savior. It may be sacrilegious for me to say it here, but it seems to me that this edifice was built more to satisfy the pride of the builders than the needs of the parishioners. I must confess that all this magnificence does not bring me closer to the Savior."

Ken couldn't believe his ears. Karen was articulating what was in his mind, but he had refrained from saying it as he thought it might appear mean spirited and hurt her feelings. After all, this building belonged to her church. He hesitated before saying, "I think I know what you mean. When my mother and father visited Christ Church Cathedral in Philadelphia, they felt the same way. Certainly church buildings should be beautiful and awe inspiring, but I believe they should also be practical. The new tabernacle on the temple block in Salt Lake City is not nearly as grand as this, but I dare say it holds many more people—about six thousand."

After a few minutes of silence, Karen said, "I'd like to ask you a question, Ken. Feel free not to answer it if you don't want to." She paused to frame her words. "Newspaper stories about your people indicate that the women are oppressed. Now that I've become acquainted with you, I can't believe that to be true."

Ken smiled. "I wish my mother were here to answer your question. Among her many other activities, mostly medical, she writes for a magazine called the *Woman's Exponent,* a semi-monthly newspaper published by Mormon women. One of its most important objectives is to get back the right of suffrage for *all* women in Utah."

Surprise filled Karen's face. "Get back the right? You mean women in Utah could vote at one time?"

"Some can now, but not those in polygamy. When the first government was established in Utah—at that time it was called the State of Deseret—women had the vote. However, when the federal government established Utah Territory in 1850 that right was taken away. Twenty years later it was restored by unanimous vote of the territorial legislature. Unfortunately, a few years ago both men and women who practiced polygamy lost the right, and there's talk that soon all women in Utah will again lose it."

"With the turmoil between your church and the federal government, it must be difficult to live in Utah right now," she said sympathetically. "Are you glad you're over here?"

"I'm glad I'm over here now that I've met you," he said.

She blushed. "Although I can hardly say that I'm an active suffragist, I do think that women should be allowed to vote at all levels. I was happy to learn a few years ago that the land-owning women of the Isle of Man achieved suffrage."

"Perhaps they should now call it the Isle of Man and Woman," Ken said with a grin.

Karen smiled and rolled her eyes. For a moment neither of them spoke. When Karen finally broke the silence, her tone was serious.

"In most ways I'm rather traditional. I would love to marry and have children." She looked him in the eye and grinned. "Perhaps I can break the curse on Gage Hall."

Ken's eyebrows arched. "The curse you don't believe in?"

She nodded and continued grinning. "That's the one. Since the opportunity of having a family has so far eluded me, I guess I'll just have to continue spending my time trying to be of some service in the parish."

Ken gazed at her with admiration. "You and my mother would get along well," he said. "You think alike."

The next day they worked on copying Ken's family records. The day after, accompanied by Maggie, they drove to the Glastonbury Station, where they would catch a train to Weston-super-Mare. At the train station Maggie asked Karen if she could be allowed to return home as she had much to do. Karen, feigning reluctance, let her go. Maggie would pick them up at the train station when they returned from the seaside.

"It reminds me a little of the Great Salt Lake—the seagulls and all," Ken said as they strolled along the beach later that morning. "But this is much prettier." He pointed at a row of small houses on wheels. "Those bathing machines, however, are a bit of an eyesore. Exactly how do they work?" He had a fair notion of their use, but he used the question to help their conversation along and to provide an opportunity to listen to Karen's cultured English accent, which gave him great pleasure.

Karen smiled and adjusted her parasol to keep the sun from her fashionably pale face. "As I'm sure you know, they're used to preserve a lady's modesty. After she enters through the back door, the machine is pulled down to the water—in this case by manpower, but on some beaches by ponies. In the privacy of the machine, she changes into her bathing costume. Then, screened from onlookers by the vehicle, she goes out the front door, down the steps, and directly into the water. After a prede-termined time of swimming with other women—as you can see there is no mixed bathing—she reenters the machine, changes back into her clothing, signals the operator by means of a flag, and is transported up from the water. Does that answer your question?"

"It does," he said. "You've explained it brilliantly. Since I wouldn't be allowed to swim with you, would it be permissible if we went wading?"

"Yes," she said. "That would be very nice. In fact, I antici-pated you and have brought a pair of rubber slippers."

After Ken rented two folding chairs from a vendor, they sat down and began removing their shoes. Karen slipped the rubber slippers over her stockinged feet while Ken took off both his stockings and shoes and rolled up his trouser legs.

"This reminds me of an excursion we made to the Great Salt Lake with my school class at the end of a term," he said. "Our teacher, Mr. Angus Reid, a dour Scot, accompanied us. Throughout our years in his class, he had always maintained his dignity, always wearing a brown, three-piece tweed suit, Black Watch tie, argyle stockings, and highly polished shoes. At the beach, though, he took off his felt hat and tweed coat and placed them on a large rock. Withdrawing his handkerchief from his pocket, he tied a knot in each corner and placed it on his head. Then to our further astonishment, he proceeded to take off his shoes and stockings, roll up his pants, and join us in the water. We couldn't have been more shocked if he had suddenly begun cartwheeling on the sand."

Karen laughed. "We don't really know people until we see them in a recreational setting."

As they waded in the cool water of the Bristol Channel, seagulls screamed above them in the cerulean sky. Ken felt as if the warm sun was nurturing their growing friendship. Later, they returned to the chairs, and Karen produced two small towels from her voluminous handbag. She gave one to Ken and glanced around. "Be right back," she said.

He watched her as she talked with one of the bathing-machine men. Then she entered one of the machines. A few minutes later she rejoined Ken. He assumed that she had changed into dry stockings, but he knew that it was not something a proper English girl would discuss with a man.

Later, strolling on the promenade, they stopped to listen to a brass band, and then continued along the promenade. "Ice cream?" Ken asked as they came to a vendor's shop.

She nodded. "I love ice cream."

Ken smiled. "Another thing you have in common with my mother."

As they ate the delicious confection from glass cups, Karen said, "Do you know that the ice that made this may have come all the way from Norway or even from America?"

He nodded. "I can imagine. I recall reading about a man in Boston who made a fortune shipping ice all over the world—even as far as Persia." He paused and looked thoughtful. "I was surprised that the man who served us has a foreign accent. He's the first foreigner I've seen since coming to England."

Karen smiled. "He's Italian. They seem to have a monopoly on ice-cream making in England."

Ken smacked his lips and held up his glass. "To Italy!"

On the way back in the train Karen curled up on the seat and fell asleep. Ken removed his jacket and tucked it under her head. As he gazed upon her sleeping form, his heart swelled within him and he prayed with all his heart that the Holy Ghost would open the way for her to become a member of the Church.

"Thank you, Karen," Ken said as, tired but happy, they parted in front of Maggie's cottage. "I'll long remember our day at the seashore."

Karen's face, full of color despite her parasol, beamed. "I enjoyed myself very much. 'A joy shared is twice a joy.'"

* * *

On the Saturday of the second week of copying and sight-seeing, they wandered the streets of Bath and visited the Roman ruins. Everywhere they went, Ken jotted down ideas for his newspaper articles. They returned from Bath in the late afternoon. Rain, which had been threatening all day, finally burst through the clouds as they entered the lane bordered by tall Lombardy poplars that lead to Gage Hall.

"You go on in, Karen, and I'll see to the pony and trap," Ken said.

"No, no," she said, taking an umbrella from under the seat and handing it to him. "You take the brolly and open the carriage-house door and I'll drive it in."

He nodded, handed the reins to her, and jumped down from the vehicle. Inside, she stood by while he unhitched the pony, rubbed it down, and filled the manger with hay. Then, laughing like children, without benefit of brolly, they ran through the rain to the main house.

"Miss Karen, Mr. Ken," Maggie said, "you're soaking wet. Let me help you off with those coats."

Later, as they sat in front of a cozy fire in a small parlor, Karen said, "By the by, I read that chapter in the *Uncommercial Traveller*. Mr. Dickens certainly wrote glowingly about your people. Please tell me more about your church. For example, why are you so interested in genealogy? Of course, many Americans come to England searching out their roots, but with you it seems to be a religious duty."

"You're really interested in my church?" he asked.

Karen smiled and crimsoned. "I'm interested in you, and your church seems to be important to you. Perhaps you have the answers I've been seeking."

Ken nodded enthusiastically. "My church is important to me, but I'm afraid I'm no authority on it." He hesitated for a moment. "I don't know where to begin. I wish my cousin Jonathan were here. He's very meticulous and really knows the gospel. He's serving at the mission home up in London."

"London?" Her brow creased in thought. "I have an idea. Stonehenge is on the way to London. Why don't we go to Stonehenge on Monday and continue on from there? We can see your cousin, and I can show you the sights. It's about time I visited my Auntie Vi. She lives in Kensington, this side of London."

Ken's face lit up at the prospect. "Great. You'll like Jonathan. His father taught my mother the gospel and baptized her in the River Barle many years ago. Our families are so close, he's more like an older brother." He paused before adding, "It's not that I don't know the gospel, mind you, it's just that I'd probably present it all topsy-turvy and confuse you. In the meantime, I'll try to answer your question about genealogy. We primarily seek out our ancestors because we believe in the ongoing link between generations. In other words, we feel that we're connected with all our ancestors and have a responsibility to provide them with the opportunity of becoming members of Christ's Church if they didn't have that opportunity while they lived on the earth."

Karen looked confused. "I don't understand," she said. "How can you do that?"

"We believe that if a person dies without having the opportunity of hearing and accepting the gospel of Jesus Christ, he or she will have that opportunity on the other side."

"You mean missionary work goes on after one is dead?"

"Exactly. However, if a person accepts the gospel in what we call the spirit world, that person cannot become a member of the Church without baptism, which is an earthly ordinance. So through genealogical research we identify our ancestors and are baptized as proxies for them."

"How curious," she said. "Of course, it does make sense. I have often wondered about those, especially babies, who pass on without baptism. It seems very unfair that they would be denied access to heaven on happenstance."

Ken felt warm all over and thrilled at Karen's willingness to learn his beliefs. "As far as little children go, we believe that they need not be baptized at all. Children before the age of accountability, which has been revealed as the age of eight years, are not capable of sin and hence don't need baptism. Somewhere in the Book of Mormon the prophet Mormon gives a discourse on that topic. Have you heard of the Book of Mormon?"

"Vaguely. Is it your Bible?"

"Not quite."

For the next few minutes Karen listened attentively as Ken described the origin of this book of scripture.

"It sounds fascinating," she said when Ken finished. "I wish we had a copy. I love to read."

Not wanting her enthusiasm to wane, Ken went to the window and looked out. "It's stopped raining. If you like, we can go over to Ainsley and get the copy my mother tucked into my valise before I left home. It's still early."

"All right. Let me check with Maggie about tea."

They had supper first and then fetched the book. On the ride to Ainsley and back Ken glowed with the Spirit. He could hardly believe his good fortune. Not only was Karen attractive, intelligent, kind, and spiritual, but she also had a sense of humor, and seemed genuinely interested in the gospel. That night before retiring, he knelt by his bed as usual, but now appreciation poured out of him in large measure.

The only fly in the ointment, Ken thought while still on his knees, was introducing Karen to Jonathan Kimball. Ken admired his cousin but always felt inadequate in his presence, like a little brother. He recalled a conversation with a friend who had returned home after years abroad. "Despite my successes in life and my maturity," his friend had said, "as soon as I am again under my parents' roof, I feel like an inadequate boy." Ken had understood completely. That is how he felt around Jonathan.

The next day Ken attended church with Karen. They sat in comfort in the Gage family pew, with its enclosed sides and embroidered cushions. The vicar took 1 Corinthians 13 for his text. On their way back to Gage Hall, Karen said, "I've always loved the text the vicar used, but it has always confused me. It seems to me that if a person bestows all he has to feed the poor, he would already possess charity. How could one be charitable without having charity? It's very confusing. Also, what are we to make of verse twelve where he talks about seeing through a glass darkly?"

"I don't really know," Ken said with chagrin, "but I think the Book of Mormon defines charity as the pure love of Christ. Let's ask Jonathan when we see him."

She nodded. "I hope you don't mind my asking all these questions. It's just that despite what I said when we were on the river, I confess my life is not as full and satisfying as I would like it to be. I have a great spiritual longing that has never been satisfied. Do you remember when Jesus was at the well with the woman of Samaria? He said that those who partake of the water He could give would never thirst again. I long for that water."

A river of warmth flowed through Ken. Silently he prayed for the proper words to say. But no words came and the opportunity passed.

When he didn't respond to her confession, she smiled and gently chided him. "It appears that we both need some instruction in what *you* believe," she said.

❧ CHAPTER 8 ❧

On Monday morning Ken awoke in semidarkness. Today he and Karen would go to Stonehenge and London. Satisfying warmth filled his breast as he lay in bed thinking about the many hours he and Karen had spent together, dividing their time between copying the Ashcroft records and touring the southwest. He loved being with her and reveled in the knowledge that she enjoyed his company too. His only regret was that he had still not told her about his mother's claim to Saladin's ring. The time never seemed right. *Oh, well,* he thought, *the trial is still in the future. I'll cross that bridge when I get to it.*

Because the room was still rather dark, he thought it must be early, but on checking his watch he found it was seven. Rising, he glanced out the window at lowering skies. Despite the gloomy morning, his soul still glowed from the events of the previous days. A delicious expectancy filled him as he contemplated seeing Karen and spending another day with her. He was dressed and waiting when Karen and Maggie drove up to the front door.

"Maggie will drive us to Glastonbury," Karen said.

At the Glastonbury Station, Ken talked to the ticket agent while Karen stood by.

"We would like to stop over at Salisbury for a few hours and go see the ruins at Stonehenge, but still get to London today," Ken said. "Would that be possible?"

"It would, sir," the agent said. "I'll book you and the missus on the nine o'clock to Salisbury and the three o'clock from Salisbury to London." At the mention of "the missus," Ken and Karen exchanged smiles.

Ken paid for the tickets, and Karen took his arm as they walked over to a wooden bench.

"I think that man over there buying a ticket was eavesdropping on your conversation with the ticket agent," Karen said after they had sat down.

Ken glanced over at the man, who quickly averted his face. He was dressed in a well-worn black suit and had a black cape over his arm.

"From the glimpse I got of his face under his slouch hat," Karen whispered, "he has a scar."

"I wonder what interest he has in us," Ken said. "Perhaps I should go over and ask him."

At that moment the train pulled into the station and the stranger quickly rose and, keeping his face averted, blended into the knot of passengers heading onto the platform. By the time Ken and Karen had reached the platform, the man had disappeared.

"I wonder who he could be," Karen said as they entered the railway carriage.

Noting a trace of fear in Karen's voice, Ken shrugged his shoulders. "Probably no one we should concern ourselves with," he said nonchalantly, although inwardly he wondered if it might be the man he saw lurking in the shadows of Gage Hall. "If we run into him again, I'll confront him."

They shared the carriage with an elderly lady, all in black, whose knitting needles clicked rhythmically.

"I found a book on Stonehenge in the library last night," Karen said after the train finished shunting back and forth and was finally underway. "I brought it with me. Perhaps it will help you with your article." Taking the book from her purse, she handed it to him.

"Thanks," Ken said. "Very thoughtful of you."

The lady ceased her knitting and gazed across the carriage at Karen. "Pardon me, miss," she said, "but did you say Stonehenge?"

"Yes," Karen replied. "Are you familiar with it?"

The woman nodded. "I went there once many years ago. A very peculiar place. Very mysterious. No one knows who laid those huge stones one atop another or why, but there's talk of Druid priests and unholy rites."

As the woman returned to her knitting, Ken glanced at Karen and rolled his eyes. "Scary stuff," he whispered as he opened the book in his hands and glanced inside. Coming across a poem called "Stonehenge" by Thomas Stokes Salmon in the introduction, he chose a stanza and in a low, mysterious voice read:

> *Here oft, when Evening sheds her twilight ray,*
> *And gilds with fainter beam departing day,*
> *With breathless gaze, and cheek with terror pale,*
> *The lingering shepherd startles at the tale,*
> *How, at deep midnight, by the moon's chill glance,*
> *Unearthly forms prolong the viewless dance;*
> *While on each whisp'ring breeze that murmurs by,*
> *His busied fancy hears the hollow sigh.*

While he read, the old woman ceased her knitting and closed her eyes. For a moment only the clickety-clack of the wheels could be heard. When he had finished reading, Ken glanced at Karen and again rolled his eyes. "Do you still want to go?" he whispered.

Before Karen could answer, the old woman's eyes blinked open. "Of course she does, young man," she said. "Despite my unease—I was truly on edge—I've never regretted, nor forgotten, my sojourn there."

The woman returned to her knitting, the sound of her needles blending harmoniously with the clickety-clack of steel on steel as the train coach swayed its way east toward Salisbury Plain.

At the Salisbury Station, Ken and Karen bade good-bye to the knitting lady and left the train. As it was near noon, they ate egg sandwiches at a pretty little tearoom with round tables covered with checkered cloths. Afterward, the waitress directed them to where they could hire a carriage to take them to Stonehenge.

"Sorry, sir," the liveryman said. "We don't have a closed carriage, only a gig. If you take it you might get rained on."

Ken glanced at Karen who raised her eyebrows and nodded. "We'll take it," Ken said. "We're going to see the ruins at Stonehenge and will be back in time for the three o'clock train to London."

"Stonehenge?" the man said. "That's curious. A coarse fellow just hired a horse to take him to that place, Stonehenge, I mean. It's not often a body goes there in such weather. Gloomy place, don't you know? All that talk of human sacrifice, Druid priests, and the like scares folks off." He noticed the concern in Karen's face. "Sorry, miss. I've misspoke." He gave Ken an accusing glance. "It's jist that it's not the place I'd be takin' a refined young lady on a day like this."

Despite the liveryman's misgivings, they rented the vehicle and were soon on their way to the ancient site. It first came into view from a long distance. Set in the boundless Salisbury Plain, Stonehenge was unimpressive.

"I'm disappointed," Karen said. "It just looks like a pile of gray rocks from here. What's scary is this vast, green plain—no trees, no houses. The site seems like a small, rocky island in a lonely, undulating green ocean." When they came closer to the giant, upright stones, however, Karen changed her mind. "Now I *am* impressed," she said. "The liveryman was right, though. It is a gloomy, scary place." She moved a little closer to him on the seat. "I'm glad you're with me. I wouldn't want to be here alone, especially on a day like this."

Ken nodded toward a horse hitched to a post where the ruler-straight road ended. "It appears that we are not alone."

Karen gazed at the horse and then at the mist-shrouded, megalithic stones forming a gigantic semicircle. Remembering the threatening talk of sacrifices, she involuntarily shivered. Ken turned to face her and put a comforting hand on her arm. "Let's go back," he said. "We can come another time when the sun is shining."

"Thank you," she said with a deep sigh. "I'd prefer—"

Suddenly, her eyes widened and a muffled cry escaped her lips. Ken looked in the direction she was staring. A dark apparition emerged from behind one of the huge, upright stones and started toward them. Their fertile imaginations, coupled with their earlier conversation, immediately assigned ominous duties to the creature.

"Let's away from this place," Karen gasped.

Ken didn't have to be asked twice. He swung the pony around and snapped the reins. The animal broke into a canter and then a full gallop. With gloved hands Karen hung on to the front rail as the two-wheeled vehicle bounced along the rough road. They didn't slow down until the crossroads, where Ken maneuvered in behind a heavily laden mail coach heading for Salisbury.

"Was it man or beast?" Karen asked.

Ken looked at her and smiled. "Man. Most likely our mysterious stranger. It's surprising how a man we would probably acknowledge with a nod on a busy street seems terrifying in a lonely place like Stonehenge."

Karen nodded. Her lips fashioned a nervous smile. "Perhaps he is the devil. After all, you defied him at the Tarr Steps."

Ken glanced at her and grinned. "I'm sure Old Nick has better things to do than ride around the country on a horse scaring tourists like us."

"Or worse things," Karen said ominously.

At Salisbury they returned the rented vehicle and boarded the train for London. This time they had the compartment to themselves.

"I'm sorry you didn't have the chance to study Stonehenge," she said when they were well on their way. "I promise if we go back again on a good day I won't panic."

"No harm done. I'll use your book to write the article, but I'll include our experience. It will make good copy. I'm sure my readers will enjoy reading about our brush with Beelzebub! And don't feel that you were the cause of our hasty retreat. When I saw the man in black come from behind that pillar, I was startled too."

After a while Karen said, "By the way, I should warn you about Aunt Vi. She's a dear soul but she has . . . well, she has a rather jaundiced view of the world—lots of petty prejudices. She doesn't hold with steam trains, foreigners, the upper class, and so forth. You'll see."

Ken smiled. "What does she 'hold with'?"

"Well, there's me, tea, her canaries, Bo and Peep, and poultices."

"Poultices?"

Karen nodded and smiled. "According to Auntie, they're the cure for all ailments."

Ken shook his head and smiled. "I can't wait to meet her," he said.

They got off the train at the Kensington Station in southwest London and walked the short distance to Karen's aunt's cottage near High Street.

"Are you sure you can handle those bags?" Karen asked.

"I guess," he said through a smile. "What do you have in yours, bricks?"

Karen smiled back. "We'll soon be there."

A small, birdlike lady answered the door of a lovely, vine-covered cottage. "Karen, my love!" she exclaimed. "What a wonderful surprise." The two women embraced and the older woman looked askance at Ken. "And who's this, then?"

"Mr. Kenny Sanderson from America, Auntie. He's over here searching his roots. We have become friends over the past while."

Aunt Vi observed Karen's beaming face and then focused on Ken. "American, you say? Well, come in anyway," she said.

They were no sooner in the door than the aunt frowned and brushed something off Karen's shoulder with a quick, bird-like motion. "Did you come on that awful steam contraption?"

Karen smiled and rolled her eyes at Ken. "Yes, Auntie, we came by steam train."

The older woman's face showed disapproval. "Steam, belching fire, soot, cinders, and all. It's the devil's invention without a doubt. Are you both staying?"

"Just me, Auntie," Karen said. "Mr. Sanderson will be lodging at Lady Brideswell's townhouse in the city."

The older woman arched her eyebrows. "Lady Brideswell's townhouse? How posh! Well, young man, take my niece's things up to the first room at the head of the stairs whilst we put on the kettle."

"Ken doesn't drink tea, Auntie," Karen said.

"Not drink tea?" the aunt said, shaking her head. "Well, I've no coffee. Americans don't know what's good for them. Ever since they dumped that tea in Boston Harbor . . ."

Karen smiled at Ken as he started up the stairs. Then she followed the little woman into the kitchen.

Ken soon rejoined them. He politely listened as the two women caught each other up on the happenings in their lives since they had last met. Ken's politeness seemed to impress the older woman, and by the time the visit ended, Aunt Vi had begun to thaw a little toward Ken.

The next morning he walked from Lady Brideswell's place to Charing Cross Station, where, by prearrangement, he met Karen. From there they walked to the mission home of The Church of Jesus Christ of Latter-day Saints.

"Ah, Ken, you're back," Jonathan Kimball said. "How was Somerset?"

Ken glanced at Karen and then back at his cousin. "Extremely pleasurable," he said with a smile. "Let me introduce

Miss Karen Gage. She would like to learn more about the Church."

The missionary's face lit up. "Well, that's a switch. Unlike the old days when hundreds were flocking to the Church, we now have to go out and hunt for investigators. They seldom come to us."

"I wondered why there are so many churches," Karen said later. The three of them were sitting in an upstairs room of the mission home. Elder Kimball had just explained that the primitive Church established by Jesus Christ had floundered after the deaths of the Apostles, eventually resulting in a proliferation of Christian churches.

"The Apostasy also explains all the horrid things, like the wars of religion, the Crusades, the Spanish Inquisition, and so forth, perpetrated in the name of Christianity," she said. "And it answers a question I've often asked about my own church. It has always bothered me that Henry VIII, a man of dubious morality to say the least, established the Church of England. But if all the Christian churches are without authority from God, what makes your church any different?"

"A good question," Jonathan said. "We believe that in 1820, God the Father and His Son Jesus Christ appeared to a young farm boy, Joseph Smith. The result of that vision was the eventual restoration to the earth of God's authority, or priesthood, and the reestablishment of the true Church of Jesus Christ."

Karen turned to Ken. "Do you truly believe that God actually appeared to Joseph Smith, Ken?"

Looking her in the eye, he said, "Yes, I truly do. I may not have as strong a testimony as Jonathan or know the doctrine as well, but here in this room, filled with the Holy Spirit, I have never been more sure of it."

Karen's eyes moistened. "I feel the Spirit too. Logic tells me that Joseph Smith's vision is myth, but the Spirit tells me it is true," she said. "Please be patient with me as I attempt to . . . to assimilate all this. I promise to keep an open mind."

Basking in the glow of the Spirit, the three young people discussed the Restoration for the next two hours. Ken occasionally added his views but left most of the teaching to Jonathan. Ken closed the meeting with prayer.

"Oh, we have a question," Karen said as she and Ken were about to leave the room. "What does the word 'charity' mean in 1 Corinthians chapter 13? And what does the phrase 'seeing through a glass darkly' mean in the same chapter? It seems to me that a man who can speak with the tongue of angels, has the gift of prophecy, has all faith and knowledge, and gives all his goods to feed the poor must already have charity."

"A wonderful question," Jonathan said as the three of them sat down again. "According to the prophet Mormon, charity is 'the pure love of Christ.' Paul's message in 1 Corinthians 13 is that the end result of truly living the gospel of Jesus Christ is the attainment of Christlike love. As Paul explains, all other attainments in this life pale before it. At the final Judgment it will not be what we've done in life that will count, it will be what we've become."

"Why then should we do good acts if we're not going to be rewarded for them?" Karen asked.

Jonathan smiled. "Because, Miss Gage, God will not reward us for the act alone, but for the motivation behind it, the intent of the heart. Let me give an example. Many years ago a certain nobleman lived a completely immoral life. Through fraud, robbery, and even murder, he amassed a fortune. On his deathbed he donated all of his ill-gotten gains to his church to build a magnificent cathedral to his memory. Donating all of his money to build such a structure would appear to be a pious act. But do you really think it will count in the Judgment?"

"That's an extreme case," Ken said, playing the devil's advocate. "What if a member of our church pays tithing, attends meetings, fasts every first Thursday, and so forth? Are you saying that he will not be rewarded for these things?"

"If he does them for the right reasons, he will," Jonathan said, picking up the Book of Mormon and thumbing through it. "Please read these words of the prophet Mormon."

Ken read, "'For behold, God hath said a man being evil cannot do that which is good; for if he offereth a gift, or prayeth unto God, except he shall do it with real intent it profiteth him nothing'."

"Thank you," Jonathan said. "In St. Matthew as well, the Savior stresses the importance of having the right motivation when doing pious acts. Miss Gage, would you please read Matthew 23:23?"

Karen took the Bible and read, "Woe unto you, scribes and Pharisees, hypocrites! for ye pay tithe of mint and anise and cumin, and have omitted the weightier matters of the law, judgment, mercy, and faith: these ought ye to have done, and not to leave the other undone."

"Thank you," Jonathan said. "Similarly, Jesus said of the scribes and Pharisees, 'This people draweth nigh unto me with their mouth, and honoureth me with their lips; but their heart is far from me.' These scriptures provide a key to 1 Corinthians 13. They clearly point out that merely doing outward pious acts is not enough; one must do them with real intent and thus be constantly working to change the inner man, to become more like the Savior, or to attain charity, the pure love of Christ."

Karen gazed on Jonathan with admiration. "Thank you, Elder Kimball," she said. "However, I still don't think that a man or woman could attain to all the attributes mentioned by Paul without having charity."

Jonathan nodded slowly. "You make a good point," he said. "It seems to me the Prophet Joseph Smith spoke on that. May I search out the answer?"

"Of course," she said.

Ken gazed at Karen in awe. "You're the first person I've ever seen stump Jonathan," he said.

Jonathan shrugged. "I'm sure Miss Gage won't be the last," he said. "In the meantime, Miss Gage, do you have a Book of Mormon?"

"I've been reading Mr. Sanderson's."

"Well, I'll get you one of your own," Jonathan said. "In the book of Moroni chapter 7, the prophet Mormon discusses faith, hope, and charity. Perhaps you could read it before our next session so we could discuss it further. As to your question about seeing through a glass darkly, as we become more like the Savior our minds will become more and more enlightened through personal revelation until eventually we will no longer just know in part, but know fully. In essence our goal as Christians is not only to know the gospel and perform its outward ordinances, but to allow it to change us internally and make us more like Christ."

Karen nodded in agreement. "I will reread 1 Corinthians 13 along with Moroni 7," she said.

Ken remained silent. The discussion had further clarified something he already knew: merely going through the motions of Mormonism was not enough to get one to the celestial kingdom.

In the afternoon Karen guided Ken to the sights of London, which established a pattern for the following week: religious instruction in the morning, sightseeing in the afternoon.

❧ CHAPTER 9 ❧

A tall man in a new suit set a valise and battered leather portfolio on the stoop and worked the dolphin knocker at the front door of Gage Hall. After a minute he knocked again. The door slowly opened and Mr. Bennett peered out.

"Mr. Jack Tolley t'see Miss Maggie Stowell," the man said, removing his hat. The elderly butler scrutinized Jack, wondering if he should ask the one-legged man to go to the servants' entrance. The man's speech dictated that he should, but his new suit of clothes seemed to advise otherwise.

"Who is it, Mr. Bennett?" Maggie asked, coming up behind the old man.

"For you," the butler said.

"Thank you, Mr. Bennett," Maggie said, and the butler shuffled off, pleased to be free from the burden of decision.

"Mr. Jack Tolley at your service, miss," the stranger said in his best speech and bowing from the waist. "Recommended by Mr. K. Sanderson and in the service of Sir Jeffrey Lyttle, barrister."

With narrowed eyes Maggie scrutinized the man's weathered face before stepping aside. "Wipe your . . ." She glanced down. "Foot," she said.

Jack nodded. "Right y'are, miss." He leaned against the doorjamb, balanced on his peg, and made a great production of wiping his one foot.

Maggie frowned and shook her head. "You don't have to wear the mat out. Follow me."

He picked up his things and stumped after Maggie, who led him across a broad hall and down the stairs to the kitchen. "Y'can warm yourself at the fire whilst I put the kettle on," she said.

Before long the two of them were sitting across the kitchen table from each other. Maggie nursed a cup of tea while Jack sampled her baking.

Jack smacked his lips. "Why, Miss Stowell, 'tis the best soda bread I ever et. 'Tis a mystery t'me that some bloke ain't made you a bride."

"Give over," Maggie said, blushing. "Call me Maggie, everybody does. And don't think I haven't had offers."

"I'll call you Maggie if you'll call me Jack and I don't doubt you've had lots of offers, Maggie. Why haven't you taken one?"

It occurred to Maggie to wonder about the man's brashness in asking such a personal question. But he appeared to be harmless, and he did seem sincere. She sighed and answered, "What it boils down to is I've never had a offer what tempted me to leave service. Being in service has its uses, you know: a roof over my head, good food, and the chance to hobnob with respectable people. If I'd wed someone of my class, I might have ended up in a hovel with a hungry brood and a man what spends all his time and brass at the pub. No, the married life's not for me. A spinster I am, and a spinster I'll stay."

Jack glanced at her speculatively as he buttered another piece of soda bread. "Maybe you just ain't found the right bloke."

"And why are you a bachelor, then?"

"Me? Oh who'd want an old cripple like me, what's lived from han' to mouth?"

She studied him. "You look right smart to me. A new suit of clothes?"

Jack nodded. "Aye. Got 'em for the occasion."

"You're an artist?"

"That I am."

"A good one?"

"Mr. Sanderson says so."

"Draw me a picture and show me."

"Right y'are." Jack opened the flat binder and withdrew a sheet of paper and a pencil. "Sit still."

Maggie blushed. "Oh, you're not wanting to draw me."

Jack didn't answer. With an economy of deft strokes he had captured Maggie's image on paper in a few minutes. When finished, he held it up. "Whatchya think?"

Maggie blushed. "Why, Mr. . . . Tolley, it's brilliant . . . but a bit too flattering."

Jack smiled. "I see more'n wi' my eyes."

Maggie blushed again and abruptly changed the subject. "You're here to draw pictures of the former Lady Ashcroft and her *proflikit* husband. Is that right?"

As his mouth was full, he simply nodded. When finished chewing, he said, "I'll start in the morning. In the meantime, is there a wee corner o' this big house where I could lay m'head for t'night?"

Maggie weighed the request. "I suppose if you come recommended by Mr. Sanderson y'can be trusted. But no funny business, mind you."

"By my mother's eyes, you'll have no call to regret putting me up."

"All right, then. I'll make up the room next to Mr. Bennett. It used to be the underbutler's in better days. Be warned that Mr. Bennett snores up a storm. He fairly rattles the windows wi' the noise of it."

By noon the next day Jack had fulfilled his assignment, and Maggie offered to drive him to the railway station at Glastonbury. She had enjoyed having a man close to her own age around the house and was reluctant to see him go.

"I could catch a later train," Jack said. "Whilst I'm here 'twould be nice to see the countryside."

Maggie leapt on the suggestion. She quickly packed a picnic lunch, and soon they were eating on the banks of the River Brue. "Will y'be coming up to London for the trial?" Jack asked, hinting that he didn't want their budding relationship to end.

Maggie nodded. "I'll be up with Miss Gage. It's always a lark visitin' London, but after a while I can't wait to get back home—just too many people there." She paused and was lost in thought for a moment. "After all my years in Ainsley, I don't think I could ever get used to livin' in a place like London."

"Maybe y'could," Jack said, "if y'had the right bloke t'look after you."

Maggie looked askance at him. "You cheeky devil! And what makes you think I need looking after? I've done pretty well on my own all these years."

"I'm sure y'have," he said admiringly, "but being alone is no kind o' life, Maggie."

Maggie began to nod her agreement and then countered with, "Like I said before, it's better'n being married to a man what spends all his time and brass in the pub."

"True enough. But what if your man came home wi' his pay packet ev'ry Saturday?"

Maggie smiled. "Is there such a man?"

"You're looking at 'im."

Maggie stared at him skeptically. "You wouldn't be askin' for my hand, would you?"

"I would!"

Her apple cheeks took on a deeper shade of red as she considered Jack's impulsive proposal. "Kind of sudden, isn't it? You hardly know me."

" 'Tis. But I know all I need to. I've a feelin' this job'll lead to more, an' I'll soon be making bags o' brass. I'll need sumun t'look after it and me."

She stared at him. "Do you want a wife or a housekeeper?"

"Both," he said with a grin. "Sumun t' keep away the cold abed o'nights."

She glanced down at his peg leg, which stuck straight out as they sat on the grass. "Does that thing come off at night?"

Jack laughed. "It does."

"Mmm. Let me think about it, then."

He nodded. "Don't take too long, though. We haven't many years left."

"Speak for yourself," she said with a toss of her head. "Myself's in the prime of life!"

"There's no mistakin' that," he said with a twinkle in his eye. "I suppose we best be off if I want to catch that steam train."

"I suppose so," she said reluctantly.

They packed up their picnic things, loaded them into the trap, and were soon on their way to Glastonbury Station.

"You haven't seen the last of me, Maggie," he called as the train pulled away.

"I've heard that before, Jack," she responded, but deep in her heart she hoped that this time might be different.

☙ CHAPTER 10 ❧

The day after Karen's first religious instruction, Jonathan was prepared to further answer her question about 1 Corinthians 13. "I talked with Brother Lewis, our mission president," he said as the three of them again sat in the upstairs room of the mission home, "and he gave me a copy of the Prophet Joseph Smith's discourse on charity. The prophet first repeats Paul's words: 'Though I have the gift of prophecy, and understand all mysteries, and all knowledge; and though I have all faith, so that I could remove mountains, and have not charity, I am nothing.' Then he explains: 'Though a man should become mighty, do great things, overturn mountains, perform mighty works, and should then turn from his high station to do evil, to eat and drink with the drunken, all his former deeds would not save him, but he would go to destruction.'"

"Ah," Karen said, "that makes sense. The hypothetical man St. Paul was talking about probably did have charity or the pure love of Christ when he was performing all those good things, but lost that love by turning to evil. Now I understand."

"Exactly," Jonathan said. "In James 1:22–27, we gain further understanding about what true discipleship means."

Karen read the verses and said, "The words 'forgetteth what manner of man he was' in verse 24 could be referring to St Paul's hypothetical man, who had charity but lost it through sin."

"Yes," Jonathan said. "I like the phrase in verse 26, 'seem to be religious.' Getting back to our discussion last time, merely performing religious duties without real intent is hypocrisy."

The word *hypocrisy* stabbed Ken's conscience. He determined it was time he told Karen of his connection with Saladin's ring. This resolution assuaged his guilt and for the rest of the meeting he participated with vigor. The session ended with Jonathan answering Karen's question about the difference between the Holy Ghost and the Light of Christ, which she'd read about in the Book of Mormon.

That afternoon, Ken and Karen attended a horse show at the Crystal Palace. In the evening, before they parted, Ken said, "Tomorrow is the first Thursday of the month—fast day—so I will not be eating the first two meals of the day."

"Fast day?" Karen asked. "Why do you have a monthly fast day?"

"We're masochists," he said with a grin. "No, actually we do it for charitable reasons. Our custom is to fast for two meals each month and donate the money we save to help the poor. We also believe that fasting and prayer, done properly, can help us come closer to God, become more spiritual. By my calculations, tomorrow's the first Thursday in June. But I could be wrong. Ever since I've been traveling, the days seem to run together."

"Yes. Thursday, June 3. What a wonderful custom," she said. "Well, if you're not eating, I'll fast too. Perhaps we can have a special meal in the evening." Her face lit up with an idea. "I know. Please come to Auntie Vi's for tea. I'll ask her to make her specialty, shepherd's pie."

"I'd love that," Ken said. "I'll see if Auntie Vi makes it as well as my mother."

Ken enjoyed his "tea" at Aunt Vi's the next evening, and by the time the meal was over he was convinced that the little woman had warmed to him even more.

By the end of the week, Ken had learned a great deal about his own faith, and with Karen's help a great deal about the capital city of the vast British Empire. After their religious instruction on the morning of their last day in London, Ken and Karen accompanied Jonathan from the mission home to the postbox at the end of the street. After Jonathan deposited the mission mail, the three of them stood chatting.

"I've thoroughly enjoyed our discussions," Karen said, "but my Aunt Vi is a little worried about me. She tends to be cynical where religion is concerned—"

"Where anything is concerned," Ken interjected with a grin.

"True," Karen said. "In this case she feels that Mormon people are very gullible. In fact she feels that people in general will believe just about anything." She chuckled. "Auntie told me an unrelated story that had me in stitches." She paused, not sure if it was appropriate to share the story so soon after a spiritual discussion.

"Go on," Ken said. "You know you're dying to tell us."

Karen glanced at Jonathan, who smiled and nodded.

"All right," she said. "In the middle of the last century the Duke of Montagu, who owned the Haymarket Theatre, got into a discussion with some of his friends about gullibility. Montagu shared Aunt Vi's cynicism. He said that people would believe anything if it were presented in the right way. But one of his friends had a more charitable view of people. They got into an argument and decided to make a wager. They would invent a character and announce to the public that he would perform impossible feats at the Haymarket Theatre. If a substantial number of people came to see the bogus act, Montagu would win the bet; if only a few attended, his friend would win.

"The 'Great Bottle Conjurer' was the character they invented. They had playbills made up announcing that among other things the conjurer would, before the very eyes of the audience, stuff himself into a quart bottle—" Karen burst out laughing and couldn't continue. This set off the other two. The three of them pealed with laughter.

Karen dabbed her eyes with the corner of her handkerchief before continuing. "Not only would he squeeze himself into a quart bottle," she said, hardly able to suppress her mirth, "but while he was in there he'd recite selected soliloquies from Shakespeare—" Again she couldn't go on and the three of them howled.

She again wiped her eyes and with some difficulty continued, "Well, on the appointed night the theatre was packed, not only with regular people but with the *crème de la crème* of London society. Clearly, the duke had won the bet, but now he had a problem: how could he inform the patrons that it was all a hoax? After much delay the audience became restless, calling for the act to begin. The duke thought that perhaps he could get away with it by appealing to the audience's sense of humor. So he sent the stage manager out to announce that the Great Bottle Conjurer was unavoidably detained, but if the people would return the next night he would stuff himself into a pint bottle instead.

"Well, the audience caught on to the hoax and they were far from amused. The Duke of Cumberland, who was on the front row, drew his sword, called out, 'Follow me!' and leapt onto the stage. The stage manager ran for his life while the audience proceeded to smash the scenery and seats and haul them outside to the street where they made a bonfire. Had the authorities not shown up the mob might have burned the building to the ground."

Jonathan wiped his eyes and shook his head. "That's one for my journal, Miss Gage," he said. "Of course, the story does make a valid point. One should be cautious about what he or she believes. But the Lord has given us an unfailing guide: the Holy Ghost. As I mentioned earlier, if you continue to pray and study the restored gospel, the Holy Spirit will testify to you that it is true."

"I shall continue to study and pray," Karen said. Then she looked thoughtful and asked, "Are one's sins truly washed away in baptism?"

"Yes," Jonathan said. "All of them."

"I can't imagine you having any serious sins, Karen," Ken said lightly.

Karen didn't reply. She looked away and for a moment no one spoke.

Jonathan ended the awkward silence that followed. "Where are you two off to today?" he asked.

"The Royal Botanic Gardens at Kew," Ken said.

Jonathan nodded enthusiastically. "You'll enjoy them, Ken. I've been there. Oh, by the way, when you mentioned the Haymarket Theatre, Miss Gage, it reminded me of a playbill I saw the other day for the Theatre Royal at Drury Lane. The play's called *The Rightful Heir.* With all this talk in the papers about the rightful owner of Saladin's ring, I thought it ironic. Perhaps you two should attend. The female lead is the renowned Nell Keene." Turning to Ken he added, "You should see at least one play while you're in London, Ken."

"Pardon?" Ken said, distracted by Jonathan's mention of the ring.

"I was suggesting that you and Miss Gage go see *The Rightful Heir,*" Jonathan said.

Karen's face lit up. "Why don't we all go?" she said. "Would it be permissible for you to attend, Elder Kimball?"

Jonathan hesitated. "I believe I could get permission," he said, "but I fear I'd be in the way."

"Of course you wouldn't," Karen said. "Would he, Ken?"

"No," Ken said, veiling his true feelings. "You get permission and we'll try to get tickets for tonight. As you know, we're heading back to Somerset tomorrow."

Ken and Karen were successful in acquiring three tickets for adjoining seats in the stalls. Afterward, they caught the train to Kew.

"It's been a long time since I was here," Karen said as they wandered among the exotic plants of every clime. "I'd forgotten how beautiful it is and the wonderful aroma. It's strange to see bananas and oranges growing in England and all these colorful birds flying around. May we sit?"

"It is beautiful," Ken agreed as they sat on a slatted bench, "but nothing I've seen is more beautiful than you."

Karen blushed. "Desist, sir, or you'll turn my head."

For a moment they wordlessly enjoyed the exotic surroundings and each other's company. Ken broke the silence. "Now that you've had a chance to study the gospel, what are your feelings?"

Karen looked thoughtful. "My feelings tell me that all that I've heard and read is true. But I'm not sure if I can trust my feelings." She paused. "I've thoroughly enjoyed our religious sessions, but there's something . . . something that will keep me from applying for baptism. I hope Elder Kimball understands. I'd hate to disappoint him. He's a fine man and an excellent teacher. Handsome too. I'm surprised he's not married. He must be in his early thirties."

Ken wondered how the topic had changed so quickly from Karen's feelings about the gospel to Jonathan's personal life. He felt a twinge of jealousy at her interest in his cousin, but he tried not to let it show.

"He's a widower," he said. "His wife died in childbirth several years ago. They were wed in a temple ceremony, so, as you've learned, they're sealed for time and eternity. In that sense he's still married."

Karen nodded thoughtfully. "He'd make a wonderful husband and father, so kind and patient—and the child?"

"She's being raised by Jonathan's mother, my Aunt Becky." Ken paused before bringing the subject back to religion. "I can understand your not wanting to make a hasty decision, but as Jonathan said, the Holy Ghost will assure you of the truth."

Karen nodded. "I believe that. The only sure way of knowing spiritual things is through the Spirit. I marked a passage in the Book of Mormon which warns against trusting in material things, in the 'arm of flesh.'" She removed her

Book of Mormon from her handbag, leafed through to a marked passage, and read: "'I will not put my trust in the arm of flesh; for I know that cursed is he that putteth his trust in the arm of flesh.'"

Ken was impressed by her acceptance of the Book of Mormon. "You obviously believe the Book of Mormon," he said. "Would you care to discuss what's holding you back from applying for baptism?"

She pursed her lips and sighed. "No—at least not yet. As I said, I have difficulty trusting my feelings. About two years ago I was betrothed to a man. My feelings told me that I loved him and that he loved me. But my feelings betrayed me. It turned out that he only coveted Gage Hall. When I confessed to him that I was in debt and had few resources, he immediately went away. I had read enough about life, especially in novels, to know that sometimes people follow the despicable practice of marrying for money. Nevertheless, it was devastating to me. I was just getting over him when I met you. I suppose that's why I told you on the river that I was in debt. I didn't want to go under false pretenses." She looked thoughtful and added, "I'm not sure if I can ever trust my feelings again."

Perhaps now is the time I should tell her about my connection with Saladin's ring, he thought as he listened to her bare her soul. *It would be dreadful after what she's been through if she found out some other way and thought I'd deceived her. I'll try to work it into our conversation.*

"I'm sorry," Ken said. "But please don't reject the gospel because of that experience. Of course, there's nothing wrong with taking your time. Some people accept the gospel readily, almost as soon as they hear it. Others take a while. Sister Eliza Snow, one of the most prominent women in our church and a good friend of my mother, took four years before she was baptized. I'm sure as you continue reading the Book of Mormon you'll gain a full testimony. When the time is right, you'll know it." For a while they sat in silence, breathing in the exotic aroma of many flowers and listening to the sweet cacophony of various birds. "By the way," he finally said, "what happened to the man you were engaged to?"

She seemed not to hear the question and asked, "What kind of questions are asked in the examination for baptism?"

"Oh, just ones about worthiness." He smiled. "From what I know about you, I'm sure you'll have no problem."

A strange, sad look clouded her face. "Perhaps if you knew more about me you wouldn't be so certain," she said, quickly rising. "I think we should be going now."

Her abruptness surprised him. It was not like her. *It has been two years. Why is she still so sensitive about him? I guess now is not the time to mention my connection with the ring.*

That evening the three of them attended the Theatre Royal. Jonathan sat on the aisle seat, Ken three in from the aisle, and Karen between them. Karen was her usual, pleasant self again. They had just settled into their seats when she chuckled.

"What are you thinking?" Jonathan asked.

She smiled. "I looked at the stage and the ridiculous image of the Great Bottle Conjurer squeezing himself into a quart bottle came to mind," she said.

The three of them laughed.

For the next hour they viewed Sir Edward Bulwer Lytton's play in silence. When the gaslights came up at the intermission, they discussed the performance.

"I've seen as good in Salt Lake," Jonathan said.

Ken agreed.

"I thought Nell Keene was excellent, though," Karen said, as if defending the London stage against that of Salt Lake City. "And very beautiful."

"She was good," Ken admitted.

"And beautiful?" Karen asked playfully.

Ken shrugged. "I hardly noticed," he said with a shrug, but the faint blush on his cheeks and smile on his lips belied his words.

She turned to Jonathan. "Elder Kimball, don't tell me you didn't notice either?"

"Of course, I didn't," he said, tongue-in-cheek. "After all, I am a missionary."

Just then a pretty young girl approached them. "Orange, sir?" she asked Jonathan. "Fresh from Seville."

Jonathan turned to Ken and Karen and lifted his eyebrows. "No thanks," Ken said.

"I just love oranges," Karen said, "but they're so messy to eat."

"We'll have two," Jonathan said to the girl.

"One shilling, sir," the girl said coyly. The price was exorbitant, but Jonathan paid without protest. "Enjoyin' the pl'y, is you, sir?"

"Yes," Jonathan said.

The girl looked wistfully at the stage. "I 'ope to be up there somed'y. D'y'know Nell Keene once sold oranges like me? Then she runs into Lord Darnley and 'e puts 'er on the styge. They're married, don't y'know?"

"I didn't know that," Jonathan said, a little embarrassed by the girl's obvious flirting. Karen and Ken looked on with amused interest.

"This the missus?" the girl asked, nodding at Karen.

"No," Jonathan said.

"Ah, so you're a single gent?" she asked, her interest increasing.

Jonathan smiled. "Yes. I'm a missionary. Would you like to hear about my church?"

The girl's expression changed. "Oh, no, sir. I must aw'y."

They laughed at the girl's quick flight.

"I should have warned you," Karen said. "Orange sellers are outrageous flirts. As the girl said, their greatest hope is that they will latch on to a rich patron who will finance their way to an acting career. I guess Nell Keene was one of the lucky ones."

While Karen was speaking, Jonathan took out his handkerchief and pocketknife. He placed one of the oranges in the handkerchief and cut the skin into quadrants. Then he peeled back the skin and carefully divided the orange into segments, all without spilling a drop of juice. "There you are, Miss Gage," he said. "Enjoy."

"Thank you, Elder Kimball," she said. "Very neatly done."

A twinge of jealousy shot through Ken. "No thank you," he said when Karen offered to share with him. Until the intermission was over, he studiously ignored the two orange eaters. His eyes roamed the theatre, fastidiously studying the building from pit to gallery to sculptured ceiling. He knew that he was being petty, but all his life Jonathan had upstaged him. In all honesty, Ken felt that he and Jonathan were probably equally good looking, or so he had been told. But Jonathan's extra four inches, sixty pounds, and muscular build gave him a much more commanding presence. In addition, in pioneer communities like those in Utah Territory, manual dexterity was greatly prized, and there were few things Jonathan couldn't do with his hands. Ken, on the other hand, was good at manipulating words, but all thumbs when it came to physical things.

When Jonathan finished eating his orange, he looked around for somewhere to deposit the peel. Noticing this, Karen took the peelings from him, wrapped them in her handkerchief, and deposited them in her purse. She whispered something to him and they both laughed quietly. Then she leaned over and whispered to Ken, "I just told your cousin that the audience sometimes use the orange peels to pelt the actors if they don't perform well."

Ken smiled. Despite his discomfort at sharing Karen's company with Jonathan, he was man enough to acknowledge and appreciate her sensitivity.

Later at Aunt Vi's doorstep, Ken said good-bye to Karen while Jonathan waited in the hackney cab.

"Thank you for a wonderful day," Karen said. "But I fear it was not all wonderful for you."

Ken smiled. "Being with you is always wonderful. Don't mind me. I should have warned you that although I admire my cousin, I've always been a little envious of him. I'm sure he doesn't mean to, but he makes me feel . . . I don't know . . . a little inadequate."

"You shouldn't feel that way. I think you're marvelous."

Karen's words sent a surge of pleasure through him. "Thanks for your confidence in me," he said. "I guess we're off to Ainsley tomorrow?"

"Yes. It will be nice to be home, but I really have had a lovely time in London, thanks to you and Elder Kimball."

Karen was still standing on the steps when Ken joined his cousin in the cab. She waved good-bye to them as the vehicle pulled away.

✤ C H A P T E R 11 ✤

During their journey from London to Somerset, Ken tried to recapture the euphoria of their first days together. But Karen's reluctance to share what was holding her back from joining the Church, her confession that she could not trust her feelings, and his suspicion that she might have feelings for his cousin, all put a strain on their relationship. Rationally, Ken could reason away all these impediments, but despite this, an invisible wall had come between them.

It was raining when they reached Glastonbury Station. They hired a closed carriage and driver to take them to Gage Hall. When they arrived, an elegant black coach-and-four sat in the drive, the matched ebony horses groomed to perfection.

Ken whistled. "Pretty fancy," he said. "A friend?"

Karen shook her head. "No one I know."

"You have a guest, Miss Karen," Maggie said as she helped Karen off with her coat. "He's cooling his heels in the drawing room. Been here over a hour."

"Who is he?" she asked.

"Mr. Stephen Langton, the late Sir Gerald's son. Very handsome and well dressed, but a mite too sure of himself." Maggie accompanied the last with a rolling of her eyes.

"Stephen Langton," Karen said, remembering. "I *do* know him, slightly. I met him at a party in London two years ago when I was . . ." She let the sentence dangle and quickly added, "He was rather charming."

They met Stephen Langton in the drawing room. "Good day, Mr. Langton," Karen said. "It is nice to see you again. This is my friend Mr. Sanderson."

The two men shook hands. Karen may have thought Stephen Langton charming, but Ken took an instant dislike to him. He wondered why Langton had not inherited his father's title, why he was "Mr. Langton" and not "Sir Stephen."

"Miss Gage, wonderful to see you again," Stephen Langton said. "Forgive me for coming unannounced. I learned from Mr. Squibbs that you were stopping in Kensington with your aunt. I went there but just missed you and continued on here."

"What you have to say must be very important," Karen said.

"It is," he said. "If I may, I'd like to speak to you in private."

Karen looked at Ken and smiled. "There is nothing you have to say that Mr. Sanderson can't hear. Please go ahead."

"I don't mind leaving the room," Ken said.

"No. I'd prefer you stay," she said. "Go ahead, Mr. Langton."

Langton glanced at Ken and then back at Karen. He was obviously displeased at Ken's presence. Nevertheless, he said, "As you may know, I, too, am contending for Saladin's ring. The court case has been moved up and will begin Thursday next. Since we're both after my father's ring, I propose we join forces. My greatest desire, Miss Gage, is to restore this object to its rightful place, and I am willing to pay whatever is necessary to do so. If you win the court case, I will buy the ring from you at a prearranged price."

"And if I don't win the ring?" Karen asked.

"Then I will pay all your legal expenses," Langton said. "You will be out nothing."

Ken could see by her eyes that Karen was interested in the proposition. She glanced at him for guidance. Almost imperceptibly, he shook his head.

"Let me say, Miss Gage," Langton added, "another claimant has entered the fray—an American, Lord Claverley's widow, estranged from him many years ago. Sir Jeffrey Lyttle is representing her, and I can assure you that he is a force to be reckoned with. You and I must unite or there is every chance that we shall both go down to defeat."

Karen again looked to Ken for advice. Noting this, Langton said, "You're an American, Mr. Sanderson?"

"Yes," Ken said evenly.

Langton's eyes narrowed. "My barrister has done research into the former Lady Claverley. It seems that she joined the Mormon Church shortly after marrying Lord Claverley, then ran off to America."

At the mention of the Mormon Church, Karen glanced at Ken. Panic seized his breast and his face reddened.

Noting Ken's discomfiture, Langton asked, "You wouldn't have any connection with this American bid, would you, Mr. Sanderson?"

Ken hesitated as Karen and Langton both waited for an answer. "Uh . . . yes and no," Ken finally stammered. "My mother is Lord Claverley's widow but—"

Karen's mouth fell open and her eyes grew wide. Langton pressed his advantage. "I see. Now we know your real interest in Miss Gage." His words dripped venom. Karen turned pale. In disbelief she continued staring at Ken, who started to speak but was again cut off by Langton. "Obviously, this revelation is news to Miss Gage. She is shocked, and I don't blame her." He tightened the screw. "Shocked to learn that you have insinuated yourself into her confidence in order to find out the strength of her position. How dare you? As her acquaintance, I am bold to say, remove yourself from these premises forthwith or get the horse whipping you deserve."

By this time Karen was reduced to tears. With her hands over her mouth, she looked to Ken for an explanation.

"I'm sorry, Karen," he said. "I can explain—"

"Of course he can," Langton interjected savagely. "His kind are full of explanations. Get out, Sanderson, before I throw you out."

Ken, his face crimson from embarrassment and anger, turned on Langton. "Look, Langton, this is Miss Gage's home. I'll not go anywhere unless she tells me to."

"Stop it," Karen screamed. "Both of you leave my house this minute." Turning her back on them, she fled the room.

"See what you've done," Langton said. "Why don't you go back where you came from? There's too many meddling Americans in England already. Your mother deserted her husband and has no right to the ring."

Ken was about to respond when Maggie burst into the room.

"What's going on?" she asked. "I heard a scream. Where's Miss Gage?"

"I think she's gone to her room, Maggie," Ken said. "She's very distraught."

Maggie turned on Langton. "I think you'd better go, sir," she said acidly.

"Miss Gage ordered us both to go," Langton said.

"Then why are you both still here? Away wi' you." Turning on her heel she swept out of the room.

Ken and Langton glared at each other, each reluctant to be the first to leave. Finally, Ken said, "I'm not going, Langton, until I see the back of your carriage go down the lane."

"I'm not leaving until you do."

Storming back into the room, Maggie broke the impasse. Pointing at Langton, she yelled, "You! Get into your fancy carriage and be gone." Turning to Ken she added, "You follow me."

Ken meekly followed her to the back door, where she thrust an umbrella into his hands.

"Thank you, Maggie," he said, as she pushed him out into the wet night.

"Don't thank me," she called out as she closed the door. "Thank Miss Gage."

Under the protection of the umbrella, he trudged back to the village full of self-recriminations. Over and over in his mind, he pondered the path that had led to his hurting the woman whose company he craved. *Why didn't I tell her the whole truth from the start? She must think I'm no better than the man who jilted her.* He fervently wished he'd listened to his parents and left Saladin's ring alone. Had he come only for the Ashcroft records, he reasoned, all would be well. *What a mess I've made of things.* His mind went back to the night he'd received the inspiration that it was his destiny to go to England and that something special awaited him there. *Have I forfeited my destiny?*

By the time he got to Maggie's cottage, his feet and legs were icy cold. But he didn't care. His mental anguish far exceeded his physical discomfort. Nevertheless, his practical side forced him to start a fire in the hearth, remove his wet trousers and stockings, and hang them up to dry. As steam rose from his clothes, he stared into the fire and cursed himself for being a fool.

As he lay in bed later, sleep wouldn't come. For a long time he mulled over a plan to win back Karen's confidence. *All I can do is go to her in the morning and beg forgiveness.* He determined that he would go back to Gage Hall at first light before Langton had time to further poison Karen against him. *I'll pry her from his clutches. Karen's a reasonable woman. Maybe she'll understand. She had Maggie give me the umbrella, so she must not be too angry with me. Tomorrow's Sunday. I'll have to go early before she leaves for church.*

It was well into the morning hours when he had this last thought. With a reasonable plan in mind, he finally felt enough solace to fall into a dreamless sleep.

He awoke to sunshine flooding the room. At first the light filled him with optimism, but when he glanced at his watch and realized that it was almost ten, he groaned. *So much for getting to Karen first thing. Langton's probably beaten me to the punch. She'll think I don't care.*

After hurriedly dressing, he took the main road to the hall, reasoning that the shortcut through the wood and fields would still be too wet from last night's rain. As he headed up the country road, the beauties of nature were all around him, but he was unaware of them. Eyes to the ground, he gingerly stepped around puddles while his mind sought words of explanation. Not far from the lane to Gage Hall, he suddenly looked up to see four glistening black horses bearing down on him. Throwing himself out of their way, he landed in a water-filled ditch. As Langton's coach rumbled past, his heart sank to see Karen through the window. Their eyes briefly met before the wheels deluged him with muddy water. Maggie was also in the coach. Ken wiped the mud from his eyes and stared in disbelief at the back of the vehicle. A knot tightened in his stomach. As the coach diminished, so too did his hope that he could ever obtain Karen's forgiveness. Mortified, dripping with mud, and in ditch water up to his ankles, he felt that nothing could ever be right in his life again.

He wondered what he should do. *Perhaps Mr. Bennett knows why Karen and Maggie went off with Langton.* With heavy heart he trudged on to Gage Hall. With some difficulty, he pried out of the ancient butler the information that Langton had offered Miss Gage and Maggie a ride to London so that they could attend the court case. The butler knew nothing more.

Afterward, Ken returned to the cottage and for the second time in as many days cleaned his soiled clothes. While working at this task his mind was full of Karen. He assumed that she must have accepted Langton's offer to buy the ring should she win it. The thought of her and Maggie riding in Langton's coach galled him, filling him with fresh recriminations. *All I can do is follow them to London and pray that somehow I can win back Karen's trust.*

⊰ CHAPTER 12 ⊱

It was late in the evening when he arrived in the city the next day. As before, Lady Bridewell's servants treated him as an honored guest, but still smarting from the events of the previous day, he hardly felt worthy of their deference.

The next day he busied himself writing newspaper articles and the following day, Wednesday, he made his way to the mission home, where he sought solace in the company of his cousin and the other Saints.

"Ken," Jonathan said with pleasure, "I thought you and Miss Gage had gone back to Somerset."

"We did, but the ring trial's been rescheduled for tomorrow, so I came back."

"You look rather down. Is anything wrong?" Ken nodded and told his story. "'Oh, what a tangled web we weave when first we practice to deceive,'" Jonathan said.

"I didn't knowingly deceive Karen," Ken said defensively. "I promised my parents not to tell anyone and I kept that promise. But, of course, in hindsight I should have explained everything to her."

Jonathan nodded. "I'm sure you didn't mean to deceive her. Don't despair. Have faith and I'm sure things will all work out in the end. Miss Gage is an intelligent, spiritual woman. Heavenly Father has set her on the path to the gospel. He will not abandon her or you."

Ken sighed. "I surely hope you're right. In the meantime, it will be unbearable seeing Karen in court tomorrow knowing she thinks me a deceiver. I must have a chance to explain."

"Well, you're among friends here and we are happy to have you."

Considering his emotional state, Ken decided that spending the day at the mission home was the best thing he could have done. He enjoyed the warm spirit and friendly association with his fellow Saints, something he had taken for granted over the years.

On Thursday Ken left for the Old Bailey early in the morning. On his way he had the sensation that someone was following him. Twice he turned around quickly but could see no one. He shook it off as paranoia. When he reached the courthouse, he was disappointed. The trial had been postponed until the next day. For a while he vacillated between going to his lodgings or to the mission home. Feeling the need for companionship, he chose the latter. Soon he and Jonathan were packaging pamphlets to be sent to various parts of the mission. While they worked, they talked.

"Did you leave a girl behind in Utah?" Jonathan asked. "I rather thought you'd have found someone by now."

"No, no one special. My parents, of course, would like me to find someone and settle down. Mother warned me about becoming involved with gentile girls over here. Maybe she was right."

The two men worked together all day and Ken appreciated the fellowship. "Will you stay for supper, Ken?" Jonathan asked late in the afternoon.

"No thanks. I don't feel like eating. I think I'll take the long way to my lodgings and soak up some of London's atmosphere for my articles. I've been told that the fish market at Billingsgate is a sight to see."

"And smell," Jonathan said with a smile. "Good luck tomorrow."

Not long after leaving the mission home, Ken once more felt that someone was following him. To test this feeling he suddenly stopped. Sure enough he heard a footstep and then silence. Looking back, he could see no one and continued on. After a while he found himself lost in the seamier side of London. Concern turned to fear as darkness fell and the fog began to roll in off the Thames. How he wished that he had gone directly to his lodgings. Pulling a map from his pocket, he moved close to a lamplight and tried to figure out where he was in relationship to the fish market.

Suddenly, he was literally lifted off his feet, dragged far into an alley, and slammed against a brick wall. Gasping for breath, he tried to struggle free, but two burly men kept him pinned to the wall. He looked up, and by the thin light from a second-story window, he saw the ugly face of a third man directly in front of him, so close he could smell his foul breath. A livid scar, starting at the right eyebrow, ran the length of the man's face. *The mysterious stranger!* The man was dressed in rough clothing and, like the other two, smelled of the sea. A knitted toque covered his head.

"Quit the case, Sanderson," the man hissed, "or suffer the consy-quences."

"What are you talking about?" Ken gasped.

"Y'know what I'm on about. Give over tryin' t'get the ring, or we'll have yer guts for garters."

Ken stopped struggling and vigorously shook his head. "Did Langton put you up to this?" he asked. "Were you the one spying on Miss Gage and following us to Stonehenge?"

The man answered with a fist in Ken's stomach, winding him and doubling him up. When he had caught his breath, he threw all his strength into getting free. But it was no use. His captors had grips of steel. Scarface's second demand for Ken to quit the case was met with sullen silence. Infuriated, the man knocked off Ken's hat, pulled his head up by the hair, and smashed his forehead into Ken's face, sending fingers of blinding pain radiating from the point of impact below his left eye. Wincing, Ken prepared for another blow. But it didn't come. Suddenly, the two men released their grips, dropping Ken to the dirty pavement. Like jackals fleeing from a kill before a lion, the three of them bolted down the alley. Painfully, Ken turned to see what had scared them off. A light was approaching from the alley entrance.

"All right, young fella, you're coming wi' me to the station," said a voice behind the light.

Ken groaned as the London bobby none too gently attempted to pull him to his feet. "That hurts," Ken said. "Can't you see I've been beaten?"

"Sorry, mate," the police constable said, lowering Ken back to the pavement. A shrill blast from his whistle brought another peeler, and the two of them managed to get Ken to the police station, Scotland Yard, where they took his wallet from him and deposited him in a holding cell. Groaning, Ken curled up on a lumpy mattress and waited. After a while he gingerly fingered his throbbing cheek. *Why did I ever get mixed up with Saladin's ring?* he thought, his former river of obsession now reduced to a trickle.

"How are you feeling now, Mr. Sanderson?" a man in plain clothes asked a half hour later. "I'm Chief Inspector Soames."

Ken painfully sat up, flexed the muscles in his face, and once more touched his left cheek. "I'll live," he said.

Soames studied Ken's bruise and half-closed eye. "Somebody surely did a number on you, son," he said. "Should I send for a physician?"

Ken slowly shook his head. "No. I'll be all right." With his good eye, he glanced around the cell. "Am I under arrest for something?"

The man smiled and shook his head. "No, no, sir. PC Walcott thought you might be a vagrant when he found you in the alley, but we see from your wallet you're an American and that you have money. Obviously, thieves didn't assault you. Have you any idea who might have done it or why?"

Ken nodded. "I have a very good idea. It was three toughs from the waterfront—they smelled like fish. Even though it was dark in the alley, I'll never forget the ringleader's face. He had a long, pale scar from eyebrow to chin. I think he's the same man who was spying on my friend, Miss Karen Gage, before I met her. He demanded I withdraw my mother's claim to Saladin's ring."

"Miss Gage from Somerset?" the policeman asked, "One of the other claimants to Saladin's ring?"

"Yes, sir."

The chief inspector nodded thoughtfully. "Your assailant sounds like Jacob Gandy, a hard case if ever there was one. Undoubtedly he was hired by one of the other contestants for the ring. Any idea which one?"

"Stephen Langton," Ken said with certainty. "We had a set-to a while back. He's obsessed with getting back the ring."

The detective nodded. "Young Langton, eh? I wouldn't put it past him. Our paths have crossed before. He's as rich as Midas and mean as ditchwater. Had scrapes with the law ever since he got out of short trousers. Killed a man once."

Ken's mouth fell open and his first thought was concern for Karen. "He did?"

Soames nodded. "A knife fight. It was ruled self-defense, but I've no doubt his father's money got him off. Yes, sir, a piece of work is Stephen Langton. You can count on me following up on this. There's nothing I'd like better than to see him behind bars." The detective thought for a moment. "There's one thing I don't understand. Men who'd hire themselves out to thrash a body wouldn't think twice about nicking his wallet. But they didn't take yours. It doesn't make sense."

"They didn't have time to rob me. Your constable scared them off."

"I suppose you're right. Well, it shouldn't be too hard to find Gandy. As soon as we do, I'll call you in to identify him. Here's your wallet. Would you like help to get home?"

Ken refused assistance. It was very late when he got to his lodgings. The butler's eyes went wide when he saw Ken's bruised face.

"It's nothing," Ken said and went straight to his room.

The next morning he looked in the mirror and groaned. His cheek was black and blue and his left eye was still half-closed. Nevertheless, nothing could keep him from the Old Bailey. Again he was there early and again he was told that the trial had been postponed, this time indefinitely. He immediately headed for Sir Jeffrey's chambers.

"Ah, Mr. Sanderson," Sir Jeffrey said. "In a brawl, were we?"

Ken's hand went to his bruise. "You could say that. At least I've learned not to wander around London by myself in the dark."

"'Experience is a good teacher, but fools know no other,'" the lawyer quoted. When it appeared that Ken didn't want to discuss his injury further, Sir Jeffrey continued, "By the by, I'm pleased with the work of your pavement artist."

"May I see the pictures?"

Sir Jeffrey shook his head. "I'm afraid not. They're under lock and key until the trial."

Ken acknowledged this with a nod. "About the trial," he said, "why has it been postponed again? No one at the Old Bailey would tell me."

Sir Jeffrey nodded. "It is frustrating for sure. The ring's been stolen!"

"Stolen?"

"I'm afraid so. That dunderhead, Twiddy, had it locked up in his study and someone broke in and nicked it. Things won't go ahead until it's recovered. But don't despair. Because of all the publicity surrounding it, it's one of the most identifiable baubles in England. It will be almost impossible to fence. Finding it's a priority for the Yard. In the meantime, all we can do is wait."

"I suppose so," Ken sighed. "Thank you, sir." He turned to leave. At the door he stopped. "Sir Jeffrey, as you know, Miss

Karen Gage has also laid claim to Saladin's ring. How are her chances?"

Sir Jeffrey was quick to answer. "Poor to none. She's engaged that incompetent but well-named Bartimaeus Squibbs to represent her. Money down the drain. No doubt about it."

"Well-named?"

"Read your Bible," the barrister said gruffly. "Is Miss Gage a friend of yours?"

Ken sighed. "She was, but we've had a falling out. I'd really like to see her and perhaps make amends."

The barrister shook his head. "Not advisable. Consorting with the enemy is always counterproductive. My advice is to stay away from her at least till after the trial."

❧ CHAPTER 13 ❧

Disregarding the barrister's advice, Ken was soon riding the new underground railway to Kensington. He knocked on the cottage door with some trepidation.

"Mr. Sanderson!" Aunt Vi said, a shocked expression on her pinched features. "Whatever happened to your face?"

"It's nothing. I should have known better than to wander around London alone on a foggy night. Is Miss Gage home?"

The little woman shook her head. "I'm afraid not. She's out with Stephen Langton." Ken's heart fell. "Maggie Stowell and a one-legged gentleman are with them. It seems Maggie's finally found a beau."

Ken nodded. "Jack Tolley," he said.

"Yes, he's the one." Her eyes focused on his wound. "That bruise needs seeing to. Come in and I'll put a poultice on it." She stepped aside to let him in.

Since he had nothing better to do, he accepted the invitation and soon found himself lying on a chesterfield in the parlor with an odorous cloth covering his face. The elderly woman left him, and after a while he fell asleep. An hour later he woke with a start. He had no idea where he was. His head ached, an evil smell filled his nostrils, he was blind, and something was crawling in his hair. With a shriek he sat bolt upright. The poultice fell from his face, allowing him to see Aunt Vi flitting into the room. She pointed her index finger at his head and said, "Bo, you cheeky boy. Let Mr. Sanderson alone." Her finger came away with a canary perched on it. "I'm sorry, Mr. Sanderson. Bo's taken to getting out of his cage of late. Peep never leaves her cage unless I take her out. I'll put this bold fellow back in the atrium."

Ken cautiously rubbed the sleep from his eyes and shook his head. "No harm done," he said.

She soon returned. "Let's have a look," she said, peering at the bruise. "The swelling's gone down. How does it feel?"

"Much better," he said, more to please her than anything else. "I take it Miss Gage has not returned?"

"No. Not yet."

"Well, I must be on my way. Thank you very much for the poultice."

"I'll wrap it up and you can take it with you. Just soak it in cold water and put it on before you go to bed."

"Thank you. I'll do that." She gave him the poultice and saw him to the door. "Please tell Miss Gage that I apologize for the misunderstanding we had and would like to make amends."

"I will." She studied Ken for a second. "If it's any consolation, young man, in spite of your being an American with questionable religious views, I find you less objectionable than the Langton fellow. He appears charming, but there's something sinister about that man. I've warned my niece about him, and I think she's coming around to my opinion."

Aunt Vi's backhanded compliment gave Ken a sliver of hope. He smiled weakly. "Thank you, Miss Gage," he said. "Would it be permissible to come back and see your niece this evening?"

"I'm afraid she'll be out again with Langton. They're dining at the new Savoy Hotel."

Despair filled Ken as he slowly nodded. "Perhaps tomorrow, then."

He thanked Miss Gage again and soon found himself slowly trudging back to Kensington Station. Sitting in the train compartment, he stared at his bruised reflection in the window and decided that the poultice really had helped. His mind then turned to his troubles. *What else can happen to me? One day I'm on top of the world, the next I'm branded a deceiver, deluged with muddy water, and beaten by London toughs.* As he idly toyed with the strap for raising and lowering the window, he contemplated the peaks and troughs of life and decided that he had nowhere to go but up.

Back at Lady Brideswell's he tried to concentrate on writing the Stonehenge article, but all he could think of was Karen and Stephen Langton. Mr. Bramley, Lady Brideswell's butler, invited him to come to supper, but he declined. *They'll be at the Savoy now. If she only knew what kind of man Langton is, she wouldn't go out with him. But how is she going to know unless someone tells her? Why am I sitting here moping when Karen's dining with a murderer?* Leaping to his feet, he was soon out the door.

Forty-five minutes later he approached the entrance to the Savoy Hotel. The doorman's eyes went to Ken's bruised face, and for a second it appeared that Ken would be denied entrance. A half crown slipped into the doorman's hand caused the huge brass door to swing open. For a moment Ken drank in the elegance of the lobby. His heart skipped a beat when he saw Karen sitting in the reception area at the entrance to the dining room. Langton was nowhere in sight. She spotted him as he rushed toward her.

"Mr. Sanderson," she said in a neutral voice, "fancy meeting you here."

"Your aunt . . . your aunt said you'd be here," Ken stammered.

Despite her attempt to be unemotional, her countenance filled with compassion on seeing his bruised cheek. "Your face," she said. "What happened?"

"An encounter in a dark alley," he said. "Aunt Vi was kind enough to make me a poultice for it."

"Did it help?"

"Like magic." He paused to draw breath, exhaled, and poured forth a stream of words: "Karen, I'm so sorry for hurting you. I should have told you about my mother. I wasn't trying to deceive you, and my friendship with you had nothing to do with finding out about your case as Langton said. I didn't tell you because I promised my parents I wouldn't get involved in the case. Except for helping Sir Jeffrey locate some pictures, I've kept that promise. The last thing in the world I want is to hurt you. Please forgive me."

Karen sighed and nodded. "I'm afraid I did take offense too readily. Maggie told me everything. When she mentioned that Sir Jeffrey wanted her to testify, I told her to go ahead. I want to win the ring fair and square or not at all."

Ken gazed on her with unabashed admiration. "You really are amazing. No wonder I . . . I think so much of you. I promise never to give you reason to doubt me again."

Her lips parted in a smile. "Don't make any promises you might not be able to keep. Nevertheless, we'll say no more of it. I should apologize to you for not forcing Mr. Langton to stop when his carriage drenched you with muddy water. Believe it or not, it pained my heart to see you standing in the ditch with such a pathetic expression on your face."

Ken shrugged. "I felt rather pathetic. To see you riding off in Langton's coach—I assume you accepted his offer."

She lowered her eyes. "I did."

"In writing?"

She nodded. "He had the papers with him. His barrister drew them up." She could see by Ken's expression that he was worried for her. She shrugged her small shoulders. "Where's the harm? If I win the ring, I will have money to pay off all my debts. If I don't win, Mr. Langton will pay my legal fees. How can I lose?"

From what Chief Inspector Soames had said about Langton, Ken could think of several ways she could lose, but he decided to treat her question as rhetorical. He simply said, "I hope the figure you agreed on reflects—"

A group of noisy people streamed out of the dining room, interrupting him. When they had passed, Karen bit her lower lip and said, "We agreed on ten thousand pounds."

Considering what he knew about the ring's value, it was obvious that Langton had tricked her, but Ken didn't dwell on it. "Oh, well," he said cheerily, "you've made the bargain, so we'll just have to see how things play out. In the meantime, may I attempt to restore your trust in me?"

She smiled. "Yes, you may—"

"Come away this minute, Miss Gage," Stephen Langton demanded as he strode toward them. "I forbid you to talk with him."

Anger flashed from Karen's green eyes as she rose to her feet. "Forbid me? Mr. Langton, I will talk with whomever I please. Just because we're partners in the ring case, it doesn't give you the right to order me around. And while we're at it, I'm having second thoughts about our agreement. Until the ring is recovered, if it ever is, we need have no further association." She turned to Ken. "Mr. Sanderson, please order me a cab."

Langton's eyes narrowed and he thrust his face close to hers. "You've signed the papers and you'll keep the bargain," he said, his voice shrill, "or I'll ruin you. I know the state of your finances."

At that moment the *maitre d'hotel* emerged from the dining room, obviously angry at the disturbance. When he saw that Langton was at the center of it, however, he quickly retreated.

"How dare you talk to Miss Gage that way," Ken said to Langton. Then to Karen, "Come, Miss Gage, and I'll get you the cab."

"Leave now and you'll regret it!" Langton warned, ignoring Ken. "A waiter will show you to my table."

Karen stared at Langton's back as he marched off. Then she took Ken's arm and they headed for the exit.

"May I see you home?" Ken asked when they were outside.

"No, thank you," she said. "I want to be alone."

He nodded. "Fair enough. I'll get you the cab."

He helped her inside the hackney.

"Thank you, Ken," she said. "Oh, one last thing. Despite all that has occurred in the past few days, you'll be happy to know that I'm still very much interested in the Church and I'm still reading the Book of Mormon."

"That does make me happy," he said, doubly pleased that she'd used his first name.

For a long moment they looked into each other's eyes, reluctant to part. Karen finally sighed. "Be assured I shan't be walking out with Mr. Langton again. I must go."

"May I come see you in Kensington tomorrow morning?" Ken quickly asked.

"Would the day after be acceptable?" she asked. "I've promised Auntie my time tomorrow."

"I'll be there in the morning with bells on," he said.

Her smile told him that she truly had forgiven him.

With a light heart he returned to Lady Brideswell's and launched into the Stonehenge article. The next day he finished it and put it in the mail. The remainder of the day was agony, counting down the hours until he would see Karen again. Somehow he got through the rest of the day and the long night. In the morning he leapt out of bed. Glancing out the window, he noted that it was dull and overcast. But the weather didn't dampen his spirits. He was humming "Come, Come Ye Saints" as he straightened his tie before a mirror when a knock sounded at the door.

"A PC Walcott's here to see you, Mr. Sanderson," the butler said. "He's in the foyer."

"Thank you, Mr. Bramley. I'll be right down." *I wonder what the bobby wants?*

"Good day, sir," the policeman said. "Please come with me to the Yard."

"I can't," Ken said. "I'm due in Kensington."

"Won't take long, sir. Chief Inspector Soames needs you."

Ken sighed. "I guess it's on the way to the underground station. All right, but this had better not take long."

By the time they arrived at Scotland Yard, the fog had turned the morning into night. "Mr. Sanderson's 'ere to see the chief inspector," PC Walcott said to an older man behind a desk littered with paper.

"Right ye are. Please take a seat, Mr. Sanderson. Sergeant Harris's the name," the older man said. "Chief Inspector Soames is over to Newgate. He'll be along directly."

After a while, Ken pulled out his pocket watch. *Almost ten o'clock. The morning's half gone. I hope Karen doesn't think I've let her down again. Hopefully, I'll get out of here soon and have time to see her while it's still morning.* As the minutes ticked by, Ken's hope of seeing Karen that morning evaporated. He tried to free himself once more. "I really must be going," he said to the station sergeant.

"Shouldn't be much longer, son," the sergeant said as he placed his teacup on the littered desk. "You young fellows are in such a hurry these days. Slow down and you'll live longer. Would you like a cup o' tea and a biscuit?"

"No, thank you. Have you any idea why I'm here?"

The sergeant brushed biscuit crumbs from his mustache and nodded. "The chief inspector's bringing over a prisoner for you to identify. He might be the one what assaulted you."

More minutes ticket by before Soames finally arrived. "Sorry for keeping you, Mr. Sanderson," he said. "I'm afraid I must further inconvenience you. Due to the fog, I thought it prudent not to transport the prisoner here and risk his escaping. Rather, I'd like you to accompany me to Newgate Prison. It shouldn't take long."

Everything takes long today, Ken thought. Nevertheless he followed the inspector out of the building and into the fog. They walked the short distance to the prison. When the steel door clanked shut behind them, Ken had the awful feeling that he was in the prison to stay and would never again see Karen. A guard handed Soames a lantern, and the inspector signaled Ken to stay close behind him. As he followed the inspector down a corridor, down a flight of stairs, along another corridor, and down yet another flight of stairs, the noise, squalor, and smells sickened him. Without breaking stride, the policeman kicked a fat brown rat, sending it squealing down the corridor. By the time they reached the cell containing the prisoner in question, it was all Ken could do to keep the bile from rising into his mouth.

"You have a visitor, Gandy," Soames said, raising his lantern a little higher. A string of profanity issued from a dark corner, the gist of which was that Soames could go to the nether regions. "Suit yourself, Gandy," Soames said in a flat voice, "but you'll be going without food for the next two days unless you show yourself posthaste."

Gandy apparently liked his food. He slowly lurched over to the bars and stared out. Ken took one look at him, quickly turned, and headed back the way he had come. Soames followed closely behind him. They were in the fog-filled street before Ken spoke. "That's him all right. It was dark in the alley, but that scarred face is indelibly etched into my mind. There's no doubt about it. He's the ringleader of the three."

"I figured as much," Soames said. "When we get back to the Yard, I'll have you fill out a report and you can be on your way. Are you going far?"

"I'm taking the tube to Kensington."

Soames nodded. "Sergeant Harris will find a constable to go with you to the Charing Cross Station. You know what happened the last time you wandered around in the fog."

Ken filled out the report and asked Sergeant Harris about an escort.

"On a foggy day like this all the constables are out on patrol, but PC Walcott should be back in a jiffy," the sergeant said. "Just have a seat."

Again the minutes ticked by. Ken could stand it no longer. "I'm sorry sergeant, but I'll take my chances alone."

At that moment Constable Walcott arrived. "Walcott," the sergeant said, "see Mr. Sanderson safe to Charing Cross Station, then."

The constable sighed. "I was 'oping to put m'feet up for a sec', Sarge, and 'ave a cuppa . . . but if I must. Come along, Mr. Sanderson."

The two were only a few hundred yards from the subway station when a shrill whistle pierced the fog. "Sumun's in trouble, Mr. Sanderson. Can you go the rest of the way alone?"

"Of course, constable," Ken said as another insistent whistle reached them. "Sounds like you're needed."

Nothing untoward can happen in such a short distance, Ken thought. But he was wrong. Suddenly he felt a sharp object at his back and the rather high-pitched words: "Yer money or yer life. Don't turn 'round."

The desperation in the demand was obvious, and Ken was more frustrated at the delay than he was afraid. *This is the last straw,* he thought. *I've been shunted from pillar to post all day and I'm not going to take any more.* Making an abrupt 180-degree turn, he came face-to-face with a young boy in ragged clothes holding a pointed stick. Surprise and fear filled the boy's pale face. He seemed rooted to the ground.

Ken shook his head. "Put away that silly weapon," he said as he withdrew a pound note from his wallet. "Here. Get yourself a good meal."

The boy grabbed the money and without a word was gone. Ken watched him go, then turned into the station. He pulled out his watch and he glanced at it. *Past noon. I've let her down again!*

The fog was not as bad in Kensington. Unsure of his reception, he knocked on the door of Aunt Vi's ivy-covered cottage. While he waited, the anticipation at seeing Karen again flowed through him, sweeping away his uncertainty. He knocked a second time, more confidently this time. Out of the corner of his eye he noticed movement at the window of the adjacent cottage. He turned his head quickly and saw a curtain close. *Nosy neighbor,* he thought. Turning back to the door, he knocked a third time. No one answered. He took a deep breath and slowly exhaled. *She must have given up waiting for me.* Taking a notepad and pencil—the tools of his trade—from his inside pocket, he tore off a sheet and jotted down:

Karen,

Sorry I missed you. Thanks for your forgiving attitude at the Savoy the other night. I'll return later this afternoon or evening—

For a moment he pondered on how to end the note, wanting to write "Love, Ken," but thinking that it might be too forward. He finally ended up with a neutral "As ever, Ken."

After sticking the note in the mail slot, he waved good-bye to the invisible neighbor and headed for the underground and back to his lodgings.

⁂ CHAPTER 14 ⁂

Later that day, Ken was back in Kensington. To his dismay the note was still protruding from the mail slot. He tried the door but it was locked. *I wonder if Karen and her aunt have gone down to Somerset?* While he was pondering what he should do next, the nosy neighbor came out her door and made a great production of sweeping the front steps. Ken went over to her.

"Excuse me, madam," he said. "Would you happen to know where the Miss Gages have gone?" *Or is it the Misses Gage?*

She stopped sweeping and looked him up and down. "And who might be askin'?"

"My name is Ken Sanderson. I'm a friend of Miss Gage junior."

"Well, I'm not one to spy on my neighbors, am I? But I did happen to see them go off in a coach just after noonday—a real posh one, don't you know?"

His heart skipped a beat. "It wasn't a black coach with four matched black horses, was it?"

"Black as pitch the coach was. Now the horses is another thing. I only saw the back of the coach, didn't I?"

Many thoughts coursed through Ken's mind. He wondered if Langton had taken them somewhere. But why would Karen go with Langton after what she had said the night before? Karen's aunt surely wouldn't go with him voluntarily. She had made it clear that she didn't trust him. Could Langton have kidnapped Karen and her aunt? Ken dismissed the idea as overly dramatic. Probably the two women went shopping or perhaps down to Somerset. But if they'd gone to Somerset, why the fancy coach? Wouldn't they have taken the train? No. Aunt Vi didn't approve of trains. But why would Karen go off when she knew Ken was coming to see her? *Of course, I said I'd be here first thing in the morning and she didn't leave until after noon.* All this went through his mind in an instant.

"Thank you, madam," he said to the neighbor. "If you happen to see them when they return, would you please tell them that I called and will return again this evening?"

The woman nodded. "Surely, I will. It's all very strange, isn't it?"

"What is?"

"Them rushing off without a word. She usually tells me, Vi does, if she's goin' away, and sometimes leaves Bo and Peep wi' me."

"Did she take them with her?"

"Must have. They ain't in the atrium. I looked. Very strange goings-on. Then there was the man yesterday."

"What man?"

"Never seen him before, have I? Looked like a banker. She went with him, Vi did. Then come back. Very strange goings-on."

"Yes. It seems strange that they'd rush off like that. Well, thank you very much for your help."

On the way back to London, Ken couldn't erase the uneasiness from his mind that Langton was somehow involved in the women's disappearance. He got off the train at Charing Cross Station and went straight to Scotland Yard. "Mr. Sanderson," Chief Inspector Soames said. "Good news. Gandy's blown his head off."

Ken eyes squinted. "He shot himself?"

Soames laughed. "No. Pardon my slang. He's talked. Confessed to attacking you and has implicated Langton."

"How'd you get him to do that?"

Soames frowned and shook his head. "I'd rather not say, but we have our ways. The bad news is, Langton's decamped. We went to arrest him this morning and he'd bolted."

"Any idea where?"

"His man Jenkins says he's gone off to Scotland. Apparently, he has a shooting lodge there. But not to worry. He'll have to come back sometime, and we'll be waiting to nick him. Jenkins—a crafty fellow who appears to have moved up the ranks—hinted that for a price he'd give us additional information, but I didn't bite."

"I saw Langton two nights ago at the Savoy. He and Miss Karen Gage got into an altercation and he threatened her. I was supposed to see her today, but she and her aunt have disappeared."

"Disappeared?" the policeman said. "Surely, you're over-reacting, Mr. Sanderson. Just because *you* can't find them doesn't mean they have vanished. Do they inform you of their every move?"

"Well, no. You're right. But I've gone to Kensington twice to see Miss Gage. She was expecting me, but neither she nor her aunt were there. And then I keep remembering that ugly scene at the Savoy. Langton seemed capable of anything that night. It's probably just silly of me, but . . . never mind. It's a foolish notion."

"Tell me anyway. As I once told you, Langton *is* capable of anything."

"Well, Miss Gage's neighbor said the two ladies rushed off in a fancy black coach around noon today. Langton has a black coach, and I can't see them going off with him voluntarily."

Soames smiled. "Most coaches in London are black."

Ken smiled back and nodded. "Of course. I did say the idea was foolish."

The policeman wondered if there might be something to the notion. "So you're suggesting Langton might have something to do with their disappearance. I'll tell you what. Why don't you go see Jenkins? Like I said, he appeared to have more information than he divulged. Perhaps if you gave him a few shillings he'd satisfy your mind that Langton went off to Scotland alone."

Ken liked the idea and agreed to follow the chief inspector's suggestion.

Langton's townhouse was in the fashionable part of London, not far from Lady Brideswell's home. A hollow-faced man answered the door. *He has a lean and hungry look,* Ken thought. "Mr. Jenkins?"

"Aye, that's me. If you're after Mr. Langton, he's not here."

"Actually, I want to talk with you. I understand Mr. Langton has gone on a trip. Do you know if he went alone?"

Jenkins drew himself up and appeared affronted. "Here, who do you think you are, coming here and asking such a question? It's none of your business if Mr. Langton went on a journey or whether he was alone. Be off with you."

Ken didn't budge. He took his wallet from the inside pocket of his coat and withdrew a five-pound note. Jenkins's eyes locked onto the money. "Do you think this might make it my business?" Ken asked.

"Put that away," Jenkins said, glancing around furtively. Satisfied that no one had seen the offer, he waved Ken inside. When they were seated in the butler's room with the door securely fastened, Jenkins said, "Now, sir, you was saying?"

"I need to know if Mr. Langton had anyone else in his carriage when he left for Scotland."

Jenkins rubbed his hands together. "And how much is it worth to you?"

Ken again withdrew his wallet. "Five pounds."

"Make it ten and you have a deal."

"Fifty dollars? You must think I'm insane. Five pounds or nothing."

"Seven."

"Five."

Jenkins sighed. "All right. Five." Ken gave him the money. The butler scrutinized the bill, folded it once, and put it in the inside pocket of his coat. "He didn't go alone. There was two ladies with him."

Ken's heart was in his mouth. He slid to the edge of the chair. "Do you know who they were?"

Jenkins shook his head. "I didn't get a good look at 'em, did I? Master Stephen was acting very funny-like, mysterious you might say. All the coach blinds was drawn, and he wouldn't let no one near it, except to put some supplies in the boot."

"Then how do you know there were two women with him?"

Jenkins narrowed his eyes and dropped his voice. "When no one was looking, I climbed up on the boot and peeked in the small back window. It hasn't got a blind."

"What did the women look like?"

"I only saw the one clear, a smallish older lady. She seemed to be asleep. The other woman was heavily veiled. She had on nice clothes."

Panic seized Ken. "How long would it take him to get to the shooting lodge?"

Jenkins's brow creased. "Here! I didn't tell you anything about a shooting lodge. Who are you anyways?"

Ken's voice hardened. "I'm a friend of Chief Inspector Soames. Now, tell me how to get to the lodge and how long it will take."

Despite Ken's hard words, Jenkins could read the desperation in the young American's face. "I've told you what you paid for," he said, a speculative gleam in his eye. "'Course, if you wanted to buy more information . . ."

Ken sighed with frustration. "All right, Jenkins, five more pounds. Now, out with it."

Impatiently, Ken waited for the butler to go through his ritual of inspecting the note, folding it once, and placing it in his inside pocket. Only then did Ken learn that the hunting lodge was on an island in Loch Lomond and that the nearest village was called Luss. He took this information to Chief Inspector Soames.

"From what Jenkins told me, I'm convinced that Langton has—for some unknown reason—kidnapped Miss Gage and her aunt and has them on his island," Ken said. "Will you send someone to arrest him? And may I go along?"

Soames shook his head. "Afraid not, lad. Langton's a wealthy man and could cause us a world of trouble. We must do things by the book. What I will do is wire the local constable a warrant for Langton's arrest on the charge of conspiracy to cause grievous bodily injury and ask him to search the island. Let's see if Luss has a telegraph office." Soames consulted a thick book and shook his head. "Dumbarton's the closest one. I'll wire them and have them get the message to the constable at Luss."

Ken processed this information and quickly came to a decision. "All this could take too long. Who knows what danger the ladies could be in? I'm going there myself."

"Where? Scotland? I wouldn't advise that, son. If Langton caught you on his island, he could shoot you as a trespasser and get away with it scot free, so to speak." The policeman smiled at his little pun.

Ken pursed his lips and shook his head. "I don't care. I've got to go. You said yourself that Langton's capable of anything. If you'd seen his face at the Savoy the other night when he threatened Miss Gage, you'd know why I must go. How do I get to Loch Lomond?"

Soames shook his head at Ken's impetuosity. Nevertheless, he took him over to a wall map of Great Britain. "It's pretty straightforward by steam train," he said, stabbing his finger at the map as he read out the various cities on the route: "London, Birmingham, Manchester; then Glasgow and Dumbarton in Scotland. There's no train from Dumbarton to Luss, so you'd have to get there some other way. From here to Luss you're looking at something around four hundred miles. Are you sure you want to do this? It could be a wild goose chase. You'd be wise to wait. I could wire Dumbarton right away."

Ken ignored Soames's advice. "By all means wire them now," he said. "I'll check in with the constable at Luss when I get there. If Langton has kidnapped them, he'd probably have them hidden away somewhere. It may take some time to find them."

The chief inspector heaved a sigh. "All right, lad, but be careful. If you're caught on that island without authorization, you could end up dead and there's little anyone could do about it." He then added wryly, "I hope you're able to understand the locals up there."

"They speak English in Scotland, don't they?"

"After a fashion," he said with a grin.

"I shouldn't have too much trouble. One of my school-teachers was a Scot. Except for his accent, which took a while getting used to, he spoke impeccable English."

"He must have been a well-educated lowlander. Those who aren't so well educated or who were raised in the Highlands are difficult to understand. Like our Cockneys, they *do* speak English but you'd hardly know it. I've had some experience up there. I go fishing up near Dundee when I can get away. At least you'll find the Scots very hospitable, especially those in the country."

❧ CHAPTER 15 ❦

From Scotland Yard, Ken went directly to his lodgings, packed a few things in a small valise, threw his greatcoat over his arm, and headed for the train station. As luck would have it, he had to wait only twenty minutes for the train to Birmingham and less time than that for the one to Manchester. There, however, he had a two-hour wait before catching the Glasgow train. The waiting was unbearable. His overactive imagination conjured up all sorts of things that could happen to Karen and her aunt on that isolated isle.

A jovial Scot, with freckled face and carrot-colored hair, enlivened the ride from Manchester to Glasgow. "Sandy Hutchison's the name, life insurance my game," he said thrusting out his hand. Ken took it and introduced himself. They were the only two in the compartment. "American, eh? I've always liked the Yanks. Now, my lad, tell me how old you are and if you're married."

Ken's first reaction was to tell the agent that it was none of his business, but Sandy's enthusiasm was infectious. "I'll soon be twenty-five," Ken said, "and I'm single."

"Twenty-five years. Oh, to be twenty-five again! I suppose you think you'll live forever?"

Ken thought about his beliefs and truthfully answered, "I know I will."

This wasn't the answer Sandy expected and it threw him off his pitch for a second. But only for a second. "Well, my lad,

you err. Actuarial charts say different. If you're lucky you'll last
another twenty-five years or so. Think of it, only two and a half
decades! Now during that time you'll marry, have children, and
die. And what happens to your missus and bairns when you're
gone? The poorhouse. Poverty and misery. That's what. But I can
have them living in luxury. For only ten shillings per month, six
pounds per annum, you can die happy, knowing that the
Caledonia Assurance Company will pay your widow the princely
sum of five hundred pounds. Twenty-five hundred American
dollars! Think of it. Are you a religious man, Mr. Sanderson?"

"I would say so."

"Good. Then you'll no doubt agree with the Apostle Paul
when he says, 'But if any provide not for his own, and specially
for those of his own house, he hath denied the faith, and is
worse than an infidel.' First Timothy 5:8. There you have it,
lad. Would you like to pay monthly or annually?"

Ken laughed. "Neither," he said, although as he thought
about the danger he might face in Scotland, he was a little
tempted to sign up. He smiled and recalled the scripture Karen
had read to him at Kew Gardens. "Let me quote you a scripture," he said. "'I will not put my trust in the arm of flesh.'"

Sandy's brow creased in confusion. He was not used to
having prospective clients rebut with their own scriptures. It
disrupted his memorized pitch. "That in the Old Testament?"
he asked.

"Perhaps. It's also in the Book of Mormon. Have you heard
of the Book of Mormon?"

Sandy hesitated. "Aye. I've heard a wee bit."

"Good. It's a long way to Glasgow. Lots of time for me to
tell you more about it and about my church," Ken said, confident that Jonathan's instructions had given him the expertise
he needed to spread the gospel.

Sandy squirmed in his seat. "Perhaps another time, laddie,"
he said quickly. "Right noo I must get some rest. Big day
ahead, don't you know?"

The Scottish salesman curled up on the seat opposite Ken and was soon fast asleep—or appeared to be.

In the early hours of the morning the train pulled into the Glasgow Central Station and stopped with a jolt, waking Ken. The salesman had disappeared. Ken stretched, rubbed his stubbly chin, and pulled his valise down from the netted shelf overhead. He had gotten some fitful sleep during the journey, but it had done him little good. As he stepped down from the train, the size and newness of the station overwhelmed him. Never in all his travels had he seen the like. On the platform he bought two oatcakes from a vendor and washed them down with water from an iron cup chained to a fountain. He then sought out the train to Dumbarton. After a long wait, he was on his way again. At Dumbarton he caught a ride on a mail coach to Loch Lomond. It was almost nine o'clock that morning when he finally arrived at Luss, a pretty village on the banks of the famous lake.

He climbed out of the coach and for a long moment stared with admiration at the magnificent, island-studded loch with Ben Lomond looming in the background. Tearing himself away from the scene, he shook the cobwebs from his sleep-deprived brain and went in search of the local policeman, whom he found at home. The man introduced himself as Constable Jock McTavish.

"I'm sorry to disturb you at home, Constable," Ken said at the door. "But I've traveled all the way from London on important police business."

The constable took only a second to make up his mind about Ken. "Never bother 'boot that, laddie," he said. "Come ben the hoose." Ken did so. "We're just finishin' up br'akfast. Will ye sup wi' us? The wifey'll put out another plate. Y'look like death warmed over."

"Och, aye," Mrs. McTavish said, coming into the hallway from the kitchen and observing Ken with motherly concern. "Sit doon and have a wee bite."

Ken was overwhelmed by their welcome. *Chief Inspector Soames was right,* he thought. *The Scottish are very hospitable.* "Thank you," he said. "I'd like that very much. Would you mind if I cleaned up a bit first?"

Mrs. McTavish showed Ken into a small bedroom, left him there, and soon returned with a basin, jug of warm water, soap, and towel. She placed them on a dressing table and left him again. When Ken was finished washing up, he felt like a new man.

"My, yer a bonnie wee lad when yer scrubbed up," Mrs. McTavish said with a smile.

During the meal of porridge followed by kippers, Ken told his story.

"Aye. I know o' this man Langton," Constable McTavish said. "Keeps t' himsel' when he's up from London. Rich, they say."

"You haven't received a telegram from London about him?" Ken asked.

"Naw, laddie. Those lads in Dumbarton are a slow lot. We'll just have t' bide our time."

"Thank you so much, Mrs. McTavish," Ken said after the meal. "I can't remember when I've had more welcome food. I surely needed it."

Mrs. McTavish smiled. "Dinna mention it. You and Jock should gae away doon tae the polis station t' check for the wire."

"Aye," the constable said. "Let's away doon."

"Would it be all right for me to leave my greatcoat and things here?" Ken asked.

"Of carse. Now you boys be on yer way," Mrs. McTavish responded.

The police station was down near the jetty and had a good view of the islands. There was still no word from Dumbarton.

Ken gazed out the back window of the station. "Can we see Langton's island from here?" he asked.

"Naw laddie," Constable McTavish said, pointing. "It's t' the south o' those two, Inchtavannach and Inchconnachan. Ye hafta go atween them t' get t' Inchmoan, Langton's island."

"I take it 'inch' means island?"

"Aye, lad. The passage atween the islands is called The Narrows."

"How will we get to Inchmoan?"

"Old Georgie Graham's got boats for hire down at the jetty. For a few bob he'll tak' us. As soon as we get the wire, we'll be awa' over. It wouldn't do t' go there wi'oot authorization." The constable glanced up at the clock on the wall. "Time for me t' make m'rounds. You wait here for the wire. I'll be back in no time."

After the policeman had gone, Ken stared out the window at the lake and islands and wondered if Karen and her aunt were really there. From his vantage point, the distance from the shore to the two islands Constable McTavish had mentioned didn't seem very far. After what seemed like an eternity, he glanced up at the clock. *Only twenty minutes.* Another ten minutes ticked slowly by. Ken heaved a sigh. "I'm sorry, Mr. McTavish," he finally said out loud to the empty room, "but I can't wait for you or the wire."

At the jetty Ken introduced himself to the boatman, Mr. Graham, and asked about getting to the island.

"Ye'r no' goin' over wi' McTavish?" the boatman asked, surprised. "He was jist here. Hired the big boat when it gets back."

"Gets back?"

"Aye. Some lads from Glasgie have it oot fishin'. It'll be back in a wee while."

"I'm in rather a hurry," Ken said. "Do you have another boat? I can row it myself."

"Aye, I've got a wee one." The boatman looked up at the sky. "Will ye be back afore lang? Rain and mist's a comin'. I wouldna want ye t'get clagged in."

A few scattered, gray-tinged clouds drifted across the blue sky, but Ken could see nothing to indicate a severe change in the weather. "Are you sure the weather's going to change? It looks fairly clear."

The boatman nodded sagely, took a long draw on his pipe and exhaled the smoke. "They say aroon here, if ye can see Ben Lomond, it's gonna rain. If ye canna see it, it is raining."

Ken smiled. "Yes, I plan to be back before long."

The boatman regarded Ken suspiciously. "D'ye ken hoo t'row, laddie?

"I've rowed before," Ken said, thinking of his one time on the River Barle.

"Awricht, then. But have a care wi' m'boat. 'Tis a tight wee craft. Built it m'sel'.'" He pointed at the two islands Constable McTavish had mentioned. "Atween those isles is The Narrows. Stay in the middle o' the channel where 'tis deep. Once yer through the channel, ye'll see Inchmoan, Mr. Langton's isle, t' the left. Ye canna miss it. When ye get close ye'll see the lodge. Mr. Langton's steam launch should be tied up t' the jetty. Bonniest boat ye'll ever see. The wee isle ye'll see on yer richt as ye come oot o' The Narrows is Inchgalbraith. It has an awld castle on it."

Ken thanked the old man and clambered into the rowboat. He tried to look like he knew what he was doing. As he zigzagged away from the jetty, Mr. Graham looked on with furrowed brow. Shaking his gray head, he called out, "Are ye sure ye dinna wan' t'wait for McTavish, lad?"

"No thanks, Mr. Graham. I'm getting the hang of it now." Just as Ken was saying this a mis-stroke sent water splashing into the boat.

The boatman took his pipe out of his mouth and again shook his head. "There's a bailin' pan 'neath the backseat," he yelled in a tone suggesting that Ken would need it.

"I see it, Mr. Graham. Thanks."

The journey to the island took longer than Ken had imagined. It was a full hour before he reached the channel between the islands and another hour before he cleared The Narrows and came in sight of the shooting lodge on Inchmoan. Except for a lot of unnecessary zigzagging, the only real trouble he had was when he entered the channel and rowed too close to the right shore, scraping the bottom of the boat on an underwater shelf of rock. Taking an oar out of the oarlock, he'd used it to push away from the obstacle, and from then on he managed to follow the boatman's advice to keep to the deep water in the center of the channel.

Mr. Graham was right about Langton's steam-powered launch. All lacquered oak and shiny brass, it was a joy to behold as it rocked gently beside the jetty. Ken tied the rowboat on the opposite side of the jetty and clambered out of it. With Soames's caution in mind that he could be shot as a trespasser, he carefully surveyed the area before moving toward the timbered lodge. He got all the way to the building without meeting anyone.

With some trepidation, he knocked on the heavy, metal-studded plank door. A smallish lady answered and stared at Ken, who knew immediately that he had made a huge mistake.

"Who is it, Marian?" asked a cultured voice from behind the woman at the door.

When Ken saw the owner of the voice, his jaw dropped and his eyes expanded in astonishment. "You . . . you're the actress Nell Keene," he stammered.

"Lady Darnley to you," the woman called Marian said.

With a motion of her well-shaped hand, the actress waved away the other woman's correction. Her lips parted in a beautiful smile. "I already know who I am," she said playfully. "The question is, who are you?"

"I'm . . . I'm Kenny Sanderson from America," he said.

The actress placed her hand on her heart. "All the way from America to visit me? I'm truly touched. Come in, Mr. Kenny Sanderson from America. This is my maid, Marian Treadwell."

"Maid Marian?" Ken said with raised eyebrows.

Nell Keene wagged a finger at him. "Say no more, Mr. Sanderson. The poor woman's teased enough about it."

The maid went off to her duties while the celebrated actress invited Ken to sit on a leather sofa in front of a huge stone fireplace, above which a mounted stag's head stared down with glassy eyes. Red coals glowed cheerily in the grate. The actress sat opposite him on an identical sofa and fingered the large, shiny pin on the side of her tartan skirt.

"Now, Mr. Sanderson," she said, "please tell me why you've come all this way. I'm sure it was not to see me."

Ken related all that had happened since his first confrontation with Langton at Gage Hall. As she listened the actress's mood changed from playful to somber. "That certainly explains Mr. Langton's deceitful behavior," she said when Ken had finished. "Had I known he was such a person, Marian and I would never have come here with him. As for you, you must care very much for Miss Gage to come all this way to rescue her."

"I do," Ken said. "Of course, I should have followed Inspector Soames's advice and done a little more checking. My mother said my impetuosity would get the better of me someday. But there was so much mystery surrounding your journey, I convinced myself that Langton had actually kidnapped Miss Gage and her aunt."

The actress smiled and studied Ken for a moment before saying, "I think I'll take a chance on you, Mr. Sanderson. You've an honest face, and I'm glad you've come. I think you can be of great service to Marian and me. The reason for the secrecy surrounding my journey is that I'm a married woman. My husband, Lord Darnley, doesn't know I'm here. He's an old man and gives me much freedom to come and go as I please. However, he would not countenance my running off with Stephen Langton to Scotland. If I'd known what Mr. Langton was really like and if I'd known there were no other guests, I of course would never have done so."

"You agreed to come here without really knowing him?" Ken asked, surprise in his voice.

"You're not the only impetuous one in the room," she said with a self-deprecating smile. "I've known Mr. Langton socially for many months. Often he would boast of the beauties of his Loch Lomond shooting lodge. He persistently invited me to see for myself. Bored with the London social scene, I finally gave in to his importunities when he told me that he'd invited several people to Loch Lomond for the shooting. I agreed to go on three conditions: that it would be handled discreetly, that Marian would accompany me, and that Mr. Langton would not try . . . well, you know."

"And how did Langton deceive you?" Ken asked.

The actress dropped her eyes briefly and then in an embarrassed voice said, "First, we arrived here to find that there were no other guests. Not only that, but he claimed that the caretaker had rushed off to Edinburgh to visit an ailing daughter. Thus, there is no one on the island but us. On top of all that, this morning early he came into my bedchamber. When I commanded him to leave, he became very abusive, calling me all sorts of foul names. Because I began my career in the theatre as an orange seller, he supposed that I was a woman of low morals." She paused for a moment and smiled sardonically. "Coming to this remote place with him, of course, lent credence to that belief. Anyway, we had an awful row. I demanded that he take Marian and me back to London. He refused and hasn't spoken to either of us since. An hour or so ago he grabbed his shotgun off the wall. He was so angry, I honestly thought he might use it on me. But rather, he flung himself out of the room, slamming the door after him. I was hoping that after venting his anger on a few innocent fowl, he'd return in a more reasonable frame of mind. Perhaps I was mistaken."

"I think you were. Chief Inspector Soames said that in a rage Langton murdered a man and got away with it."

A gasp exploded from her lips and her hand went to her mouth. "That settles it. We must get away from here. How big is your boat? Would it have space for all three of us plus a large portmanteau?"

Ken pursed his lips. "Perhaps, but it would be a tight squeeze—"

Suddenly the front door flew open and Langton burst into the room, a shotgun over his arm, breach open. Ken leapt to his feet.

Immediately recognizing Ken, Langton snapped the breach closed and pointed the gun at him. "Sanderson," he bellowed, "how dare you set foot on my island and enter my lodge! I ought to shoot you down where you stand."

"I invited him in," the actress said bravely. "You'll have to shoot me too."

Langton glared at her and then turned his attention back to Ken.

Realizing that there was no way he could adequately explain his presence on the island, Ken went on the offensive. "I'm taking Lady Darnley and her maid back to London," he said.

"Over my dead body," Langton answered.

"Don't try to stop us," Ken said. "You're already in a world of trouble. Gandy has informed on you."

Langton sneered. "No one would take Gandy's word over mine."

"Ah, so you admit to knowing him," Ken said. Langton ignored the insinuation and Ken pressed further. "I'm prepared to testify that Gandy's the one who assaulted me, and Gandy's already testified that you're the one who paid him to do it. You've made a powerful enemy in Chief Inspector Soames in the past, Langton. He won't rest until you're behind bars. Refusing to let these women go will only add kidnapping to the charges against you. Furthermore, Chief Inspector Soames knows that I'm here. If anything happens to me or these ladies, you won't get away with it, no matter how much money you have."

Ken's words hit home. Langton glanced around like a trapped animal. Then his eyes narrowed and it appeared that he had come to a decision. Locking eyes with Nell Keene, he said, "All right, you and your maid may go, but *I'll* take you to Luss. Then you're on your own and good riddance." He headed for the door. "It'll take twenty minutes to get up steam," he said over his shoulder. "Don't keep me waiting."

⚓ CHAPTER 16 ⚓

Mr. Graham was right. The sky had already begun to cloud over, and mist clung to the islands when Ken helped the maid carry the actress's large traveling bag down to the jetty. Lady Darnley followed with a hooded cloak over her arm and a large purse dangling from her hand. Langton, an oily cloth in his hand, fussed with the controls of his fashionable launch as Ken and the maid maneuvered the traveling bag up the ramp and into the boat. Ken turned to help the actress onto the boat, but she had moved to the other side of the jetty and was inspecting the hired rowboat.

"Get out of my launch, Sanderson," Langton bellowed, "and you, Nell, get in before I change my mind."

The actress ignored Langton and addressed Ken, who had climbed back onto the jetty. "I've decided to go in your boat, Mr. Sanderson," she said.

Ken hesitated and glanced at Langton, who suddenly looked worried. The latter left off wiping his hands on the rag and stared at the actress. "Absolutely not!" he roared. "You're going with me in the launch."

Marian Treadwell glanced at Langton and shook her head as much as to say that he was using the wrong tactic if he wanted her employer to board the launch.

The maid was right. Nell Keene drew herself up and said firmly, "Well, that settles it. I'm going with you, Mr. Sanderson."

Seeing her determination, Langton moderated his words. "You can't go with him, Nell. I'm responsible for your safety and I don't trust small boats on the loch, especially with the weather changing. You could get caught in a squall or fogged in before you reach Luss. Stop this foolishness and get into the launch."

The actress tossed her head dramatically. "I'll take my chances," she said.

Although flattered that this beautiful woman wanted to accompany him, Ken's conscience told him that she should go with Langton, both for her own safety and for the sake of propriety. After all, she was a married woman and Ken a single man. "Perhaps you should go with him, Lady Darnley," he suggested weakly. "I'm really not a very good boatman and the fog is rolling in."

She smiled. "All the more reason I should go with you, Mr. Sanderson. I trust you, and I have no fear of small boats. I'm going with you and that's all there is to it."

Suddenly the decision was out of Ken's hands. Langton threw down the rag he was holding and pointed at Marian, who stood by the portmanteau, wide-eyed, silently taking in the altercation. "You're my witness," he said to the maid. "I tried to get your mistress to go with me, but she refused. I wash my hands of her. It's on her own head if she finds trouble." The maid was speechless as Langton turned to Ken. "Sanderson, cast off that line." Ken didn't know what to do. He resented being pushed into a situation not to his liking. "Cast off the line," Langton repeated with more volume. Ken shrugged and complied. Thrusting a lever forward, Langton backed the sleek vessel into the bay.

"Go to the inn, Marian," the actress called to her maid. "I'll be there directly."

Marian Treadwell waved a reply as the launch made a wide turn and chugged toward the channel between the islands.

"What was all that about?" Ken asked. "Langton insisting that you go with him, I mean?"

She shook her head. "I have no idea. But I don't think it was because he craved my company. Knowing what I do now about his duplicity, I wouldn't be surprised if he were up to something." Having said that, she nonetheless dismissed the topic with a wave of her hand and asked, "May I row?" Ken's brow creased with surprise. "Please," she added. "I wasn't always a pampered lady."

Ken shrugged. "If you insist. You couldn't be any worse than me."

She slipped into her hooded cloak, climbed into the rowboat, deposited her handbag on the bow seat, and took her place in the middle beside the oarlocks. Ken sat astern facing her. Taking up the oars with authority, she skillfully maneuvered away from the jetty and with swift, sure strokes drove the boat across the dark water. Ken stared at Nell with astonished admiration.

She answered his unspoken question. "Before he drank himself to death, my da made a precarious living scavenging on the Thames in a rowboat. When I was old enough, I worked the oars."

"I can't believe how easy you make it look," Ken said. "At this rate we'll be at Luss in no time."

She thanked him with a smile, and for several minutes they traveled in silence.

"Your father's profession does sound rather . . . rather precarious," Ken said after a few minutes. "What kind of things did you find?"

"Oh, lots of interesting stuff, mostly fallen off ships. Once we found a large waterproof box of tea. Da got good money for it. The times I hated most were when we came across a corpse."

Ken screwed up his face. "I don't blame you. Did your father actually pull them into the boat?"

"No, thank goodness. He'd put a line around them and drag them to shore."

"Why?"

She smiled at Ken's curiosity. "Sometimes there was a reward on them and sometimes they had money in their pockets." She paused for a moment. "As you can imagine, I was eager to get away from such work and was overjoyed to get on at the theatre, even if it was just selling oranges."

Before they were halfway to The Narrows, the clouds began to spit rain, and patches of fog somewhat obscured the islands on either side of the passage. Nell regarded Ken's worried look. "Relax," she said. "Once we're through the channel it's clear sailing to Luss."

Ken did relax, but only for a moment. He had been so fascinated with her rowing and so concerned about the weather, he hadn't noticed the water pooling at his feet. Now he felt the cold through his boots and glanced down. "Oh, no," he said, "we've sprung a leak. Except for the water I splashed in with the oars, it was dry on the way over."

With Ken sitting at the rear, the boat was stern-heavy and the water had not yet reached the actress's fashionable shoes. "You'd better start bailing," she said with only a trace of concern.

Ken felt under the seat for the bailer. "It's gone! The bailer's gone, and the water's rising fast."

As she tucked her feet up under her, she said, "I know. It's beginning to slosh around me now. You'd better bail with your hands." Despite his frantic bailing, the water continued to rise. "We'll not make it to Luss," she said, studiously keeping the panic out of her voice. "I'm afraid I'll have to beach it—if we can find a beach."

The water in the boat continued to rise, slowing the vessel as the actress desperately sculled it toward the channel. Soon the islands disappeared in the gathering fog and they were traveling blind. "Don't worry," she said loud enough to be heard above Ken's noisy bailing. "I've been in worse fogs on the Thames. We'll be in the channel soon. Keep bailing and keep your eyes peeled for a good landing place."

Ken said a silent prayer and kept bailing. He wondered if she could swim and whether either of them could keep afloat in sodden clothes. *How long would we last in this icy water? And where could we swim to now that the fog's blotted out the islands?*

"We're in the channel," she said, interrupting his thoughts.

He could see nothing but fog and wondered how she knew. But he was too busy bailing to ask. Suddenly a window in the fog opened and he saw what appeared to be land. "To the left," he yelled. "I think it's a beach."

She turned to look. "I think you're right," she said triumphantly.

With all her strength, she pulled on the oars, driving the boat onto the shingled shore. Ken leapt into the shallow water and pulled the craft farther onto the beach. Then he held up his hands to her. Clinging to her cloak and handbag, she climbed into his arms and he deposited her on dry land. "Thank you, Mr. Sanderson," she said with a smile. "I'm hardly wet at all."

"Thank *you*," he said. "If you hadn't insisted on coming along, I'd be fish food by now."

She smiled mischievously. "All part of my master plan to get you alone on this deserted island."

He shook his head and could feel his face redden. Putting out his hand, palm up, he felt the increasing raindrops. "Please find some shelter," he said, "and I'll see if I can patch up the boat."

She saluted. "Aye, aye, sir," she said with a grin and headed for the mist-shrouded trees paralleling the shore.

He had no sooner begun to examine the boat than her terrified shriek sent him dashing to her side. Doubled over, her hand on her heart, she took a huge breath and straightened up. "I'm sorry," she said sheepishly. "I must have scared the wits out of you." She pointed to a huge fir tree. "I leaned over to look under those branches and three deer jumped out—a doe and two fawns. Just about scared me to death."

He smiled. "No harm done. Let me have a look." Bending down, he examined the nook under the spreading lower branches of the tree, then crawled under. "At least you've found shelter," he said. "This is great. It's dry and the ground's soft from the needles. It's even still warm where the deer were lying. You've done very well."

"Thanks," she said as she joined him under the needled canopy and sat a respectable distance apart from him. She pulled her cloak around her. "I should be fine, but you have no greatcoat."

"Don't worry about me. I'd better get back to the boat and see if I can fix it."

"It's raining harder. Leave the boat until it lets up."

He hesitated and then said with a smile, "Okay, I'll stay with you for a while in case you're attacked again by ferocious fawns."

Her pretty face formed a mock frown. "That's not fair, Mr. Sanderson—do you mind if I call you by your Christian name?"

"No. It's Ken, short for Kenny."

"Mine's Eleanor, but you can call me Nell. As I was saying, you are unfair to tease me about the deer. I'm sure you would have screamed too, if they'd leapt out at you."

"I'm sure you're right."

She glanced around their evergreen haven. "This is fun. It reminds me of when I was a child and we'd make shelters and pretend we were lost on a desert island. I'm very comfortable. I've sheltered in much worse places growing up poor. Will you be all right? Your feet and legs are soaked. They must be awfully cold."

Ken pulled his jacket tight around him and leaned against the bole of the tree. "Don't worry about me. I'll brazen it out. I'm suddenly exhausted. Except for a little on the train, I've hardly slept in two days."

For a few minutes neither of them spoke. Except for the soft patter of raindrops on the boughs and the gentle lapping of the water against the shore, all was silent on the fog-bound island. Ken used the time to say a silent prayer, thanking his Heavenly Father for sparing them a watery grave. A huge sigh from Nell prompted his response.

"You okay?" he asked.

"I'm fine—very comfortable, actually. I was just thinking about the poor mother deer and her two babies. I drove them out of their snug little house into the cold rain. I'm sure I scared them as much as they scared me."

What a tender heart she has, Ken thought. A poem he'd memorized as a child came into his head and, affecting his best Scottish brogue, he impulsively quoted the first two lines aloud: "Wee, sleekit, cowrin', tim'rous beastie, O, what a panic's in thy breastie!"

"Are you talking about me or the deer?"

"Both," he said with a chuckle. "Those are the first couple of lines of a Robbie Burns poem, 'To A Mouse.' One of my schoolmasters steeped us in Scottish poems. Burns wrote the poem after having had an experience similar to yours when he was plowing, only it was a mouse, not a deer, that he drove out of its home into the cold."

"I've heard of it. Isn't that the one that has the line, 'The best laid plans of mice and men . . .'?"

Ken nodded. ". . . 'gang aft agley.' My plan of rescuing Miss Gage has certainly gone *agley.*"

"Maybe if you win Saladin's ring, you'll be able to rescue her financially. You mentioned at the lodge she was in dire straits."

"Actually, my parents don't want any money from the ring. If we do win the case, the money will go to charity. However, I did promise to see about paying Miss Gage's legal bills." He sighed. "Perhaps the ring will never be recovered and Miss Gage will lose her home."

Nell didn't comment and was lost in thought for a while. He turned to look at her in the murky light. She had averted her head. A suppressed sniffle told him that she was crying.

After a long pause, she said with heavy voice, "One's best laid plans often do go *agley*."

Ken didn't know how to respond and for a long time neither of them spoke.

"Thanks again for saving my life," he finally said in a low voice.

"Don't mention it, Ken. Tell me something. Do you believe in fate?"

"I believe in God."

"Do you think He intervenes in our lives?"

He thought for a moment. "I believe He does, but only for our ultimate good. What I mean is, He knows what's best for us in an eternal sense, so sometimes we think He isn't answering our prayers but He actually is." Neither of them spoke for a moment. Then he added, "I have a question for you. What made you decide to come with me rather than go with Langton?"

She shrugged. "I'm not really sure. Perhaps I wanted to show off my rowing ability to someone who I thought would appreciate it. Of course, when Langton forbade me to go with you, I got my back up. I can be stubborn. Why do you ask?"

Ken didn't answer right away. "It may seem strange to you, but perhaps God prompted you to go with me."

"God? That does sound strange. I'm sure God has better things to do. Do you really think He gets that involved in our lives?"

"Actually, I do. Before I left home for England, my father gave me a blessing, you know, like the patriarchs in the Old Testament blessed their children. He promised that God would protect me and bring me safely home. So you see, you could well have been the instrument in God's hands to realize that blessing."

Nell wasn't convinced. "Oh, you probably could have swum ashore if the boat had gone down."

"What shore? I couldn't see anything in the fog. No. You saved my life and that's all there is to it."

"It's strange talking with you about such things," Nell said after a moment's silence. "Except for my mother, I haven't discussed God or fate with anyone for a long time. She's a religious person. She grew up Chapel, of course—"

"Chapel?"

He could hear the smile in her voice. "People of the established church, the Church of England, are called 'Church.' Dissenters, like my mother and grandparents, are called 'Chapel.' My mother was a Wesleyan."

"I see," he said. "I believe Miss Gage is 'Church'."

"Most likely. Upper-class people usually are. And you are?"

"A Mormon."

"Oh," she said evenly. "I'm afraid I know very little about your church."

He looked at her with surprise. "You don't read the newspapers?"

"As a matter of fact, I don't. All they have is bad news. Of course, I've inadvertently overheard some bad things about the Mormons, but I simply refuse to believe gossip. I prefer to accept people on face value. Of course, as in the case of Stephen Langton, it sometimes gets me in trouble, but all in all I prefer my way to being overly suspicious of everyone."

Ken smiled. "That's a refreshing attitude. I'm sorry, I interrupted you. What were you saying about your mother?"

"Oh, I was just saying that she's the only one I talk to about religion. I was going to ask you how God decides when to get involved in our lives and when not to."

Ken pondered the question. "I don't really know, but I'm sure it has a lot to do with what He wants us to accomplish on this earth."

"You mean we're supposed to accomplish something? We're not just here on earth to muddle through until death catches up with us?"

Ken shook his head. "I don't believe so. That's why faith is so important. Often life doesn't make much sense. Burns is right that the best laid schemes of mice and men do often go awry. Although I'm no theologian, I truly believe that we're here for a purpose and that we'll find and fulfill that purpose if we stay close to God."

"But what is that purpose?"

"I guess we all have somewhat different goals to reach, but generally speaking, I believe God has sent us to earth to gain experience and learn faith and obedience. We'll be judged according to how well we did—how well we did according to what we were given."

"I wonder how I'll be judged?" she said tentatively and then changed the subject. "Are you warm enough? Your feet are awfully wet." She dug into her handbag. "Take off your stockings and boots and wrap your feet in this. I brought it because I knew Scotland's weather is rather changeable." She handed him a scarf.

"This is mohair," he said, fingering the softness. "You don't want me to foul it with my feet."

She laughed. "Don't worry. I have dozens more. My husband is a very wealthy and generous man."

After he had done what she suggested, she asked, "Is that better?"

"Much better. Now I'm warm all over. For some reason when I discuss religion it warms my blood. But I am very tired. As I mentioned, I haven't slept much in the last two days."

"Feel free to have a nap. I'll wake you when the rain stops."

"Thanks, Nell. Maybe I will."

The cadence of water lapping on the shore finally lulled him to sleep and to dream. He was back in Utah in the fragrant English garden his father had laid out for his mother to help her adjust to the arid West. In his dream he was about six years old. With the aroma of many flowers—marigolds, snapdragons, heartsease, violas, feverfew, camellias, irises, roses, clematis—filling his nostrils and the sun's warm rays on his face, he soberly went about the task of catching bumblebees in a jam jar.

❦ C H A P T E R   1 7 ❦

Suddenly Ken's eyes opened to the sun's rays filtering through the needled boughs. An intoxicating floral scent filled his nostrils and warmth blanketed him. He wondered if he were still dreaming. Sitting up, he realized that the warmth and scent came from Nell's cloak, which now covered him. He looked over to where she had been sitting—she was not there. Crawling out from under the fir boughs, he stood up and stared, transfixed at the sun-drenched beauty of the misty islands and patches of bright water. To his surprise the boat was bobbing gently in the water. Nell, like some enchanted princess, was sitting on a log combing her long, ebony hair. A vague guiltiness spread through him as he gazed on the exquisite picture before him. Seeing him, she smiled and waved.

Quickly putting on his stockings and boots, which Nell had laid out to dry in the sun, he soon joined her. "Thanks for covering me with your cloak. It was very kind of you."

She smiled and with nimble fingers did up her hair and fastened it with tortoiseshell combs. "You were shivering and I took pity on you," she said. "You must really have been tired. The sun's been out for some time, but I decided not to wake you. It was strange sitting here watching the world appear. As the sun began to burn off the mist and the sky lightened, shrubs, trees, and rocks began to appear. It was marvelous—oh, by the way, I bailed out the boat and found the hole. I'm sure

Langton made it. I plugged it with a piece of stick hammered in with a rock."

He stared at her with admiration. "You really are a very enterprising woman."

A hint of rose colored her cheeks. "When one grows up poor, one needs to be enterprising."

Ken didn't know what it was like to grow up poor, but he nodded his agreement. "Let's take a look at your handiwork," he said.

After pulling the boat up, stern first, onto the beach, they inspected the inch-wide hole somewhat concealed at the bottom of an overlapping plank in the stern. "It's just above the waterline," Ken said. "When we got in at the jetty, our weight drove it below and the water rushed in. I'll bet Langton bored it when he was waiting for the steam to get up in the launch. He must have taken the bailer, too. I guess we can add attempted murder to his other crimes."

Nell touched her lips with her fingers and nodded thoughtfully. "So that's why he insisted I go with him. He knew I couldn't swim. I mentioned it on our way over in his launch when I first got here."

Ken leaned against the boat and nodded. "Your decision to go with me upset his murderous scheme."

Nell shuddered. "I can hardly think that he'd attempt to kill you. But I guess your testimony could send him to prison." She took a deep breath and added thoughtfully, "I've got to be more careful with whom I associate."

He took one more look at the plugged hole. "You did a great repair job. It should keep the water out till we get back to Luss. I'm afraid Mr. Graham will not be pleased with my stewardship of his 'tight wee craft.' I suppose we should be on our way."

Nell slowly surveyed the area and sighed. "I suppose so, but now that the sun is out I hate to leave this pretty place. In spite of everything, I'll always remember our Loch Lomond adventure."

He helped her aboard and she took the seat in the stern. He looked at her quizzically. "You're not rowing?"

She shook her head and smiled. "It's time you learned. You row; I'll instruct."

"Fair enough," he said as he pushed the boat fully into the water, turned it around, and climbed in. Taking up the sculls, he clumsily maneuvered the boat into the deeper water of The Narrows. As Nell looked back wistfully at the large fir tree, Ken wondered what she was thinking. She then turned around and looked down the channel. "How wonderful," she said, pointing to a ruined castle seemingly floating in the air. "It looks like a fairy castle floating on a fluffy, white cloud."

"I think that's Inchgalbraith," Ken said. "Langton's island is called Inchmoan. But you probably know that. The islands on either side of us have unpronounceable names. Loch Lomond surely is a mystical place. No wonder there are so many poems and songs about it."

Nell nodded her agreement, and turned to look at him. Impulsively, in a sweet, stage-trained voice she sang,

By yon bonnie banks,
And by yon bonnie braes,
Where the sun shines bright on Loch Lomon',
Where me and my true love were ever wont tae gae,
On the bonnie, bonnie banks of Loch Lomon'—

Ken shipped the oars and listened, enraptured. Her song ended abruptly. "Please don't stop," he said. "It's lovely."

She turned away her face, but not before he saw the moisture in her eyes. Surreptitiously, she dabbed it away. After a while she turned back, chagrin on her face. "I'm not always the shallow flirt," she said softly.

Ken wondered if her response to the sentiments in the song was linked to the emotion she had shown when he had quoted from Burns's poem, but he decided not to ask her. If she wanted to share her feelings, she would do so when the time was right.

Except for Nell's occasional word of instruction, neither of them spoke for many minutes. "I think I'm getting the hang of this rowing," Ken finally said.

"You're doing brilliantly. Of course, you have an excellent—It's Langton!" she cried, staring wide-eyed over Ken's right shoulder. "He's going to ram us."

Ken turned to see a launch darting toward them out of a patch of mist a few hundred yards away. With his new skills he tried to maneuver the boat out of the way of the oncoming launch. But his effort proved unnecessary. Constable McTavish waved as he slowed the engine of the sleek launch and pulled up alongside the rowboat.

Ken heaved a sigh of relief as he held tight to the oars while the small boat rocked in the waves created by the larger vessel.

"Y'all richt?" Constable McTavish called, looking down over the launch's gunwale.

"We are now," Ken said. "We thought you were Langton coming to finish us off. He's already tried to drown us."

"Sorry. I came up a wee bit fast," the constable said. "Not used t' the controls. Throw me the line an' I'll tow you in."

Ken and Nell hardly spoke on the ride back to the village, preferring to drink in the beauties of Loch Lomond in silence. At the Luss jetty, they related their adventure to the constable and the boatman. While Nell looked on, the three men hauled the boat onto dry land. With an ancient penknife, Mr. Graham pried out the plug and inspected the hole. "Made a wee while ago," he said. "Wi' a dirk, no doot. Mr. Langton did this, ye say?"

"Who else?" Ken said. "There was no one else on the island."

Mr. Graham nodded. Taking his pipe out of his mouth he glanced admiringly at Nell. "Mr. Sanderson's lucky t've had ye along, lassie. The loch's over six hundred feet deep in places."

"By the way," Ken said to Mr. McTavish, "where's Langton? We didn't hear his launch return to the lodge."

"In the lockup at Dumbarton," the constable said with a satisfied smile. "The lads from Dumbarton brung the wire from London, and the three o' us nicked your man as soon as he landed." Turning to Nell, he added, "Your maid and bag're safe at the inn."

"Thank you, Constable," Nell said.

That night Ken stayed with the McTavishes, and Nell and Marian lodged at the inn. The next morning, Ken woke up to the sound of voices from somewhere in the cottage. He immediately recognized Nell's voice. He was soon up and dressed.

"Ah, there you are, Mr. Sanderson," the constable said. "Miss Keene and Miss Treadwell are here t' sup wi' us. Got them early. Nobody puts on sich a grand br'akfast as the wifey."

Mrs. McTavish blushed and motioned Ken to a seat at the table. The meal started with oatmeal. The constable rolled his eyes and a small explosion of rolling *r*'s issued from his mouth as he good-naturedly chided Ken about ruining his porridge with brown sugar and cream. After the oatmeal came kippers, fried eggs, and black pudding. Nell knowingly avoided the latter but Ken had a slice.

"Do you know what that's made of?" Nell whispered after Ken had sampled the pudding. He shook his head. "Mostly pig's blood and suet."

Ken screwed up his nose and winced. Oatcakes with lots of butter and jam helped clean his palate of the taste of suet and pig's blood.

"I couldn't eat another thing," he said as Mrs. McTavish urged more of everything on him.

"And you, luv?" she asked Nell. "You've supped like a wee birdie."

"No, thank you, Mrs. McTavish. But it was all so delicious."

"Well, if yer sure," Mrs. McTavish said. "I'll redd-up now."

"I'll help," Miss Treadwell said, rising.

"Will you be wantin' t' go back to London right away, or will you have a wee holiday whilst you're here?" the constable asked Ken and Nell.

Ken answered for himself. "I must get back immediately. There's a certain person I have to do some explaining to."

Nell looked at Mrs. McTavish and sighed. "I'd love to stay for a while. It's so lovely here. That's the one thing Langton didn't lie about. But I must return too. I'm starting a new play soon. How Marian and I are going to get back to London, I don't know."

Constable McTavish chuckled. "Well, I commandeered Langton's launch in the name o' the law. I canna see the harm in commandeering his coach to tak' you hame. He'll no' be needin' it for a wee while. His drivers are o'er t' the Highland Inn. I'll go wi' you an' order them t' tak' you hame."

"Thank you very much, Mrs. McTavish," Nell said at parting. "You've been very hospitable."

"Come again, luv," the policeman's wife said. "As they say in these parts, 'lang may yer lum reek.'"

"Long may your chimney smoke," the constable said in answer to Ken's unspoken question. "In other words, long life."

❧ CHAPTER 18 ❧

The luxurious, well-sprung coach headed south carrying Ken, Nell, and Miss Treadwell. The latter soon fell asleep. Nell placed a lap blanket on the older woman and adjusted her pillow. She smiled with chagrin, almost embarrassed to be so solicitous of her servant. "The poor dear's hardly had any sleep at the lodge," Nell said. "She claimed she couldn't sleep at the lake because of all the quiet."

To Ken, Nell's action was another evidence of her basic goodness. He leaned back in his seat, a satisfied grin spreading over his face.

"What are you thinking?" Nell asked from her seat across from him. "You look like the Cheshire Cat."

His smile broadened. "I was just thinking about what happened a week ago."

He told her about being drenched with muddy water from the wheels of Langton's coach as he watched Karen and Maggie riding off, leaving him in ditch water up to his ankles.

Nell laughed. "You must have been a sight."

"I'm sure I was. But now I'm riding in the coach and Langton's cooling his heels in jail. How ironic."

"'He laughs best, who laughs last,'" she quoted.

"He who laughs last," Ken added with a grin, "didn't get the joke!"

Nell smiled and then grew serious. She studied him for a long moment.

"What?" he asked.

"Sorry for staring," she said. "It's just that you're different from most men of my acquaintance. I'm trying to figure you out."

"I'm not sure if that's a compliment or a criticism."

"Oh, it's a compliment," she said, nodding approvingly. "Most men of my acquaintance would have tried to take advantage of the situation on the island—our close quarters under the tree, I mean. What makes you different?" Ken shrugged and lowered his head modestly as if to say he was no different from other men. "But I insist you are different."

Ken thought for a moment before saying, "Well, if I am different, perhaps it's the way I was raised—the beliefs my parents instilled in me. Joseph Smith, the founder of our church, summarized those beliefs in thirteen articles. The thirteenth reads in part, 'We believe in being honest, true, chaste, benevolent, virtuous, and in doing good to all men'—and, of course, to all women."

Nell's eyes expanded and she nodded. "If we all believed and lived those principles, what a wonderful world it would be. Unfortunately, many people just give lip service to such."

He nodded. "Yes. Hypocrisy abounds. There's a tendency in society to think of words such as *virtuous* and *chaste* as feminine, but my church teaches me that they apply equally to men and women." He smiled sheepishly. "Do I sound like I'm preaching? I'm probably coming across as some sort of prude."

She shook her head. "You're not. I asked, and you've given me an honest answer. I think it's wonderful that you believe so. I can assure you, after my experience with Stephen Langton, I wouldn't have gone on the boat alone with you had I not felt that you were a good man."

"Thank you. I hope Miss Karen Gage thinks so. As I mentioned, she forgave me once and I let her down again. She's probably down in Somerset wondering where I've gotten to." He thought fondly of Karen and smiled.

"Now what are you smiling about?" Nell asked.

"Oh, I was just thinking about the first time we saw you. It was at the Theatre Royal when you were in *The Rightful Heir.* Miss Gage remarked on your beauty and asked if I agreed. I tried to ignore the question, but she wouldn't let me off the hook."

"And?" Nell asked.

He grinned. "I told her I hadn't noticed."

Nell threw her handbag at him. He caught it and they both laughed. For a while they enjoyed a companionable silence. Then Ken said, "You certainly have a lovely singing voice. Why didn't you continue with 'Loch Lomond' yesterday?"

She sighed. "To explain that, I'd have to tell you my life's history."

"It's a long way to London. Fire away," he said encouragingly.

She hesitated as if not sure how to start. Then she began, "When my mum was eighteen, she fell in love with a handsome young man. As I mentioned yesterday, she was raised in a religious family and she was warned not to marry him because he was rather feckless. But she loved him very much and they ran off together. In time they had six children. I'm the eldest. The warnings about my da were not unfounded. He couldn't support his large family, and Mum had to take in washing to support us. As time passed Da turned more and more to drink. He died young and except for what we children could earn, Mum was our sole support. I loved my father, but when he died I vowed I'd never marry a man like him no matter how handsome or how much I loved him. With him gone I, being the eldest, tried even harder to help my mother. Ever since I can remember I've worked. First with Da on the river, and then when I was fourteen as an orange seller at the theatre. Do you know much about orange sellers?"

Ken nodded. "A little. When I was at the Theatre Royal, I noticed that they are all rather pretty, and the one who approached us was extremely flirtatious with my friend."

"They're expected to do that," Nell said. "Although many of the girls go beyond flirtation, I want you to know that I never did. My greatest desire was to become an actress so I could make bags of money and make Mum's life easier. The opportunity came when I was sixteen. Lord Darnley, an avid patron of the theatre, took an interest in me and got me a small part in a play. This led to other parts. But I was hampered by my poor speech and had to leave London to get leading roles. Eventually, my patron paid for diction lessons and introduced me to London society."

"From a diamond in the rough to a polished gem," Ken said.

"You could say that. Soon I was taking on leading roles on the London stage. Lord Darnley even financed a play for me. Gradually, I was achieving my dream. In the meantime I fell in love with David Norris, a young Welsh actor, and he with me. He was wonderfully handsome but had very little talent.

"When I told Lord Darnley that Davy had asked for my hand, he was aghast. He warned me that Davy would never amount to anything and reminded me of my vow, which I'd shared with him, never to marry only for love. Then he surprised me by also asking for my hand. A year earlier his wife had passed away, so he was a widower. Two proposals: one from a young, handsome man with few prospects, and one from an old, dignified man of wealth and high station—what a tizzy I was in. Should I marry for love or security or not at all?"

Nell stopped talking and looked for Ken's reaction. He shrugged. "Obviously, you chose security," he said.

She nodded. "But it was not without much struggle. I really loved both of them in different ways, and I was afraid what Davy might do if I threw him over. In the midst of this dilemma I came home late from the theatre one night and found my mum asleep in a chair by the fire. I was shocked to see how old and tired she'd become—not yet forty years, but caring for us children had sucked the life out of her. There and then, I decided to accept Lord Darnley's offer." Her face clouded as her mind went back to that day. She sighed. "Davy took it hard. He pleaded with me to reconsider, but I was like flint. Shortly thereafter he left the theatre and joined the army."

She stopped speaking and tears formed in her eyes. She dabbed at them and said in a husky voice, "He was killed in a far corner of the empire called Afghanistan. It broke my heart to know that I had sent him to his death." Again she was silent as she dabbed her wet eyes.

Neither of them spoke for a few minutes, during which time Ken pondered Nell's words. "I think you're being hard on yourself, Nell," he finally said. "Did you persuade Davy to join the army?"

"Oh, no. I tried to talk him out of it."

"Then it seems to me you have no responsibility for his death."

"But if I'd married him, he might be alive today."

"Or he might be dead for some other reason. We're not responsible for other people's choices in life. He made the choice and he suffered the consequences. You are blameless."

She smiled sadly at him. "I wish I could believe that. Thanks anyway for your kind words and for listening to me."

He acknowledged her words with a nod and a tight smile. "I'm sorry to have dredged up such painful memories."

She dismissed his apology with a wave of her hand. "I wanted to tell you because I knew you'd understand. When I began to sing last night I suddenly thought of Davy. The song's beautiful but sad. As you probably know, it's about a young soldier who goes off to fight and never returns. Do you know all the verses?"

Ken thought for a moment. "I don't think so. I would ask you to sing them, but I think it would be too emotional for you."

She smiled sadly. "I'll try, but I can't promise I'll finish." She took a moment to compose herself, then sang:

By yon bonnie banks and by yon bonnie braes
Where the sun shines bright on Loch Lomon'
Where me and my true love were ever wont tae gae
On the bonnie, bonnie banks o' Loch Lomon'

During the first stanza Marian awoke and nodded at Ken as if to say, "Doesn't she have a lovely voice?"

Oh you tak' the high road and I'll tak' the low road
An' I'll be in Scotland afore ye,
But me and my true love will never meet again
On the bonnie, bonnie banks o' Loch Lomon'—

Nell suddenly dissolved into tears and fell into her maid's arms. The carriage was south of Glasgow and the maid had fallen back to sleep when Nell picked up the threads of her story. "If someone asked me if I'd made the right choice between Lord Darnley and Davy, I could hardly say with confidence that I had," she said. "But, as you pointed out, I made my choice and must accept the consequences. My husband is a kind, indulgent man, but he is in his late seventies now and has little interest in the things I like to do. On the other hand, I live a secure, pampered life and move in the best company. There's truth in the old saying, 'Better be an old man's darling than a young man's slave.' Having grown up poor, though, I always feel like an impostor when I attend fancy affairs."

Ken smiled and attempted to lighten the conversation. "That reminds me of the story of a young man from a poor family who fell in love with a rich girl," he said. "He was invited to a high-class social function and felt out of place. Mistaking him for one of their own, a highbrow asked him what line of business his family was in. He replied, 'Iron and steel.' He was then asked the name of his family's business. 'No business name,' he replied. 'My mother irons and my father steals!'"

Nell pealed with laughter, waking the maid again. "Mr. Sanderson just told a funny story," Nell said by way of apology for waking Miss Treadwell.

The maid smiled and promptly went back to sleep.

"Do you still enjoy the theatre?" Ken asked.

Nell hesitated before answering. "I do, but not as much as I did in the early years. Now I only take parts that appeal to me and, of course, are in keeping with my status as the wife of a nobleman. As I mentioned yesterday, for some time my speech held me back from getting leading roles in London, but out in the country producers were not so picky.

"One summer, Davy and I toured the country towns with a small company of limited players, scenery, and wardrobe. We'd basically use the same costumes for each play, and at each little theatre we'd adapt whatever scenery was available. As for extra cast members, we'd hire as much local talent as we needed." A smile came to her face as her mind went back to those days. "They were rather unprofessional presentations, and more often than not something would go awry, to the delight of the audience. Once in a small town in the Midlands we had a corker of a mix-up. It's become part of theatre history in England."

"I'm all ears," Ken said.

A wistful smile played on her lips as she began the story. "The program consisted of three one-act plays. The first was a domestic drama set in a London drawing room. The second, according to the playbill, was a 'marrow-freezing thriller' set in the darkest jungles of Africa, and the third, a romantic comedy set in a pretty English garden."

"What parts did you and Davy play?"

"We played the leads in all three. In fact, we basically played the same role in each—young lovers. The love comedy and the domestic drama required very little to stage, but the African thriller required a lot of work. Jungle scenery had to be painted, a dozen extras had to be hired to play 'cannibal savages,' and suitable costumes for the latter had to be made up."

Nell again smiled in remembrance. "Since no one seemed to know how cannibals dressed, it was left to the wardrobe lady to come up with suitable costumes. She solved the problem by dressing the extras in chocolate-colored tights and feathered headdresses—the feathers acquired at a local chicken farm. Spears, clubs, and shields were all improvised in one day."

Ken laughed. "I wished I'd been there," he said.

Nell laughed and nodded. "You'd have enjoyed it. A dress rehearsal in the afternoon preceded opening night. The domestic comedy rehearsal went off without a hitch. For my soliloquy at the end of the jungle-play rehearsal I was overjoyed to get a standing ovation. Despite my later success on the London stage, I don't think I've ever felt more excitement than I did at that standing ovation."

She smiled as she recalled the rehearsal and, taking a mock-serious tone, she described her triumph: "The climactic scene was set in a jungle clearing. Davy, dressed in a morning suit, the same outfit he'd worn in the domestic drama except for a pith helmet the wardrobe lady had scared up somewhere, took me in his arms and in a loud, wooden voice—he really wasn't a very good actor—promised to protect me with his life from marauding lions, tigers, and crocodiles. His action of taking me in his arms was the cannibals' entry cue. In they rushed whooping like madmen. Unmoved, the hero coolly drew his six-shooter and dispatched all twelve of them."

Ken's loud laugh awakened Miss Treadwell, who stayed awake long enough to hear the rest of the story.

"Amid the carnage," Nell continued, "I had my big scene. In five minutes worth of eloquent dialogue and with all the passion I could muster, I in essence informed my hero that his bravery had convinced me that he was worthy of my undying love. As the curtain slowly closed, the audience of producer, wardrobe lady, stagehands, and several local layabouts who had infiltrated the theatre leapt to their feet in the aforementioned standing ovation." Reverting to her usual voice, she concluded, "Except for some of the scenery being damaged by the overly exuberant cannibals, the rehearsal went perfectly, which caused the producer to begin worrying."

"Good rehearsal, bad opening night," Ken said.

"Exactly," she said. "The rehearsal of the romantic comedy went like clockwork, except for the garden bench tipping up when I slid over to let Davy sit beside me. It was one of those benches with protruding ends, and one had to be careful to sit in the middle or it would tip. If two people sat on it they'd have to balance each other to keep from having an upset. This was rather difficult as my hooped skirt took up most of the bench. After a few tries, however, we learned to execute the maneuver perfectly.

"When the dress rehearsal was over, it was almost teatime. The performers were charged to stay in costume. The dozen cannibal savages went next door to the Running Footman Pub for their tea, and, as it turned out, other liquid refreshment. Meanwhile, a crew were put to work repairing the jungle scenery. This job took longer than expected and the producer decided to change the order of the plays to give the crew more time to fix the scenery. The jungle play would now go last rather than in the middle. Unfortunately, the change was not properly communicated to the extras, still next door at the Running Footman.

"That night, near the end of the second play, Davy and I were sitting on the bench in the tranquil English garden, bathed in moonlight. The hero lovingly took me in his arms and we shared a lingering kiss. Suddenly, a dozen inebriated savage cannibals in chocolate-colored tights staggered onto the stage whooping like madmen and brandishing spears and clubs, shattering the romantic mood. In their condition they apparently could not distinguish an English garden from the African jungle. Davy leapt to his feet, upsetting the bench and sending me backward into the artificial flowerbed, my pantalooned legs in the air. Not having a prop gun for which to dispatch the savages, Davy lashed out with his fists and inadvertently connected with a feathered head, sending one cannibal crashing into another. To the delight of the audience, who by this time were in hysterics, a general brawl ensued.

Believing that discretion was the better part of valor, I remained ensconced in the flowerbed until the curtain closed. Then I crawled off stage to safety."

Like the country audience, Ken and Marian were in hysterics by the time Nell finished her narrative. Ken had not laughed so hard since Karen had related the story of the Great Bottle Conjurer. The Langton coach had crossed the English border and was well on its way to Manchester before the three of them fully regained their composure.

"Another benefit of having married Lord Darnley," Nell said, again picking up her life story, "is that my family, especially my mum, are no longer in straitened circumstances. She has a cottage all to herself on our country estate where she often entertains her two grandchildren—my sister's children."

"You have no children?" Ken asked.

Nell sighed and shook her head. "Not that I wouldn't welcome them. My husband has two married children, a boy and a girl, both older than I. At first they saw me as a threat. But, of course, even if I had a male child, he could not inherit my husband's title or possessions. Ours is called a morganatic marriage—the union of a noble person with a commoner."

"Morganatic," Ken repeated. "I'm not familiar with the term."

"It comes from a Latin word meaning 'morning gift.' Since a morganatic bride cannot succeed to her husband's possessions, it is customary for the groom to give her a gift on the morning after the wedding."

"May I ask what your gift was?"

Nell smiled. "Lord Darnley showered me with gifts: the deed to our London townhouse, an annual allowance to begin after he passes, the occupancy of the aforementioned cottage for my mother until she dies; those are only a few examples of his generosity. As I mentioned, his children were not pleased when he married me, but over the years I've been able to win them over. We get along well now." She paused. "Do you mind if I have a little nap? I'm suddenly very tired."

Ken said that he didn't mind, and she was soon asleep. He too tried to sleep but his mind wouldn't let him. He thought of Nell's choice between Davy and Darnley. *Life is full of choices,* he thought. He heaved a sigh as he thought of his impulsively running off to Scotland, leaving Karen to wonder what had happened to him. He resolved to be more circumspect in the future. His thoughts continued with Karen, who had never been far from his mind during his whole adventure. *What a wonderful woman she is, much more forgiving and Christlike than I.* He wondered what in her past was bothering her and surmised that it had something to do with the man who had jilted her, since she had evaded Ken's question about him. *Well, whatever it is, it won't change my feelings for her. How inspired my parents were to let me come to Britain! While Heavenly Father may have sent me to England to introduce Karen to the restored gospel, I am learning the gospel from her and from my experiences here. God works in mysterious ways.*

* * *

Except for several stops at inns along the way, Langton's carriage traveled through the night and arrived in London at mid-morning. In an attempt to protect Nell from scandal, Ken directed the driver to go to Lady Brideswell's townhouse. There, he arranged for a carriage to take her to her own home.

"Thank you for being such a gentleman," Nell said as she was about to leave for home. "Men like Langton destroy a girl's faith in chivalry, but men like you renew it. I'll always remember with fondness our Scottish adventure. Cheerio for now, and, since I'll probably be called upon to testify against Stephen Langton, I'll see you in court." She climbed into the carriage and slid open the window. "Miss Gage is a very lucky girl," she added as the carriage pulled away.

As he waved good-bye, Ken thought about Langton's trial, and involving Nell in it weighed on his mind. Ken's father had said that trials often became sordid affairs. He shuddered to think about what Langton's lawyer would do to Nell on the witness stand. *She's had enough challenges in her life,* he thought. *Can I be responsible for putting her in the witness box?* He thought of her life with Lord Darnley and concluded that it must be difficult for such a young, vital woman to be married to an old man. But she had made her choice, and, as she said, the consequences were not without benefit. He thought of her desire for children. *She's still young. Perhaps she'll have another chance at love and the children she desires when her husband passes on.* He sincerely hoped so.

⊰ CHAPTER 19 ⊱

After running off to Scotland on scanty evidence, Ken decided to take a more cautious approach to finding Karen. At his lodgings he bathed and shaved, changed into clean clothes, and headed for Kensington. To his dismay, the note, now rain-soaked, still stuck from the letter slot. From Kensington he went directly to see Sir Jeffrey.

"Mr. Sanderson," the lawyer said, "where have you been? Langton's purchased the mortgage on Gage Hall and turned Miss Gage out."

"Oh no," Ken said, a knot forming in his stomach. "Miss Gage must be devastated. Is there anything we can do for her?"

Sir Jeffrey shook his head. "I'm afraid not. My sources tell me that Langton had an altercation with Miss Gage at the Savoy, and the very next day he bought the mortgage on Gage Hall and immediately served a foreclosure notice at her aunt's home in Kensington."

Ken felt sick to his stomach when he realized he had failed Karen when she needed him most. Had he gone to Kensington in the morning as he'd said he would, he could at least have been able to console her. How could he ever look her in the face again?

"Sit down before you fall down, Mr. Sanderson," the barrister said. "You're as white as a sheet." Numbly, Ken obeyed. "The one positive thing is that Langton served the notice prematurely."

"Prematurely?" Ken asked, a glimmer of hope in his voice.

The barrister nodded. "I understand that he didn't sign the final mortgage papers before going out of town. But it's just a formality. He has a week to sign them. Apparently he didn't have time to wait for the documents to be made up because he was so eager to get away. When he returns he'll finalize the purchase."

Ken's face brightened. "What if he doesn't get back in time to sign the papers?"

"The purchase would be canceled. Have you any reason to suppose that he won't get back in time?"

"Perhaps. You asked where I've been. Would you believe, Scotland?"

"Scotland? What were you doing there?"

Ken recited his story and Sir Jeffrey shook his head. "So that's why Langton was so eager to leave town. Who wouldn't want to go away with the lovely Miss Keene? But more to the point, I'm delighted that the law's finally caught up with the scoundrel."

Ken nodded. "Yes. Chief Inspector Soames will be ecstatic to learn that Langton's locked up. I assume the inspector will send someone to collect Langton right away."

"Hmm. I wonder . . ."

Ken guessed what the barrister was thinking. "You're wondering if perhaps you could influence Chief Inspector Soames to delay Langton's return and keep him from signing the papers?"

Sir Jeffrey took on a shocked expression and stared sternly over his spectacles. "Perish the thought," he said. "Me, an officer of the court, conspire to retard the wheels of justice? To cause the tide of law to ebb? To dam the river of jurisprudence? Never!" He paused and winked. "You, on the other hand, Mr. Sanderson, have no such professional restraints. Perhaps you could influence the good chief inspector. I understand you're almost on a first-name basis with him."

Ken was in no mood to appreciate Sir Jeffrey's attempt at humor. He stood up. "I'll go there directly. And then I must be off to see Miss Gage. That is, if she'll see me after I've let her down. I assume she's in Somerset."

Sir Jeffrey nodded. "Most likely. I imagine she went there as soon as she got the foreclosure notice and is packing up her things. Don't look so glum. It's not the end of the world. Please close the door on the way out. I must get to work on other matters." Ken paused at the door and the barrister glanced up. "Is there something else?"

Ken hesitated before blurting out, "If we're successful in blocking Langton from getting the mortgage, do you think St. Swithins might be interested in the estate? I think they could get it at a bargain price."

"St. Swithins?" the barrister said, his face full of surprise. "How do you know about my connection with St. Swithins?"

Ken grinned. "A newspaperman never reveals his sources."

Sir Jeffrey's lips moved in what could pass for a smile. "Sit down again and tell me all about the estate," he said.

By the time Ken had finished, Sir Jeffrey showed definite interest. "I'll take it up with the board," the closet philanthropist said.

Ken again arose to leave. "In the meantime, Sir Jeffrey, please don't mention to anyone that Nell Keene was in Scotland. It'll start tongues wagging to her hurt."

The barrister nodded. "Good luck with Miss Gage," he said.

"Thanks. I'll need it!"

* * *

Ken went directly from the lawyer's office to Scotland Yard. "Is Chief Inspector Soames about?" he asked the desk sergeant.

"He'll be along directly, sir. Please take a seat."

Ken obeyed, closed his eyes, and thought of Karen. *I wonder if she's already moved out of Gage Hall?* Again he regretted running off to Scotland and not being there to help soften the blow of the foreclosure notice. He fervently hoped that his apparent abandonment would not destroy her interest in the Church. The fact that she had continued her study of the gospel the last time they had a falling out, however, did give him a little hope. That Jonathan was blameless also increased his hope that she would continue studying. *I wonder what her real feelings are for Jonathan? Maybe I should be on my way to Somerset rather than sitting here cooling my heels.*

His thoughts turned to Nell. He was certain that when her going away with Langton became known it would cause a scandal. Could he in good conscience risk causing Nell embarrassment by having her testify in an attempted murder charge?

"Mr. Sanderson," said Chief Inspector Soames, entering the waiting room. "You're back. I understand from McTavish's telegraph message your trip to Scotland was successful."

"Successful?" Ken asked, feeling that for Karen it had been a complete disaster.

"Langton's behind bars, isn't he? That's certainly success. Other than that, how did you like Scotland?"

Ken answered noncommittally. "Loch Lomond's a place I'd like to visit again under more propitious circumstances."

The policeman sighed. "Unfortunately, this life has very few propitious circumstances," he said sardonically as he waved Ken into his office and pointed to a much-abused wooden chair. "I also understand from McTavish that you have some new charges against Langton. Tell me all."

Once more Ken related his Scottish adventure.

"All alone on a Scottish isle with the lovely Nell Keene," Soames said, leaning back in his chair and closing his eyes.

"Inspector?" Ken said after a long moment, bringing the policeman back from Scotland.

Soames smiled sheepishly. "Oh, I was just thinking of assigning myself to fetch Langton. I could take my fishing gear along and . . . perhaps not. There's too much to do. I'll send PC Walcott and another constable up to collect him and have them take depositions from the boatman and McTavish. With conspiracy and attempted murder, we should be able to put Langton away for a long time. I hope you're prepared to take the stand."

Ken inhaled and exhaled slowly. "On the first charge, yes. But I'm afraid I won't be of much help on the second one, sir. I've decided not to bring attempted murder charges against him."

Soames's forehead crinkled as he sat forward in his chair. "In heaven's name, why not?"

Ken shrugged. "I'm sorry, but we'd have to bring Lady Darnley into it, and I don't want to cause a scandal. As you know, she's a married woman and the press would have a field day with the fact that she went off with Langton. I just don't want Nell involved. She's going to confess to her husband and that's enough."

"Very gallant of you," Soames said, not unkindly, "but I'm afraid the choice is not yours to make. The Crown will prosecute and you will testify whether you like it or not. This is our chance to nail Langton. We'll not get a better one."

Ken felt trapped. "You mean I have no say in the matter?"

"Not really."

"Will you at least discuss the case in advance with Lady Darnley to allow her the time to prepare her husband?"

"Of course. Don't look so worried, Mr. Sanderson. Nell Keene's a survivor. She'll take this in stride. Besides, scandals are part and parcel of the theatre world. It can only enhance her career."

"I don't think her career needs enhancing," Ken said glumly. After a moment he added, "Well, if it has to be, I'm sure she'll be sensational on the witness stand."

"That's the spirit. We must nail Langton on the attempted murder charge because I doubt if the conspiracy charge will hold up. Gandy is a most unreliable witness. Once on the stand, who knows what he'll do. Of course, Langton's no better. The man's an animal."

Ken smiled sarcastically. "Gandy or Langton?"

Soames shrugged. "Take your pick! They come from different classes, but there's not a ha'penny's worth of difference in them." The chief inspector stood up. "So, I'll send two bobbies to Scotland to take the statements and collect Langton right away."

"That's the other thing," Ken said, also rising. "Would it be possible to wait a week?"

Ken explained why, and the chief inspector shook his head. "Sorry, Mr. Sanderson. We must go by the book on this one. One deviation and Bradford Rampling, Langton's barrister, would be all over us." The policeman paused and then added, "Of course, there are several ways I can keep Langton from signing the mortgage papers once he gets here. Leave it with me."

"Thank you, sir," Ken said. "I'll be so glad when all this is over."

The policeman sighed. "I wish I could say that it will be all over with Langton sentenced and locked up. But life is seldom as neat as that. Langton has a long memory."

Ken considered Soames's words. "What I can't understand," he said, "is why Langton is so . . . so mean spirited. To use an old expression, what's stuck in his craw?"

Soames smiled and seemed pleased at the opportunity of enlightening the younger man. He motioned for Ken to sit again. "My years on the force have made me somewhat of an authority on the criminal mind," he said, settling back into his chair. "I've come to a few conclusions about those who run afoul of the law. What it boils down to is this: criminals crave something they can't legally have more than they crave respectability. The desire for respectability, shored up by religion and the rules of society, keeps the vast majority of us in check. But there are those at the bottom of society, such as Jacob Gandy, whose lack of this life's goods drives them to satisfy their brutish physical desires by committing crime. And those at the top of society, like your man Langton, who have more intangible motivations."

"But he has all the money he could wish for," Ken said. "Why does he need to go outside the law? You'd think his wealth and all the trappings that go with it—his mansion, his elegant carriage with matched horses, and so forth—would be enough to satisfy him."

Soames nodded and heaved a sigh. "You'd think so, but as I'm sure you know, there are some things money can't by. The way I see it, Langton craves notoriety, fame, standing, status, celebrity—call it what you will—that intangible desire to be 'somebody.' And I think I know the source of his craving: he didn't inherit his father's title and it galls him."

"Did his parents have a morganatic marriage?" Ken asked.

Soames stared at Ken, surprised that he knew the term. "Yes. They did. From what I understand, as a youth Sir Gerald fell madly in love with a maid in his father's household. His parents absolutely forbade the relationship and threatened to disinherit him. Heedless of the threat, he ran off with the girl to Gretna Green and married. Gerald and his parents reconciled and he eventually succeeded to his father's title and estates. His wife, however, died young, leaving him a bitter, disillusioned man. Ironically, to marry his true love he had risked losing all and ended up losing her to death. Life certainly can be capricious. Their only child, Stephen, grew up without a mother and with the galling knowledge that because of his mother's low station he would not inherit his father's title."

Ken shook his head. "People have grown up with a lot worse trials and turned out all right," he said. "I can't see why so much emphasis is put on titles anyway."

Soames smiled indulgently. "You Americans, I'm sure, have difficulty understanding social distinctions in England's class-conscious society. But it's no secret that many American *nouveau riche* have taken to sending their girls to England and the continent for 'finishing' and, I dare say, in the hope that they'll latch on to a titled husband.

"Getting back to Stephen Langton, I truly believe that he's sick in the mind. He suffers from a lack of identity and will do anything to shore up his feelings of inadequacy. In his mind, possessing and flaunting the ring of the great Saladin would have helped raise his status. Similarly, establishing a connection with such a beautiful and renowned actress as Nell Keene, the wife of a nobleman, would have in his estimation elevated his position in society. But you, my friend, have been involved in frustrating his lusts in both cases. If we do manage to incarcerate him, he'll eventually get out and there's no telling what he'll do. I'll warrant he'll spend his whole time in jail plotting your destruction. We may have the upper hand now, but we've made a rich, powerful enemy."

Ken shrugged. "I'm not worried. I'll soon be returning to America. I doubt Langton would cross the ocean for revenge."

"Don't count on it, son. And don't leave town. I intend to do all in my power to get Langton in court as soon as possible. In fact, I'm hoping to set up an appointment for tomorrow morning with the Crown counsel, Sir Wilfred Pilley, who'll be prosecuting Langton, and I'd like you there. Are you still lodging at Lady Brideswell's?" Ken nodded. "Good. I'll send someone to get you if I'm successful."

Ken was about to tell the policeman that he was going to Somerset, but he changed his mind. Soames would only try to talk him out of it, and Ken was determined that nothing would stop him from seeing Karen this time. Besides, he was sure he could go down to Somerset and return on the evening train.

❧ CHAPTER 20 ❦

A satisfying lightness filled Ken's being as the back of his head touched the antimacassar and he settled into the leather-covered seat in the railway carriage. At last he would be with Karen again, and if all went well he would declare his love for her and assure her that despite how things looked, all would be well financially. He wondered if he should tell her that there was a chance that the foreclosure might be reversed. After some thought, he decided not to. No use getting her hopes up prematurely.

As the green countryside rolled by, he was glad he had come to England, but at the same time he looked forward to returning home to the Salt Lake Valley—returning home with Karen at his side. He had no doubt that if she accepted his love she would also accept membership in the Church.

The train crossed a bridge over a river, and Ken smiled to see several children splashing in the shallows. They reminded him of Karen's desire to have children. He pressed his forehead against the cool glass as trees, hedge-bordered meadows, and the occasional farmhouse glided by. Telegraph poles paralleling the tracks counted off the seconds to Somerset.

At the Glastonbury Station he hired a pony trap and driver to take him to Gage Hall. His heart beat wildly as the trap left the main road and started up the lane between the parallel lines of Lombardy poplars standing tall and regal like sentinels guarding the approach to the ancient manor house. Alighting from the trap in front of the building, he paid the driver and sent him on his way. Taking a deep breath, he bounded up the stone steps two at a time and worked the dolphin knocker. A hollow sound greeted him, sending an icy current down his spine and dampening his ebullient spirit.

Impatiently moving his weight from one foot to the other, he waited. Again he worked the knocker and listened. A sound from within made his heart race. Slowly the door opened and the ancient butler stood before him. "Ah, Mr. Sanderson," the butler slowly said. "You have returned. We thought you had gone home to America."

"No. May I come in and see Miss Gage?"

The butler's face fell. "She has gone, sir."

"Gone? Gone where?"

"I'm not at liberty to say, sir. She and her aunt and Maggie was here for a time packing. The bank's taken the hall." The old man sighed and hung his head. "Miss Gage told me to look after the place till the bank tells me otherwise. Then . . . who knows? Who would want a useless old crock like me?"

Ken empathized with the old man. "Don't worry, Mr. Bennett," he said, "I'm sure Miss Gage will make provision for you. Are you sure you can't tell me where she is? I must see her."

The ancient butler shook his head. "I'm sorry, sir."

Ken persisted. "But it's imperative that I see her. And I know she would want to see me. I have some information that might—" Ken realized he had no right to get the butler's hopes up about the future of Gage Hall.

"Sorry, sir," the butler repeated.

Heartsick, Ken trudged back down the long tree-lined lane. *What should I do? Perhaps she's at Maggie's cottage. That's it. Since she's not here or in Kensington, she must be at Maggie's.* With quickening steps he headed down the road to Ainsley Village. As he passed by the church, the front door opened.

"Mr. Sanderson," the vicar called, "I have something for you. Please wait." The clergyman went back inside the building. Ken didn't want to stop, but politeness constrained him to do so. Minutes later the vicar reappeared, smiling broadly and holding a sheaf of papers. "These are for you. You've just missed Miss Gage. She finished not an hour ago. My, she has been a diligent copyist."

Ken stared at him nonplussed. "Miss Gage has finished copying the Ashcroft genealogy?"

"She has . . . over the last few days. You didn't know?"

Ken shook his head as a seed of hope took root in his heart. *She hasn't given up on me completely. Why else would she continue to fulfill her promise?* "How long ago did you say she left?" he asked.

"About an hour."

"She's at Miss Stowell's, I presume?"

"Oh, yes. Awful, her losing the hall. But she's an enterprising young woman. I have no doubts she'll rise above this misfortune."

Ken quickly took the papers and stuffed them into his valise. "Thank you, sir. Thank you very much," he said, wheeling around and dashing down the road.

With some trepidation Ken knocked on the rose-bordered cottage door. A noise from within heightened his spirit. The top half of the door opened.

"Well, well, the *protical* returns," Maggie said, with more than a trace of displeasure in her voice. "We thought you was off to America now that the ring's stole."

Ken smiled sadly. "That's what Mr. Bennett thought too. I've just come from Gage Hall. May I see Karen?"

Maggie answered with a question. "Where have you been since you saw Miss Karen at the Savoy?"

"It's a long story, Maggie. May I talk with Karen?"

Maggie shook her head. "I fear not. She's in the village posting a letter. I told you not to trifle with her *affectations,* and you wouldn't listen. The poor girl's suffered enough hard lines . . . the awful threats of Stephen Langton, the loss of her home, your desertion—"

The word *desertion* pierced his heart and his conscience. "But I didn't desert her, Maggie. If I could only see her and explain."

"I'm sorry, Mr. Sanderson. I don't want to see her hurt again. When you didn't come to Kensington like you promised, she took it hard, very hard. But she's over it now. This morning the roses was back in her cheeks. I've never seen her more happy and excited. It's like she's in love. I'm sure it's got to do with the man she's writing to. Please let her alone. I'll tell her you called, and if she wants to see you she'll let you know. Are you still at Brideswell's?"

Ken nodded as Maggie started to close the door. "I'm not leaving until I see her, Maggie, if I have to search all of Somerset."

Maggie shook her head. "That's up to you. I must say I'm disappointed in you, Mr. Sanderson. I thought better of you. But then you are a man and don't know no better. Think on what you've done to Miss Gage and mend your ways, my lad." Without waiting for a reply, she shut the door on him.

Maggie's words cut him deeply. He stared at the closed door. The sweet scent of the roses framing the door contrasted sharply with his feelings and seemed to mock him. The knot in his stomach tightened. He reached out and touched a delicate petal and thought of Karen. Then with a sigh he turned and trudged down the flagstone path and through the gate. There he paused, not sure where to go next. *The post office! Maggie said Karen was posting a letter.*

"Was Miss Gage here a few minutes ago?" he asked the bespectacled old woman behind the wicket at the back of the dry-goods shop in Ainsley Village.

The postmistress scrutinized him for a second. "You're the American chap what was stayin' at Maggie's cottage," she said.

"Yes, ma'am," he said. "A while back."

She nodded. "Awful what happened to Miss Gage. A darling girl she is. But she seems to have taken it in stride. Happy as a lark she was only minutes ago when she was here. In fact, this is her letter I'm stampin'."

Ken's eyes dropped to the envelope, and before the woman whisked it out of sight, he glimpsed the name "Kimball." His heart fell. *Jonathan! So he's the one who's put the roses back in her cheeks.* For a long moment he hesitated, paralyzed with indecision.

"You feelin' poorly lad?" the woman asked. "You look like you've lost a shilling an' found a sixpence."

Ken smiled sadly to hear an expression his mother often used. He shook his head. "I'm fine," he lied.

Outside he sat on a bench in front of the shop. If it had been anyone else but Jonathan, he would not have hesitated to fight for Karen, but if she truly loved his cousin, who was he to stand in the way of their happiness? He thought of the glow on her cheeks as she discussed the gospel with Jonathan. He recalled her heaping praise on him at Kew Gardens. He even remembered the camaraderie they shared as they ate oranges at the theatre. Checking his watch, he sighed. Despair had settled over him like fog on the Thames. Despite what he had said to Maggie about scouring Somerset, he decided to return to London.

Going back inside the shop, he secured directions from the postmistress about hiring a vehicle and driver to take him to the train station.

He was on time for the London train and shared the carriage with a young married couple, who sat opposite him. They introduced themselves as Mr. and Mrs. Dodson of Cornwall. As ever, the train shunted back and forth for a while before it finally made up its mind to lurch toward London. Ken's thoughts were full of Karen as he casually glanced out the window. Amazingly, there she was standing on the platform! He blinked several times to clear his vision and make sure his eyes were not deceiving him. Then, leaping up, he grabbed the strap, lowered the window, and stuck out his head.

"Karen!" he called.

At that very moment, thick, sooty smoke engulfed him. "Shut the window!" Mr. Dodson yelled. Ken frantically fumbled with the strap before he finally managed to raise the window. He turned to see the compartment full of smoke. Mrs. Dodson was coughing uncontrollably into her handkerchief, and her husband was on his feet peering out the other window. He then lowered that window and signaled for Ken to lower his. The cross-draft quickly cleared the compartment of the worst of the smoke, and the two men raised the windows again and sat down.

With his handkerchief Ken wiped his eyes, moist from more than the smoke, and looked out the window on the chance that he could see Karen again. But the train had rounded a curve, obscuring the platform. After a moment he sighed and pulled his eyes from the window. He glanced across at Mr. and Mrs. Dodson. A hankie still covered the latter's face.

"Sorry," Ken said. "I've traveled enough on trains to know better."

Mr. Dodson accepted Ken's apology with a nod and a grin. "Doubtless, you had other things on your mind," he said in a friendly manner. "Woman troubles?"

Ken sadly nodded. "I'm afraid so," he said.

"Don't fret," Mr. Dodson said. "There's lots more fish in the sea. I was turned down my first time."

Mrs. Dodson pulled the hankie from her face and, mouth open, stared at her husband. "You didn't tell me that. I was your second choice, then?"

The man smiled sheepishly and crimsoned. "I . . . I wouldn't put it that way, dear."

"What way would you put it?" Before he could answer, she said angrily, "'Twas Ethel Lawson, weren't it?"

"No. It weren't Ethel Lawson."

"Who then?"

The man glanced apologetically at Ken, who was trying to ignore the altercation by again staring out the window. Turning back to his wife, the man, finding his backbone, said firmly, "It's not important who it were. And I'll thank 'ee to be still, woman, and stop annoying Mr. Sanderson."

Mrs. Dodson's eyes narrowed and her face tightened. "Either you tell me who it were, or I'll never speak to you again." Her husband mumbled something under his breath. "I beg your pardon?" she demanded.

"I said, that'd be a relief," he said, sliding to the far corner of the seat and glaring out the window.

Mrs. Dodson retreated to her corner and for long time neither of them spoke, giving Ken time to reflect on his own challenges. He stewed with self-recrimination and self-pity, and he asked himself if he had truly lost Karen or never really had her in the first place. *How could I let such a good thing go bad?*

He closed his eyes and reviewed the chain of events that had led to his misery. Despite his promise to his parents, he should have told Karen about his mother's bid for the ring, he decided. But even when she had frankly forgiven him for not telling her, and wanted to resume their friendship, what had he done? He'd let her down again. He should have told Chief Inspector Soames that he would identify Gandy after he'd been to Kensington. Why didn't he? *Why do we take for granted those we love most?* Why did he feel obligated to treat acquaintances, even strangers, better than those he loved?

His thoughts then led him to pondering destiny. If he had done everything right, would it have made any difference? Were Karen and Jonathan destined to be together regardless? He had no answer.

"It was Mildred Braithwaite," Mr. Dodson finally said from his corner, rescuing Ken from his negative thoughts.

"Mildred Braithwaite?" Mrs. Dodson said, incredulity in her voice. "I played second fiddle to Mildred Braithewaite? Why ever'd you asked her to marry you?"

He gave her a conciliatory glance. "Why ever, indeed," he said. "Had I met you first, dear, it goes without saying I'd never've asked her."

Her face softened as she studied him. "All right, then," she said, "you're forgiven."

As the chasm between the Dodsons shrank, Ken closed his eyes and let his thoughts drift to his whole English adventure. He wondered about his motivation in coming to England. Was it pure? Did he have the proper intent? Could he truly say that he sought after the money from Saladin's ring "for the intent to do good," as he had told his parents? Or was he using this whole adventure to get away from his responsibilities in Utah—his employment perhaps, his family, or, more likely, the not-so-subtle importunings for him to find a wife and settle down? *No,* he decided, *I truly was inspired to come. It's strange how when things go wrong we begin to doubt previous inspiration.* He concluded that his parents were inspired to give him their blessing, knowing that he needed to experience the world away from their presence. Perhaps the experience was changing him. Perhaps his trip to England would help him grow. *Despite all the ups and downs I've had in England,* he decided, *I know it's right for me to be here.*

Surely, Maggie must be wrong. Surely, Karen is not in love with Jonathan, although she obviously has great respect for him. Of course respect often turns to . . . Enough!

He opened his eyes to banish the thought from his mind. The gap between the Dodsons had closed completely, and they were smiling fondly at each other. He took this as a good omen. *Perhaps Karen will someday smile at me that way again.*

He heaved a heavy sigh, curled up, and slept away the rest of the trip to London.

❧ CHAPTER 21 ❧

It was late when Ken arrived at Lady Brideswell's town-house. A note from Sir Jeffrey lay on the dresser, inviting him to a meeting the next morning at ten o'clock in the barrister's chambers to prepare for Langton's trial. Ken wondered about Sir Jeffrey's role in the trial. *Surely he won't be defending Langton.* Dismissing the thought, he fell into bed and slept through the evening and night.

The sun had long been up when he was awakened by a servant calling him to breakfast. Glancing at his watch, Ken groaned to see that it was almost ten. Foregoing breakfast, he quickly dressed and headed for Gray Street.

At twenty of eleven Mr. Nuttall ushered him into the law chambers, where he found Sir Jeffrey, Chief Inspector Soames, and a third man.

Ken was mortified at having kept the three men waiting. "I'm sorry, gentlemen," he said. "I'm afraid I overslept."

Sir Jeffrey acknowledged the apology with a gruff nod. "You know Chief Inspector Soames," the barrister said. "This is Sir Wilfred Pilley, Crown counsel. Sir Wilfred will be prosecuting Langton and has asked me to be co-counsel. Tell us everything you know that might help us prepare the case, especially about what happened in Scotland."

Ken nodded at Chief Inspector Soames and then at the prosecutor. He sighed and said, "As I told Chief Inspector

Soames the other day, I don't look forward to a trial that'll subject Lady Darnley to scandal. However, if I must, I'll do my best. As much as anyone, I'd like to see Langton behind bars."

"Your testimony will be crucial," Sir Wilfred said. "Without it Langton could go free. We still have Gandy's statement, but who knows if it will hold up in court."

Ken sighed. "I just wish we could avoid dragging Lady Darnley's name through the muck."

The two lawyers exchanged satisfied looks and nodded at Soames. "Lady Darnley," the policeman said, "has already agreed to testify. When I told her about your reluctance, she was very appreciative of your trying to protect her; however, she wants to put an end to Langton's flouting the law and readily agreed to testify. Her husband, still smarting from the way Langton treated his wife, supports her decision."

"The trial is scheduled for the day after tomorrow," Sir Wilfred said to Ken. "Unfortunately, we have Sir Cedric Ellsworth, a friend of Langton, on the bench. He's a fair man, but if there's a benefit of the doubt, he'll throw it Langton's way. He's also a friend of Lord and Lady Darnley, so things could get interesting."

For the next two hours Ken rehearsed in minute detail the assault in the alley and the happenings in Scotland. When he was finished, Sir Wilfred looked worried. He nodded thoughtfully and pursed his lips. "It's all very circumstantial," he said. "You have no witnesses to your assault. I imagine it will come down to whom the jury believes—you, Mr. Sanderson, or Langton. Fortunately you have an honest face. The other charge is also highly circumstantial. No one actually saw Langton steal the bailer and put the hole in the boat. I assume that you and McTavish looked for the bailer on the launch?"

"We did," Ken said. "Perhaps Langton got rid of it before we got down to the jetty."

"I'll wire McTavish and have him search the launch again," Soames said, rising to leave, "and if it's not there, I'll have him go over to the island and look for it. I'll get on it right away. I'll also get a statement from Lady Darnley's maid, though I doubt she'll have much to add."

"To summarize," Sir Wilfred said after Soames had gone, "Langton is charged with one count of conspiracy to cause grievous bodily harm and two counts of attempted murder."

"Two counts?" Ken asked.

"Two counts," Sir Wilfred said. "When he didn't warn Lady Darnley that he had rendered the rowboat unsafe, he in effect would have been guilty of her murder had she drowned." Ken nodded and Sir Wilfred went on. "We'll call PC Walcott, Lady Darnley, and you, Mr. Sanderson, to testify. I don't think it would do much good to bring McTavish and the boatman here. We have their depositions. As for the maid, we'll hold her in reserve. All right, gentlemen, let's meet again tomorrow for another session. Would late afternoon, say four o'clock, suit you both?"

Ken and Sir Jeffrey agreed and the meeting was adjourned. Ken left alone and was soon standing on the pavement outside Sir Jeffrey's chambers wondering what to do with himself until the next meeting. Glancing down at Jack's handiwork, faint from many rains but still discernible, he wondered how Jack and Maggie were getting along and hoped that their relationship was progressing more smoothly than his and Karen's. Thinking of Jack and his talent, so long underrated, Ken experienced a momentary epiphany. With clarity that had been absent for some time, he realized that he had been playing his weak suit rather than his strong suit. He had succumbed to moping and negative thinking. Suddenly it occurred to him to write Karen a letter and explain everything. *Why didn't I think of that before? After all, I make my living with my pen. That's my strong suit.* Going back inside the office, he acquired what he needed from Nathaniel Nuttall.

Pen in hand, he wondered if he should declare his love for her. *Maybe not. Until she joins the Church we have no future. I guess I'll just stick to the facts about why I didn't show up at*

Kensington that morning and tell her about Scotland. Those were his intentions, but once he had given the facts, he couldn't help rehearsing their many happy times together: boating on the River Barle, sightseeing in Somerset, and walking on the beach at Weston-super-Mare. He ended his letter with the hope that more good times for them were yet to come. He didn't mention Jonathan.

Later, he posted the letter and felt a little better about himself, but as he stood at the postbox, he momentarily visualized Jonathan's name on the envelope written in Karen's neat script. Was a relationship really developing between the two? Could he allow himself to just sit idly by? After a few minutes of indecision at the postbox, he made up his mind to visit Jonathan.

He found his cousin plunking away on a Remington typewriter. Jonathan looked up and smiled. "Ken. Good to see you again." He nodded at the new writing machine. "Ever try one of these?"

Ken shook his head. "No. They have them at the newspaper but I'll stick to good old longhand. I'm not as dexterous as you."

Jonathan arose and shook his cousin's hand. "I'll finish this up later. What have you been doing since I saw you last? How is Miss Gage?"

Apparently he hasn't received Karen's letter, Ken thought. "She's fine, but we are on the outs again. Once more she thinks I let her down."

Jonathan shook his head. "You've got to stop doing that to my investigator. As they say over here, 'Awfully bad form, old chap.' What was it this time?"

Ken told of his Scottish adventure and of his trip to Somerset, omitting his faux pas at the train station.

"Too bad you weren't able to talk to her when you were in Somerset," Jonathan said. "If she knew you'd gone all the way to Scotland for her, I'm sure she would have forgiven you for not getting to Kensington on time."

Ken nodded. "Perhaps," he said. "I did write her a letter of explanation. Now, I don't know what else to do."

Jonathan nodded empathetically. "I've written to her as well, asking about how her study of the gospel is progressing. I haven't heard from her yet." He paused and smiled. "Maybe you could get back in her good graces by following the example of the Holy Roman Emperor Henry IV. He stood in the snow in Canossa under Pope Gregory's window pleading for absolution. It took three days, but it worked!"

"If it would work for me, I'd do it."

Jonathan looked at Ken askance. "Did you tell her in your letter that you spent time alone on an island with Nell Keene?"

Ken frowned. "Yes, I did. Why is it that that's the only part of my story people remark on? It wasn't as if Nell and I planned to be stranded on the island."

"Nell, is it? Sounds like you two got rather chummy. I hope you behaved yourself."

Ken pursed his lips and shook his head. "No, I completely kicked over the traces. Nell and I had a torrid love affair!"

Jonathan regretted his remark. "Sorry."

"You should be. Despite what people say about orange sellers and actresses, Nell is an honorable woman who's devoted to her family, especially her mother."

"Speaking of good people," Jonathan said, eager to change the subject, "I would surely like to see Miss Gage baptized before I go home. I know she has a testimony. The Spirit was so strong in our meetings."

"It was," Ken agreed. "The last time I saw her she said she was still reading the Book of Mormon and interested in the Church. And, amazingly, despite everything, she has fulfilled her promise to copy the Ashcroft records."

"She's an elect young woman, no doubt about it. I wrote to her in care of Gage Hall, Ainsley, but, as I mentioned, I haven't had a reply yet. Now if you would only stop deceiving her . . ."

His sentence ended when he felt Ken's knuckles against his arm.

After a long silence, Ken asked, "By the way, Jonathan, where's the name 'Bartimaeus' found in the Bible?"

Jonathan thought for a minute. "Ah, I remember. He was a blind man."

Ken smiled. "So that's why Sir Jeffrey said that Mr. Squibbs was well named."

"Pardon?"

"Never mind. I guess I best be going."

"Oh, I almost forgot. There's a letter for you from Utah."

"All's well at home," Ken said after reading the letter from his mother. "Although it's made me a little homesick, I certainly feel better about things. As soon as Langton's trial is over, I'll be off to Somerset to straighten things out with Karen."

"That's the spirit," Jonathan said. "Good luck in court."

Lying in bed that night, Ken mentally reviewed the meeting he'd had with Sir Jeffrey, Sir Wilfred, and Chief Inspector Soames. He wondered if he should have told them that Karen did not find out that he was the son of the American claimant until Langton made the connection. *They probably assumed that Karen knew.* Now, a vague feeling of guilt spread through him. *Perhaps I should have told them.* Then it hit him! *Once I'm on the stand, Langton's lawyer will use this apparent deception to blacken my name. Why didn't I think of this before?* His guilty feeling was no longer vague, and he couldn't wait until the next meeting to rid his soul of the feeling. He had promised his parents not to get involved in the ring court case, and now inadvertently he was involved in another one. *I guess there's no help for it. I'll soon find out why the prophet and my parents have counseled us to stay out of gentile courts.*

* * *

At the meeting in Sir Jeffrey's office the next day, Ken immediately confessed to the three men.

"Why didn't you tell us this before?" Sir Jeffrey thundered.

"I'm sorry," Ken said. "I didn't think it important."

"Not important?" Sir Jeffrey said. "By the time Langton's barrister's through with you, Gandy will look like a saint in contrast."

"Well, at least we have this information in time to do something about it," Sir Wilfred said evenly. "Let's see where we stand. We could drop the conspiracy charge, but it would hurt the more serious charge since the two of them are linked together. We need the one to show Langton's motivation for the other. Also, if the Crown drops the first charge, it will reflect poorly on us."

"What if I drop the conspiracy charge against Langton?" Ken proposed. "Then it will not reflect on the Crown."

"This is not America, Mr. Sanderson," Sir Jeffrey said, having calmed down considerably. "Once the Crown knows that a crime has been committed they are obliged to prosecute whether or not a victim wants them to, providing, of course, that the evidence warrants it. If the Crown drops the conspiracy charge against Langton, it will be tantamount to admitting that no crime took place, and, as Sir Wilfred said, it will remove Langton's motivation for trying to drown you."

For several minutes there was silence in the room as the three men of the law mulled over the pros and cons of continuing the conspiracy case.

"If we could somehow connect Langton to Gandy," Soames said, "we might have a chance. I wonder if Gandy's ever been Langton's myrmidon in the past?" The policeman smiled at Ken's quizzical expression. "Hired ruffian," he explained.

Ken nodded his thanks. "Langton *does* know Gandy," he said, eager to redeem himself. "He as much as admitted it at the lodge. Jenkins should know if there's a connection. Maybe we could get Jenkins to testify."

"Jenkins?" Sir Wilfred asked.

"Langton's butler," Soames said. "I doubt if he would testify against his master, although he does have a mercenary streak a mile wide. Perhaps he could be induced—"

"I don't want to hear it, Chief Inspector," Sir Wilfred said quickly. "By all means get him to testify if you can, but I don't want to know how you do it. It goes without saying, of course, that if you do get him to testify, it will have to be in a way that there'll be no comebacks. We can't give Rampling ammunition to use against us."

"Let me handle it," Sir Jeffrey said. "Mr. Sanderson's told me about the avaricious Mr. Jenkins. I know how to handle his type."

The meeting ended with the unanimous decision that if Sir Jeffrey could induce Langton's butler to testify to a connection between Langton and Gandy, the case would go ahead. Otherwise, the conspiracy charge would be dropped. The four agreed to meet at the Old Bailey the next morning at eight sharp.

⊰ CHAPTER 22 ⊱

The next morning Ken caught an early omnibus and was on time for the meeting. The three men were all smiles when Ken entered the room. Sir Jeffrey had been successful with Jenkins, and the conspiracy charge would stand. After a few minutes, Sir Wilfred and Soames left, and for the next hour Sir Jeffrey groomed Ken on how to withstand Bradford Rampling's expected attack.

Just before ten o'clock, Ken walked into the witness room at the Old Bailey to find Langton's butler sitting gloomily on a hard wooden chair. "Mr. Jenkins," Ken said, "we meet again. I understand that you and Sir Jeffrey had a mutually beneficial interview."

The butler nodded gravely. "You could say that, sir."

Ken dearly wanted more information on their pact, but Jenkins would say no more. A minute later the usher called for Ken to enter the courtroom.

"Mr. Sanderson," Sir Wilfred Pilley said, after Ken had sworn to tell the truth, "opening statements have been presented, and it is now time for the testimonies of witnesses regarding the charge against Mr. Stephen Langton of conspiracy to commit grievous bodily harm. Please acquaint the court with what transpired between you and the accused on the afternoon of June seventh last at Gage Hall in Somerset and what befell you three days later near Billingsgate."

Having never before been a witness in a court case, Ken felt intimidated by the trappings of the English judicial system, especially by the judge high above him in his robe and wig and the similarly dressed barristers. Langton's scowling at Ken increased his discomfiture. Taking a deep breath, he began his testimony with the altercation between him and Langton. He emphasized that Langton had made it clear that Ken's mother had no right to Saladin's ring and that Ken should give up the quest for it and go back to America. He also emphasized that except for Miss Gage, Langton was the only other claimant who knew that Ken had any connection with the ring case.

"Was this when Miss Gage learned that your mother was also a claimant for Saladin's ring?" Sir Wilfred asked in an attempt to draw the sting out of Rampling's expected assault on Ken.

"Yes, sir," Ken said.

"Why did you not acquaint her with this fact earlier in your relationship?" the prosecutor asked.

As he had been coached, Ken spoke clearly and without emotion. "I had promised my parents not to get involved in the trial in any way. This included not revealing to anyone except Miss Maggie Stowell that my mother is a claimant."

"Was Miss Gage angry when she found out?"

"More hurt than angry, sir. However, she subsequently forgave me."

"Thank you, Mr. Sanderson. Would you now relate what happened in the alley near Billingsgate."

Ken testified that several days after the confrontation with Langton he had been accosted by Gandy and two other men. He explained that they dragged him into the alley and threatened him with bodily harm if he did not withdraw from the Saladin Ring case, and that when he refused to cooperate, Gandy and his henchmen carried out their threat. He pointed to the bruise under his eye. "My face is almost completely healed now, but this bruise resulted from the attack."

When Ken finished testifying, Sir Wilfred called for Jacob Gandy to be brought into the courtroom. The convict entered the room, shackled and under guard.

"Is this the man who attacked you, Mr. Sanderson?" the prosecutor asked.

"It is," Ken said. "I previously identified him in Newgate Prison."

Sir Wilfred turned to the judge. "Your Honor, this man, Jacob Gandy, has put his mark on a deposition acknowledging his guilt and implicating Mr. Langton in the assault. With the court's pleasure, I will read the deposition."

The judge, Sir Cedric Ellsworth, nodded assent and the prosecutor read Gandy's confession. He then yielded the floor to Langton's lawyer, Bradford Rampling.

"Your Honor, distinguished colleagues, and gentlemen of the jury," the barrister began, "on behalf of my client I would like to state that we do not contest that Mr. Jacob Gandy did in fact assault Mr. Sanderson on the night in question. We contend, however, that Mr. Sanderson's notion that the assault was in any way connected with the Saladin Ring case or my client is patently false. We will prove that the assault was perpetrated for the sole purpose of robbery." Turning to Ken, who was still in the witness box, the lawyer asked, "Mr. Sanderson, during the assault did a policeman carrying a lantern enter the alley, thus driving off your assailants?"

"Yes," Ken said.

"Thank you, Mr. Sanderson," Rampling said. "Your Honor, I have no further questions for this witness at this time but I would like to reserve the right to recall him. I would now like to call Mr. Gandy to the witness box."

The exchange was made and Ken, happy to have a reprieve from Rampling's questions, found himself on a chair behind Sir Wilfred and Sir Jeffrey. He glanced up to the balcony and saw Jack Tolley, who waved to him. He acknowledged Jack's wave with a nod. He then turned his attention to Gandy, who sat in the witness box gawking around, obviously delighted to be the center of attention.

"Your Honor," Mr. Rampling said, "may I have Mr. Gandy's deposition shown to him?"

The judge nodded and the usher took the document to Gandy.

"Do you recognize this document, Mr. Gandy?" Rampling asked. With squinted eyes the felon scrutinized the paper from all angles for a full minute. "Mr. Gandy," the barrister repeated, "do you recognize this document and is that your mark at the bottom?"

Gandy looked up. "Aye, gov, that's ma chicken scratch," he said. "I ain't nivver learned ma letters."

"Then you are unable to read the contents?" Rampling said. "Is that right?"

"Right, ye is, guv. Cain't make heads nor tails o' it."

"Well, let me acquaint you with its contents. It says that you assaulted . . . thrashed . . . Mr. Sanderson. Please arise, Mr. Sanderson." Ken stood up and the barrister pointed a bony finger at him. "Did you attack that man in an alley, Mr. Gandy?"

Gandy squinted at Ken for a moment before saying, "Aye. That's the one awright."

"Why did you do it?"

"Needed the sausage and mash. A man's gotta eat, don't he?"

"So you assaulted him for money to buy food, is that right?"

"That's it, guv."

"If that is true, why did you and your two accomplices not take Mr. Sanderson's wallet?"

"Run off, wasn't we? Didn't want t' be nicked by the peeler."

"Are you saying that one policeman scared off the three of you?"

Gandy appeared affronted as he unconsciously ran his thumb down the scar on his face. "One blow on 'is whistle and there'd be a whole pack of 'em," Gandy said defensively. "Me 'n' me mates wuz after some easy brass, not another st'y in Newgyte."

Rampling nodded thoughtfully. "Let me fully understand, Mr. Gandy. Before you and your associates—your mates—were able to take Mr. Sanderson's wallet, you were run off by the policeman."

"That's it, guv."

"Thank you, Mr. Gandy. Gentlemen of the jury, please note that Mr. Gandy's assertion that a policeman drove him and his associates off before they could take Mr. Sanderson's wallet is consistent with Mr. Sanderson's previous testimony." Rampling turned back to Gandy. "Now, Mr. Gandy, in the document in front of you it states that you were paid by Mr. Langton to thrash Mr. Sanderson. Were you in fact paid money by Mr. Langton?"

"Who?"

"Mr. Langton," the barrister repeated, pointing at his client. "Have you ever seen that man before?"

Gandy squinted at Langton as he had at Ken. Then he said, "Can't say's I has. Course one toff looks the same t'me as a t'other."

"And you never took money from anyone to attack Mr. Sanderson?"

"Nivver."

"Then why did you sign a document stating that you had?"

Gandy frowned and twisted his lips. "What?"

"In the piece of paper you marked it says that you took money from my client as payment for attacking Mr. Sanderson. If that's false, why did you sign the paper?"

"Hungry, weren't I?"

Rampling feigned a shocked expression. "Are you saying that you were denied food in prison until you signed the document?"

"That's it. Starvin' I was. A man's gotta eat, don't he?"

The barrister shook his head. "Let's be clear on this point, Mr. Gandy. You are saying that you signed this document under duress?"

Gandy frowned and screwed up his face. "Naw. I warn't under nuthin'. Marked it on table, didn't I?"

Snickers from the audience brought the usher's command of, "Quiet in the court!"

When all was quiet again, Mr. Rampling, his face full of righteous indignation, turned toward the bench. "Your Honor, I move that this so-called confession be stricken from the record. It was obviously signed under duress."

The judge looked skeptical. "Either that, or Mr. Gandy's been coached to pull the wool over our eyes," he said. "Nevertheless, the deposition is stricken. Sir Wilfred, have you any questions of this witness?"

"Yes, Your Honor," the prosecutor said. "Mr. Gandy, have you or have you not had dealings with this man, Stephen Langton?"

Gandy squirmed in his seat for a moment before saying, "I've 'ad nowt t'do wi' 'im."

"You've never spoken with him before?"

"That's about the size o' it, guv."

"Thank you, Mr. Gandy." Turning to the bench the prosecutor said, "Your Honor, I would now like to call Mr. Langton's butler, Mr. John Jenkins, to the witness box."

From Ken's position he could only see the side of Langton's face, but it was enough for him to know that Langton was completely taken off guard. Rampling leapt to his feet. "Your Honor, before this new witness is called, may I exercise my right to recall Mr. Kenny Sanderson?"

The judge allowed Rampling's request and Ken found himself back in the box. "Mr. Sanderson," Rampling said, "how long did you keep the fact from Miss Gage that your mother was also a claimant to Saladin's ring?"

"Relevance, Your Honor?" Sir Wilfred said. "Mr. Sanderson has already testified regarding this."

"If I may have the court's indulgence," Rampling said, "I will show relevance."

The judge nodded. "I'll allow it, Mr. Rampling, but no fishing for information. Please answer the question, Mr. Sanderson."

"About two weeks," Ken said.

"And during that fortnight, how often did you see Miss Gage?"

Ken hedged. "Quite often."

"Can you be more specific?"

"Almost every day."

"During those fourteen days, did the subject of the Saladin Ring trial come up?"

"Yes."

"Yet you never revealed that your mother was also after the ring?"

"No."

"Did you not feel guilty discussing the trial and withholding such important information from Miss Gage?"

Sir Wilfred stood up. "Your Honor, Mr. Sanderson's feelings have no bearing on this case. As we learned earlier, Mr. Sanderson had good reasons for not revealing this information to Miss Gage."

"Sustained," Sir Cedric said. "Show relevance, Mr. Rampling, or cease this line of questioning."

Rampling nodded to the bench. "How did Miss Gage react when she found out that you had deceived her?"

Again Sir Wilfred intervened. "Your Honor, it has not been established that Mr. Sanderson *did* deceive Miss Gage," he said.

"Sustained. Please rephrase your question, Mr. Rampling," the judge ruled.

Again, Rampling bowed to the bench before turning back to Ken. "How did Miss Gage react when she found out that your mother was also contending for Saladin's ring?"

Ken paused before saying, "She asked Mr. Langton and me to leave her house. Then she left the room."

"Would you say that she was angry?"

"Yes. She was angry with Mr. Langton and me both."

"Yet the very next day, Miss Gage accompanied Mr. Langton in his coach to London and partnered with him for the upcoming trial. Is that not right?"

"Yes."

"Obviously, she was more angry with you than she was with my client." Addressing the judge, he continued. "Your Honor, I will now show the relevance of these questions. Mr. Gandy has testified that he and his companions assaulted Mr. Sanderson for the sole purpose of getting money to buy food. However, before they could attain Mr. Sanderson's wallet, a policeman chased them off. Mr. Sanderson has also testified to the latter.

"It is our contention that when Mr. Gandy attacked Mr. Sanderson, who was still smarting at having had his duplicity exposed, the latter erroneously equated the attack with my client. We contend that it is mere coincidence the attack followed shortly after the altercation between my client and Mr. Sanderson, and that there is not a shred of evidence connecting the two incidents."

Rampling sat down and Sir Wilfred declined the invitation to further question Ken.

"I see that midday is upon us," Sir Cedric said. "We will recess until two o'clock, at which time we will hear from the Crown's next witness."

As the courtroom cleared, Ken turned to Sir Jeffrey. "Are we winning?" he asked.

Sir Jeffrey shook his head. "Based on this morning's proceedings, we wouldn't have a prayer. But our esteemed colleague, Mr. Rampling, has boxed himself in with his last comment. If we can prove a connection between Langton and Gandy, the case is ours. Here's hoping the avaricious Mr. Jenkins will perform well in the box and provide that proof."

During the recess Ken sought out Jack. "I was pleased to see you in the balcony, Jack," Ken said, glancing at the battered portfolio under Jack's arm. "Have you an interest in Langton's trial?"

Jack nodded. "That I have, lad. Thanks to Sir Jeffrey—and you—I'm movin' up in the world. The *Illustrated Press's* hired me t'make sketches o' the proceedin's. I've never made such brass in m'life!"

"I couldn't be more pleased for you," Ken said, shaking Jack's hand.

Jack invited Ken to a pub for lunch. Ken, however, wanted to go to a tearoom. They compromised by having their meal in the dining room of the Winchester Hotel.

"So you don't drink spirits, Mr. Ken?" Jack asked while they were waiting for their order.

"No. Mormons don't drink liquor, tea, or coffee. And we don't use tobacco."

Jack nodded thoughtfully. "I can't imagine life wi'out my pint. I wonder if Maggie takes a drink now and then?"

"I don't know. Miss Gage is a teetotaler, so perhaps Maggie is too. She worked many years for my mother and grandfather and they both practiced abstinence." Ken smiled. "Miss Gage's aunt said that you were walking out with Maggie. Is something going on that I should know about?"

Jack shrugged. "I thought there was, but the other day I gets a note at the paper saying she's off to Somerset. Maybe I'll take a run down there when the trial's over. She's a fine lass."

Ken thought of his last meeting with Maggie. "She certainly is," he said, "but I wouldn't get on the wrong side of her. She can be . . . stubborn."

* * *

When the case resumed in the afternoon, John Jenkins was called to the witness box. While he was being sworn in, Langton's eyes never left him. At one point, Ken observed Langton surreptitiously run his index finger across his throat, signaling Jenkins that it was worth his life to testify. Ken wondered what kind of bargain Sir Jeffrey had made with the butler. What would make a man like Jenkins risk his life by testifying against his master?

"Mr. Jenkins," Sir Wilfred said, "I will ask you only one question. To your knowledge has there ever been a connection between Mr. Stephen Langton and Mr. Jacob Gandy?"

Jenkins did not hesitate. "I'll say. There most definitely has been a connection. Gandy's been the Langtons' cat's paw for a ton o' years. Whenever any dirty work needed doin', old Sir Gerald or Master Stephen would say, 'Get Gandy!' Course, he never come to the house. But I've seen him together with Sir Gerald or Master Stephen time and again."

"Thank you, Mr. Jenkins. Your witness, Mr. Rampling."

Rampling had an animated conference with his client before turning accusing eyes on the witness and asking, "How long have you served in the Langton household, Mr. Jenkins?"

"Forty years. Started out as a stable boy and worked my way up."

"Forty years." Rampling drew out the words. "Yet you seem to have no compunction in testifying against your employer."

"Ex-employer. My notice is on his desk, isn't it? Of course, he's been in Newgate and hasn't seen it. I hope they keep 'im there. Like his late father, he's an evil man, and I'm glad to be shut of the whole breed of—"

Rampling appealed to the bench and the judge cautioned Jenkins, "Please restrict your answers to 'yes' or 'no,' Mr. Jenkins."

Before continuing, Rampling, through narrowed eyes, observed Jenkins the way one would gaze on a loathsome insect. "Yours is not a very charitable attitude, Mr. Jenkins," Rampling finally said, "not charitable at all toward a family who have kept you for so many years. But laying that aside, I am going to ask you an important question and I remind you that you are under oath. If you do not answer it honestly, it is *you* who will be in Newgate Prison. Have you or have you not accepted money for bearing testimony against your employer? Think very carefully before you answer."

Ken held his breath as Jenkins cleared his throat. Then the butler spoke clearly. "Not likely, sir. I's doing my civic duty being here."

Rampling was visibly shocked. "Are you saying under oath that you did not accept any compensation for your testimony?"

"No sir. Not a brass farthing."

Rampling didn't know what to say next. After a long pause, he finally mumbled, "No further questions."

"You may step down, Mr. Jenkins," the judge said. "As there are no further witnesses, we will give each counselor time for summation. Sir Wilfred, please lead off."

Sir Wilfred stood up, adjusted his wig and ran his eyes over the twelve men who would decide Langton's fate. "Gentlemen of the jury," he began, "we are not here to determine whether or not Mr. Gandy assaulted Mr. Sanderson. Mr. Gandy has confessed to this crime and will be duly punished for it. We are here to determine whether or not Mr. Stephen Langton conspired with Mr. Jacob Gandy to commit this crime. Let me review the facts that have come out of these proceedings. Fact one, in an altercation with Mr. Sanderson prior to the assault, Mr. Langton in so many words demanded that Mr. Sanderson withdraw from the Saladin Ring case. Fact two, Mr. Gandy threatened Mr. Sanderson with violence if he did not withdraw from the case in question. Fact three, Mr. Sanderson refused and was cruelly beaten. Fact four, Mr. Gandy has admitted to assaulting Mr. Sanderson. Fact five, the accused's butler, Mr. John Jenkins, has testified that Mr. Gandy has been doing the Langtons' 'dirty work' for many years.

"I'm sure that you will agree, gentlemen, that these facts lead to the unmistakable conclusion that Mr. Stephen Langton did in very deed instruct Mr. Gandy to intimidate Mr. Sanderson, with force if necessary, into withdrawing from the Saladin Ring case. When Mr. Sanderson refused to cooperate,

Mr. Gandy and his two associates attempted to beat him into submission. There is no doubt, therefore, that Mr. Langton is guilty of conspiracy to do grievous bodily harm. Gentlemen of the jury, you have no alternative but to find Mr. Langton guilty as charged. The Crown rests."

Langton's lawyer then took the floor. "Gentlemen of the jury," he said, "the guilt or innocence of my client rests on the testimony of a disgruntled servant, Mr. John Jenkins, a man who, by his own admission, has an ax to grind. For forty years the Langton family have fed and clothed this man and provided a roof over his head. Now, for reasons inexplicable, he has turned on his employer. Can we take the word of such a miscreant? Can we take the word of a man who bites the hand that has fed him lo these many years? I think not. And I am confident, gentlemen, that you think not also. Without Mr. Jenkins's testimony the Crown has only the word of Mr. Sanderson, who, as has been proven in this court, is not beyond deception. The prosecution has failed miserably to prove beyond doubt that my client has had anything to do with this sordid affair, and I would ask you to find my client innocent of these charges. The defense rests."

"Gentlemen of the jury," the judge said, "do you wish for time to confer?"

The foreman stood up. "Aye, Your Honor."

Sir Cedric nodded. "We will recess until you have made your decision." The judge then rapped his gavel authoritatively.

Ken leaned forward between Sir Jeffrey and Sir Wilfred. "How will the jury rule?" he asked.

Sir Jeffrey nodded smugly. "Guilty as charged. No doubt about it."

"If there's no doubt about it," Ken asked, "why did they retire to deliberate?"

The two barristers exchanged amused looks. "To get one last meal out of the Crown, of course," Sir Jeffrey said. "They'll drag it out till teatime and then announce a guilty verdict."

"I see," Ken said. "Another question. How did you get Jenkins to testify, Sir Jeffrey? It was obvious that he was telling the truth when he said you didn't pay him."

"As I indicated before," Sir Wilfred said quickly, "I do not want to hear this. So, if you'll excuse me, gentlemen, I'll see you back here anon."

After the prosecutor had left, Sir Jeffrey glanced around the room. As it was emptying fast and as there was no one within earshot, he said in a low voice, "Jenkins, of course, demanded money. But I explained to him that under the circumstances it was impossible. I asked him what he wanted the money for and he informed me that he and his wife had their hearts set on a house in Blackpool. They wanted to retire there and hire out rooms to bathers. Their problem was that Jenkins didn't have enough money to buy it outright and no one would give him a mortgage. This knowledge gave me the lever I needed. I simply promised to use my influence with the bank to get him a mortgage."

"So that did it?" Ken asked. "It seems too simple."

Sir Jeffrey shook his head. "It was not that simple. Jenkins, of course, was afraid that if he testified Langton would retaliate. If anyone knows Langton's murderous nature it's Jenkins."

Ken nodded. "I wondered about that. So how did you convince him?"

Sir Jeffrey smiled smugly, obviously pleased with himself. "I convinced him to take out some insurance. After forty years' service in the Langton household, he has a wealth of dirty linen on the family, including the fact that Langton actually is a murderer even though he got off with self-defense. From what he told me, there'll be enough evidence to put Langton away for life. I instructed him to write down all of Langton's dirty secrets and deposit the document in my safe. If anything untoward happens to Jenkins, I promised to deliver copies of the document to Smollett over at the *Times* and to Sir Wilfred. In short, once the current trial is over Langton will be informed that the thread holding the Sword of Damocles over his head will snap if anything happens to Jenkins."

"Brilliant!" Ken said.

The courtroom was even more crowded when the trial resumed to receive the verdict. Despite the throng, all was quiet when Sir Cedric Ellsworth asked the jury if they had reached a verdict regarding the charge of conspiracy to commit grievous bodily harm.

"No, Your Honor," the foreman said. "We can't agree."

Ken glanced at Sir Jeffrey, whose face had turned white. The barrister shook his head back and forth in utter dismay. From the audience bedlam ensued, and it took the usher several minutes to restore order. Then the judge, with a satisfied look on his face, addressed the jury, "Will more time lead to a unanimous decision?"

"No, sir," the foreman said. "It's ten against two and the two won't budge."

"Sounds like Langton's money has won again," Sir Wilfred whispered to Sir Jeffrey.

"In that case," the judge said. "We will adjourn for today and resume tomorrow morning to consider the second and more serious charge against Mr. Langton. Court adjourned."

⊰ CHAPTER 23 ⊱

"Lady Darnley, Miss Treadwell, it's good to see you both again," Ken said the next morning as he entered the small witness room at the Old Bailey. Nell, wearing a flaming red, high-collared frock with a cameo broach at her throat and a matching feathered hat, warmly returned his greeting. The maid nodded but didn't speak.

"You look rather . . . theatrical," Ken said to Nell.

Nell smiled. "Give the public what they want," she said, striking a pose. "Glamour, fashion, novelty—they eat it up!"

Ken smiled and glanced around the seedy, windowless witness room. "You certainly look out of place here in the Black Hole of Calcutta," he said.

Nell laughed. "You'd think the court facilities of the seat of empire would be a little more accommodating," she said. "Hopefully, we won't be penned up long."

Nell had no sooner finished speaking than the usher called Ken to testify.

"Here I go again," he said as he got up to leave the room. He smiled at Nell. "Good luck when it's your turn." She answered him with a nod and a wave. Miss Treadwell had curled up in a wooden chair and appeared to be asleep.

The courtroom was filled to capacity. *No doubt most are here to get a glimpse of Nell,* Ken thought as he mounted the stairs to the witness box and was sworn in.

"In your own words, Mr. Sanderson," Sir Wilfred said, "please acquaint the court with what transpired on June thirteenth last at the shooting lodge of Mr. Stephen Langton on Inchmoan Island in Loch Lomond, Scotland."

Ken nodded. "Yes, sir. I went to Scotland on the mistaken assumption that Mr. Stephen Langton was holding, against her will, a friend of mine at his shooting lodge. In the Savoy Hotel in front of witnesses, he had threatened her, and I thought he had carried out his threat. As it turned out, I found that my friend was not there. Instead, I found Lady Darnley and her maid, Miss Treadwell, at the lodge. Lady Darnley invited me inside. She told me Mr. Langton had induced her to go to the lodge under false pretenses and that they had an altercation earlier in the day. When she had asked to be transported back to London, Mr. Langton had refused. In essence she and her maid were being held on the island against their will. She asked me if I would take them to Luss, the nearest village, in my hired boat. Before I could answer, Mr. Langton charged into the room and threatened me with a shotgun. After an exchange of words, he reluctantly agreed to transport Lady Darnley and Miss Treadwell off the island. He went off to prepare his steam launch. Then about twenty minutes later Lady Darnley, Miss Treadwell, and I went down to the jetty. After Miss Treadwell and I placed Lady Darnley's portmanteau aboard the launch, Miss Treadwell stayed aboard. Lady Darnley, however, decided to go in my hired boat rather than in the launch."

"Why was that, Mr. Sanderson?" Sir Wilfred asked.

Ken shook his head. "I'm not sure. She was certainly angry with Mr. Langton. When she asked to go with me, Mr. Langton exploded and commanded her to go on the launch. When she still refused, he called on Miss Treadwell to witness that he had tried to get Lady Darnley to travel on his boat, but that Lady Darnley had refused. He stated that if Lady Darnley got into trouble in the small boat with the fog rolling in, it would be upon her own head."

"Do you think he was truly concerned with Lady Darnley's safety, or had he another reason for not wanting her to go in your boat?"

Before Ken could answer, Langton's barrister was on his feet. "That calls for conjecture, Your Honor," he said. "Mr. Sanderson could not read Mr. Langton's mind."

"Sustained," Sir Cedric said. "Please avoid leading the witness, Sir Wilfred."

The prosecutor bowed his head toward the bench and then turned back to Ken. "Please continue, Mr. Sanderson."

Ken continued his testimony. When he began narrating the incident about beaching the boat and spending time on the island with Nell, a loud buzz spread throughout the courtroom.

The usher, a beefy fellow whose broken nose hinted that he was once a prizefighter, loudly called for order. Unfortunately, the man had the peculiar habit of some Englishmen of adding *h*'s to words, so it came out as, "Horder in the court! Horder, I say!"

"Now let me get this clear," Sir Wilfred said when the room was quiet. "On your way across to the shooting lodge, the hired boat was dry. But on the return trip it filled with water?"

"Yes, sir. There was a little water in the boat on the way over, but it was only from my splashing some in. I am not very adept at rowing. On the way to the lodge the boat definitely did not leak."

"And you are sure that there was a bailer in the boat when you left for the lodge?"

"Yes, sir. Mr. Graham pointed it out to me, and I saw it with my own eyes."

"And it was not in the boat on your return voyage when you desperately needed it?"

"That's right, sir."

"Did you discover the cause of the leak?"

"Yes, sir. Someone, and I can only assume it to be Mr. Langton since there was no one else on the island, had punctured the rear of the boat just above the waterline."

"More conjecture!" Mr. Rampling cried out as he rose from his chair. "Unless I am mistaken, there is no evidence to show that the hole was even made by a person, no less my client."

"Sustained," the judge said. "Please rephrase your answer, Mr. Sanderson, avoiding assumptions."

Ken chose his words carefully and spoke slowly and deliberately. "Lady Darnley found a hole in the boat after we were forced to beach it on the island because it had filled up with water. The hole was just above the waterline when the boat was empty, but under this line when occupied."

"And how did you and Lady Darnley get off the island, Mr. Sanderson?"

"She plugged the hole with a stick before we started back. On our way we met Constable McTavish in Mr. Langton's launch, and he towed us to Luss."

"Thank you, Mr. Sanderson. I have no more questions," Sir Wilfred said, yielding the floor to Langton's lawyer.

Bradford Rampling unfolded his long legs and slowly rose. "Mr. Sanderson," he said, "you stated that you traveled all the way from London to Scotland on the mistaken assumption that a friend was being held captive there. Is that true?"

"That is true." Ken said firmly. "I would have gone to the ends of the earth for her if I thought she were in trouble."

"Very noble of you, I'm sure," the barrister said, his words dripping sarcasm. "However, the fact remains that you came to your erroneous conclusion on very flimsy evidence. Similarly, on very flimsy evidence, you have concluded that my client had something to do with your boat springing a leak. First, let me say that it is not unusual for rowboats to leak. Those of us who have spent a Sunday afternoon on the Serpentine can attest to that. Second, you have admitted that you are not an experienced boatman. Is it not possible that because of your incompetence you could have bumped the boat against a jagged rock or perhaps a submerged tree trunk with jagged branches sticking from it and thus punctured it? Is that not possible?"

Ken shrugged. "It is possible, but—"

"Thank you, Mr. Sanderson," the barrister said quickly. "No further questions."

"You may be seated in the chairs provided for witnesses, Mr. Sanderson," Sir Cedric said. "Usher, please call Constable Walcott to the witness box."

PC Walcott, one of the two constables who had gone to Scotland to collect Langton, was sworn in, and Sir Wilfred rose to question him.

"Constable Walcott," Sir Wilfred said, "I have before me the deposition you took from Mr. George Graham, the owner and builder of the rowboat in which Mr. Sanderson and Lady Darnley almost lost their lives. In your own words, please tell us what Mr. Graham said regarding the hole found in the boat."

The policeman opened a small notebook and studied it before saying, "He said the hole were made deliberate, like, sir. It were too smooth t'be made accidental. He were most definite 'bout this. In his opinion it were made with a dirk, sir, or a dagger as we call it, a two-edged one wi' a sharp point. It's all in the report."

"Thank you, Constable," Sir Wilfred said.

"Your witness, Mr. Rampling."

"Constable Walcott," Rampling said, "was a dirk or dagger found on the launch, or anywhere else for that matter?"

"No, sir."

"Then Mr. Graham's opinion is pure speculation. Is that right?"

"I suppose, sir. But Mr. Graham were most definite."

Since Rampling had no more questions for the policeman, Lady Darnley was called to replace him in the witness box. A buzz arose and many necks craned to get a glimpse of the celebrated actress. The cynosure of all eyes, Nell entered with a flourish and made the most of her walk to the witness box, where she was sworn in. Sitting demurely in the box, she answered Sir Wilfred's questions in a clear, controlled voice.

She confirmed all that Ken had said, laying special emphasis on the fact that Langton had strenuously objected to her going on Ken's boat rather than his.

When it came time for her cross-examination, Rampling went for the jugular. "Is it customary, Lady Darnley," he sneered, "for you to go off to a remote island with a single man, such as my client?"

"No, sir," she said calmly. "Is it customary for you to attempt to besmirch a lady's reputation?"

Amid snickers from the audience, Rampling appealed to the judge. "Your Honor . . ."

Sir Cedric suppressed a grin. "Quiet in the court," he said. Turning to Nell he added, "Please answer the questions without commentary, Lady Darnley."

Nell bowed her head to the bench.

"Did your husband approve of this assignation, Lady Darnley?" was Rampling's next question.

Sir Wilfred jumped to his feet. "Your Honor, I must protest this line of questioning. Lady Darnley is not on trial."

"I am only attempting to establish the credibility of this witness, Your Honor," Rampling said.

Amid boos from the audience and stern glances at Rampling from some members of the jury, the usher called for quiet. Sir Cedric fixed Rampling with his eyes. "Mr. Rampling, I am well acquainted with Lady Darnley," he said sternly, "and I will personally vouch for her credibility. Let us have no more of such questions."

Realizing that Nell had the sympathy of the judge and the jury, Rampling decided he'd better get her off the stand as fast as possible. However, he had one more question.

"Lady Darnley," he said, "in your testimony you make my client out to be a desperate character. However, you seem to have had no qualms about sending your maid alone with him on the launch. It seems to me that your actions belie your words. Can you explain this discrepancy?"

"I can," Nell said with confidence. "At first I was concerned about sending my maid alone with Mr. Langton. However, when he made such a production about Miss Treadwell being his witness that he had tried to dissuade me from going on the small boat, I realized that she was in no danger. One does not harm one's witness."

Nell's answer, so logical and so well delivered, caused Rampling to instantly dismiss her, which elicited a sigh from the audience as if the main act of a play had suddenly been canceled. To Ken's surprise, Stephen Langton was then placed in the witness box and sworn to tell the truth.

"Mr. Langton," Rampling said, "please cast some light on what actually happened at your shooting lodge and dispel all these unfounded assumptions."

Langton nodded and assumed the demeanor and voice of a vicar. "Over a period of time," he began, "I became acquainted with Lady Darnley at social functions. Once or twice I happened to mention my shooting lodge in Scotland and the beauties of Loch Lomond. Many times she expressed her desire to go there. Eventually I gave in to her importunities. However, hardly had we gotten there when she demanded to be taken back to London. Since I had gone to Scotland for a spot of shooting, I told her she'd have to wait. I then took my gun and went after ducks. When I returned, she was entertaining Sanderson in my home. As you can imagine, I was shocked at this intrusion and an argument ensued. The result was that I agreed to take Lady Darnley and her maid off the island. At the jetty she demanded to go in Sanderson's hired boat. Concerned for her safety, I objected, but she was adamant. What happened after that, I do not know. I took the maid and Lady Darnley's travel bag to Luss as I had promised."

"Thank you, Mr. Langton," Rampling said. "And you have no knowledge about how Mr. Sanderson's boat sprung a leak or what happened to the alleged bailer?"

"None," Langton said.

"Thank you, Mr. Langton," Rampling said. "Your witness, Sir Wilfred."

"Mr. Langton," the prosecutor said, "is it true that you were down at the jetty alone for approximately twenty minutes preparing the launch?"

"Yes."

"Did you go near Mr. Sanderson's boat during that time."

"No."

"Was there anyone else on the island other than you, Lady Darnley, Miss Treadwell, and Mr. Sanderson?"

"I don't know."

"Did you see or hear anyone on the island other than those mentioned?"

"No."

"Then how do you account for the hole in Mr. Sanderson's hired boat?"

"I believe that Mr. Rampling's idea has merit. Sanderson probably knocked a hole in it through incompetence."

"No further questions," the prosecutor said.

Stephen Langton was the last witness and the judge directed the opposing counsel to sum up. In his closing argument, Sir Wilfred insisted that the evidence clearly pointed to Langton as the only one who could have made the hole in the boat and remove the bailer. He then spoke to motivation:

"Gentlemen of the jury, Mr. Langton's reasons for attempting to drown Mr. Sanderson are manifold. But I will cite only two. First, he resents Mr. Sanderson because the latter's family is contesting the ownership of the so-called Saladin's ring, which had been in the Langton family for six hundred years. Second, he wanted to stop Mr. Sanderson from testifying against him in court regarding charges that he hired three thugs to force Mr. Sanderson to withdraw from the Saladin Ring case. Had the small boat sunk in deep water and Mr. Sanderson drowned, Mr. Langton would not now be facing possible incarceration for conspiracy to cause grievous bodily harm. Furthermore, by insisting that Miss Treadwell be his witness that he had tried to stop Lady Darnley from going in the small rowboat, he tried to cover himself in the event that Lady Darnley also drowned.

"To conclude, gentlemen, the evidence is overwhelming that Mr. Stephen Langton did in fact attempt to commit the murder by drowning of Mr. Kenny Sanderson by boring a hole in his boat and removing the bailer. Furthermore, by not warning Lady Darnley that he had rendered the boat unsafe, he in effect is guilty of an attempt to murder her also. You, gentlemen, have no alternative but to find Mr. Stephen Langton guilty as charged. Thank you."

In his summation, Rampling insisted that since there was no physical evidence that his client had had anything to do with Ken's hired boat, all was circumstantial and the case should be dismissed. Once again the jury elected to have time to deliberate. Ken hoped that, as Sir Jeffrey had suggested the day before, it was only because they wanted to have one more meal on the Crown.

That afternoon court resumed. Once again the jury was deadlocked at ten for guilty and two for not guilty. Sir Cedric Ellsworth declared a mistrial and released Langton on bail.

❈ CHAPTER 24 ❈

Later that afternoon Ken lay on his bed in his luxurious room at Lady Brideswell's, deep in thought. Disappointed at the mistrial, he wondered what more he could have done to help convict Langton. His mind then turned to Karen. *I wonder if Jonathan's received Karen's letter? I wonder what it says? Should I go see Jonathan? Should I try again to see Karen?* Despite his previous resolve to go to Somerset again once Langton's trial was over, he decided against it. If either Jonathan or Karen had anything to say to him, they knew where he was. In the meantime, he would not be idle. It was time to set aside his personal life and immerse himself in writing articles for his employer. *Hard work is what I need right now.* With this resolve he launched into a travel piece on Loch Lomond.

Two days later he was busily working on the article when Mr. Bramley brought him a copy of the *Times*. "You may be interested in the lead article, Mr. Sanderson," the butler said.

Ken was very much interested in the headline: "Saladin's Ring Back!" He learned from the article that a minor burglar had tried to fence the ruby ring and had been turned in to Scotland Yard. The article also said that after several postponements, the much-anticipated trial would begin in two days.

That would be Monday the twenty-second, he thought. *When it's over I hope I never see the inside of a court again. Oh, wait. There's still Langton's retrial. Well, after that, then.* As he thought about the ring trial and realized that Karen would be there, his disgust with the Old Bailey lessened. *Perhaps I'll have a chance to explain in person why I didn't show up in Kensington as promised. I hope the fact that we're both vying for the ring won't be an obstacle to rebuilding our friendship.*

* * *

Ken again entered the Old Bailey. As the lower floor was filled, he climbed to the balcony. The ancient building was crowded with people of all classes. *Where have all these people come from? Don't they have employment?* As he glanced around the windowless room, lit by flickering gaslights, a sense of panic enveloped him. *What if a fire breaks out? We'd all be burned alive.* Making his way to the railing, he looked down to the main floor. An involuntary gasp escaped his lips when he saw Karen sitting next to Stephen Langton. It pained Ken that she was going ahead with their partnership. Then he remembered that she had signed an agreement with Langton and had no choice but to honor it. Despite his revulsion at seeing them together, his admiration for Karen increased. The wide space between her and Langton testified that the partners had not resumed cordial personal relations, giving Ken great satisfaction. As he stared down at her, she was glancing around the courtroom expectantly. Ken fervently hoped that she was looking for him.

Next to Karen was a little, round man in a ratty wig. Ken assumed that he was the "well-named" Bartimaeus Squibbs, Karen's barrister. *Bartimaeus the barrister. I wonder if he is as blind as his namesake.* Ken recognized Sir Wilfred Pilley and assumed that he was representing the Crown. As he gazed down at Karen, a great sense of loss swept over him. *How could I have been so foolish as to let her slip away from me?*

"Over here, Mr. Ken," said a voice.

Ken's eyes followed the sound. Jack Tolley was waving him over to a front-row seat. The artist had a sketch pad on his knee and a pencil in his hand.

"Jack," Ken said, "do you attend all the trials now?"

"Whenever I'm sent," he said as he moved over to give Ken room.

Ken glanced down at Karen and then back at Jack. "If you have the time, would you make me a sketch of Miss Gage?"

Jack nodded. "Consider it done, Mr. Ken. She's a real charmer in that blue frock. Did you see Maggie? Sir Jeffrey's sent for her."

"To testify?"

"Aye. Miss Gage is all right wi' it."

Ken nodded, remembering what Karen had said. "She's no doubt sequestered. Witnesses aren't allowed into the court until they testify."

Jack nodded. "I'm lookin' forrard to seein' 'er again."

Ken smiled inwardly but didn't comment.

"Quiet in the court," cried the usher. "All stand."

The bewigged and berobed judge, Sir Lionel Bradbury, took his seat behind the bench, the audience resumed sitting, and the proceedings commenced. Addressing the jury, Sir Lionel charged them with the task of deciding the lawful ownership of the so-called Saladin's ring. He hoped that they could clear up the matter in one day, and his demeanor indicated that he'd rather the jury were deciding the fate of a thief or a murderer than wasting its time on a piece of jewelry.

"Since this is not a trial in the regular sense," Sir Lionel said, squinting over his wire-rimmed spectacles, "I will allow some latitude. However, I warn council not to abuse my generosity. This is how we shall conduct the proceedings: each barrister will be granted time to argue his case. After each presentation, I will instruct the jury. When all counsel have had their say, each will have the opportunity of a summation. It will then be up to you gentlemen of the jury to decide the disposition of this article. I repeat that I would very much like to get this over with in one day so that we can get on to more important matters. We have already drawn lots as to the order of the presentations and Mr. Squibbs will lead off.

"However, before calling on Mr. Squibbs, I think it appropriate to acquaint the court with the happenings leading to these proceedings. Therefore, we will first hear from Mr. Solomon Levi, an expert in all things pertaining to jewelry. Mr. Levi will also comment on the ring's value."

A small, elderly man with wispy white hair protruding from under his skullcap was ushered to the witness stand and sworn in.

"I have examined the ring in question," he began in a surprisingly firm, clear voice, "and can state without doubt that it is of ancient origin. It features an exquisite square-cut ruby set in solid gold. An interlaced crescent moon pattern extends from shoulder to shoulder. Inside is inscribed in Arabic, *Salah ad-Din*, an honorific that means 'Righteousness of the Faith.' As a piece of jewelry I would estimate its worth at ten thousand pounds sterling." A gasp from the audience. "However, its real value far exceeds that figure. What makes it so valuable is its provenance. I have no reason to doubt the information supplied by one of the claimants, Mr. Stephen Langton, and recorded in the press. I am satisfied that the ring once belonged to Saladin the Muhammadan Sultan of Egypt. During the Third Crusade in the twelfth century, it is written that he awarded the ring to King Richard the Lionhearted in token of a truce. After King Richard died, his brother King John inherited it. Later, King John ran afoul of the Pope and his representative in England, the Archbishop of Canterbury, Stephen Langton, ancestor of the claimant. This, of course, was long before the Act of Supremacy separated the English Church from Rome. The altercation between King John and the Church led to the king's excommunication. Eventually, however, the king and archbishop came to an accommodation and the king was readmitted to the Church. As a token of this reconciliation, King John awarded Saladin's ring to the archbishop, who eventually willed it to a relative. The ring then passed down in the Langton family until thirty years ago when Sir Gerald Langton lost it to Lord Eustas Claverley in a game of chance." The old man paused to drink water from a mug and then continued. "In assessing the ring's true value, therefore, its history must be taken into consideration. Thus, I would conservatively estimate the value at five times the real value or fifty thousand pounds sterling."

A second gasp rose from the audience followed by an animated buzz. Ken turned to Jack. "I can't believe it," he said, converting the English pounds to American dollars in his head. "That's . . . that's a quarter of a million dollars."

"A pricey little bauble, for sure," Jack said.

"Horder in the court," the usher yelled.

The audience eventually obeyed and the judge spoke: "Thank you, Mr. Levi. Please step down. We now yield the floor to Mr. Bartimaeus Squibbs."

Mr. Squibbs rose to his full height of five-foot-two and said, "Your worship, members of the jury, and distinguished colleagues, I acknowledge Your Honor's desire for a hasty conclusion to these proceedings, hence I will be short—"

"He already is short!" Jack said, poking Ken in the ribs.

Ken smiled and inclined his head toward the diminutive barrister, directing Jack to pay attention.

"Over a score and a half years ago," Mr. Squibbs was saying, "Mr. Reginald Gage, of late memory, purchased the estate of Lord Eustas Claverley, lock, stock, and barrel. I say again, lock, stock, and barrel. However, he did not take possession of one very valuable item. No indeed, he did not. Unbeknownst to Mr. Gage, at the time of his death Lord Claverley owned a priceless item of jewelry, even a ruby ring, the very item at the center of these proceedings."

The barrister glanced at the jury to make sure that the members were paying attention. Satisfied that they were, he continued, "And why did Mr. Gage not take possession of this ring, you may ask?" He paused for effect. "I will tell you. For the very reason that Sir Gerald Langton had stolen it, leaving the murdered peer in his gore." The lawyer again paused. "This fact is uncontested. And now to the crux of the matter. Since the object in question was part of Lord Claverley's estate, and since Mr. Reginald Gage purchased the Claverley estate in its entirety, *ergo* Saladin's ring is the property of Miss Karen Gage, the daughter and heir of the late Mr. Gage. That is our contention in a nutshell, plain and simple with no horns on it. Therefore, I would humbly suggest that the ring be turned over to Miss Gage forthwith and that these proceedings be summarily terminated."

Mr. Squibbs sat down as a buzz filled the court.

The audience finally came to "horder" and the judge, scratching his left ear under the long side of his wig, which looked very much like a beagle's ear, glowered down at Mr. Squibbs. "I'll decide when these proceedings cease, Mr. Squibbs," he said sternly. "However, in point of law your reasoning is sound, and I see no call to comment further."

Ken looked down at Karen and saw the satisfied smile on her pretty face. Despite everything, he was pleased for her. As much as he had coveted—yes, actually coveted, he admitted—the ring, his feelings had definitely changed and he knew that he would not be disappointed if she were the victor. This magnanimous thought, however, was quickly replaced by another realization: *Because of the agreement Karen has signed, if she wins, Langton wins.*

"D'ya think she'll get it?" Jack asked, interrupting Ken's thoughts.

"I don't know," Ken said. "The judge seems to think she has a case. Let's see how the other claimants do."

When Ken refocused on the action below, Sir Wilfred Pilley was speaking.

"Her Majesty's government's position is simple," he said. "The ring should never have been awarded to His Grace the Lord Archbishop of Canterbury by King John in the first place. Those who know their history will recall that King John was severely derelict when it came to England's treasures. Besides losing all of England's continental possessions to the French, the king's incompetence also led to the Crown Jewels sinking into quicksand while he, fleeing from his enemies, was crossing The Wash in East Anglia never to be seen again—the Crown Jewels, that is, not King John." The lawyer's gaff brought a titter from the audience. Sir Wilfred ignored it and went on. "This ring, given to King Richard the Lionhearted so many years ago in consequence of the Peace of Ramla, is part of our history, a veritable national treasure. King John had no right to relinquish it, and it is Her Majesty's government's contention that it should be returned to the Crown forthwith and lodged with the present day Crown Jewels. Thank you."

"While we appreciate the history lesson, Sir Wilfred," the judge said, "let me point out to the jury that the Crown Jewels belong to the Crown and hence can be disposed of according to the will of the sovereign. It is well known that Edward III pawned them to finance an overseas campaign, and that Charles I again pawned them in Holland at the beginning of the English Civil War. Had King John not given this ring to the archbishop, it would no doubt have been lost with the other Crown Jewels in East Anglia and we would not be wasting the court's time on this matter. Next, we will hear from Mr. Stephen Langton's counsel, Mr. Bradford Rampling."

" 'Ow many acts in this 'ere play?" Jack asked Ken.

"I think there's only two more after Langton. The Church of England and my mother."

Jack sighed. "Good. I can't wait t'see Maggie."

Ken glanced down at Karen just as she glanced up at him. To his surprise and delight she did not turn away or frown. Rather, she had a small smile on her lips. A morsel of hope entered Ken's heart. She modestly lowered her eyes, and Ken reluctantly pulled his gaze from her and focused on Langton's lawyer. The latter was fulminating on the injustice of the ring's ownership being called into question when it had been in the Langton family for over six hundred years.

"Admittedly," Mr. Rampling added, "Sir Gerald did make an error of judgment when he wagered it in a card game. But are we to hold an inebriated man responsible for one rash act? Are we to deprive the Langton family of a treasured heirloom because of one hasty decision? On behalf of my client, let me appeal to the mercy of the court to restore this priceless object to its rightful owner, Mr. Stephen Langton."

"In response to your 'error of judgment' argument, Mr. Rampling," Sir Lionel interjected, "let me quote Lord Salisbury: 'To defend a bad policy as an error of judgment does not excuse it—the right functioning of a man's judgment is his most fundamental responsibility.' Are you through, Mr. Rampling?"

"Not quite, Your Honor," Rampling said. "Mr. Langton has instructed me to make it known that if the jury in their wisdom decide against him, he will support the claim of Miss Karen Gage. If the ring is not to be returned to the Langton family, where it belongs, my client would prefer that it stay in England rather than risk having it end up in America. Thank you."

Sir Lionel looked over his spectacles at Karen and Langton sitting far apart. "It appears that this *entente cordiale* is no longer very cordial," he said wryly, "but the court acknowledges Mr. Langton's support of Miss Gage's claim."

Karen's face was expressionless, and Ken was pleased to see that she moved even farther apart from Langton.

Sir Lionel made a great show of holding up a pocket watch and squinting at it. "It is almost noon," he said. "This court is recessed until two o'clock, at which time we will hear arguments from the representatives of the Church of England and our American claimant."

"I'm off t'ask Maggie t'pop around the corner wi' me t' St. George and the Dragon," Jack said. "The pub's got the best steak and kidney pie in town. Will y'join us?"

Ken shook his head. "No thanks, Jack. I think I'll just go for a walk." Secretly, Ken hoped that in his walking he'd run into Karen.

"Right y'are. I'll go find Maggie. See you in four bells."

"In two hours, then."

❧ CHAPTER 25 ❧

Jack found Maggie at the entrance to the Old Bailey. It was obvious that she was pleased to see him. "Dinner at St. George and the Dragon?" he asked.

Maggie hesitated and then shook her head. "I'm sorry, Jack. I guess there's lots we don't know about each other. I'm not the sort what frequents pubs. Never have been and don't intend changing now. Will you join Miss Gage and me at the Swan Tearoom? It's just 'round the corner—the best watercress sandwiches in London."

"I ain't the sort what frequents tearooms," Jack said with a twinkle in his eye. "Come, now, Maggie, a pint w' steak and kidney pie never hurt a body."

"Sorry, Jack. I took the pledge when I started service at the vicar's years ago. Like the saying goes, 'Lips that touch liquor will never touch mine.'"

"Your lips or your liquor?" Jack asked in an attempt to humor her.

She was not amused. "Be serious, Jack. You'll have to choose—my company or your ale."

A frown crossed Jack's weathered face. "You're in earnest? You'd deny a man one o' the simple pleasures o' life?"

Maggie nodded. "Sorry, I am, Jack. But I won't budge."

"So that's it, then?"

"I'm afraid so."

Jack shook his head, turned, and stumped away. Maggie heaved a mighty sigh, resisting the urge to run after him.

* * *

During the break Ken wandered the streets of London without succeeding in his quest to see Karen. Reluctantly, he returned to the Old Bailey and was again sitting beside Jack in the balcony when the court was called to order. Right away Ken noticed that Jack was out of sorts, but he decided not to pry. Ken turned his attention to the judge, who was making an announcement.

"Upon sober reflection," the judge said, "the Church of England have withdrawn their claim to the ring. The next and final presentation, therefore, will be that of Sir Jeffrey Lyttle, counsel for Lord Claverley's widow."

"Thank you, Your Honor," Sir Jeffrey said. "First let me say to the jury that my esteemed colleagues have spoken eloquently on behalf of their clients. I have no doubt whatsoever that according to their lights these claimants are sincere in their motives. However, I will show without doubt that my client, the former Elisabeth Ashcroft, a vicar's daughter, is most deserving of Saladin's ring."

Karen glanced up at Ken and gave him an encouraging smile that sent shivers of joy through him. He acknowledged her with a nod and a broad smile. Langton noticed the exchange and shot a menacing frown at Ken.

"Let me acquaint you with the facts of the matter," Sir Jeffrey continued. "Miss Ashcroft grew to young womanhood naïve and untutored in the ways of the world in the confines of her father's vicarage. Allow me to present a likeness of this young woman as rendered by the eminent artist Mr. John Tolley." As he pointed to the covered picture with his cane, Mr. Nuttall dramatically uncovered the twice life-size pastel portrait to the ooing and awing of the crowd.

"You did a wonderful job, Jack," Ken said, squinting to see the picture. "It is innocence and vulnerability personified. But my mother looks about sixteen. I believe she was over thirty when the tintype was taken."

"Artistic license, lad," Jack said morosely. "I followed Sir Jeffrey's orders to a T. Always give the customer what he wants is my motto. Wait till y'see Claverley. Old Nick has nothing on his lordship."

Ken wondered again why Jack seemed so depressed, but he didn't inquire. When they refocused their attention on Sir Jeffrey, the latter was well into an oration on Ken's mother that was moving the jury almost to tears. "This virtuous young woman—"

"Will you get on with it, Sir Jeffrey," the judge interjected. "We haven't got all week. Let me remind you that this case is about the disposition of a piece of jewelry, not the beatification of the former Miss Ashcroft!"

The judge's words brought a sprinkling of laughter from the audience and broad smiles from the opposing barristers.

"Duly noted, Your Honor," Sir Jeffrey said, bowing to the bench. "In conclusion, let me say that this virtuous young woman entered the marriage with all the hopes and dreams of her kind, only to realize that she had bound herself to a monster. Yes. I say again, a monster in the guise of a peer of the realm, Lord Eustas Claverley."

He pointed his cane once more and the covering on the second picture was removed, revealing a pen-and-ink sketch of evil and decadence. Sir Jeffrey moved closer to the picture and said, "Knowing that Miss Ashcroft was set to inherit a fortune upon her marriage, this man—"

He thumped the portrait with his cane, almost knocking it off the easel.

"—this man hoodwinked her into believing that he truly loved her and carried her off to the altar, all the while harboring in his heart vile deception, and in his London flat a woman of low morals."

Ken looked around the courtroom. It was obvious that the audience and jury were hanging on Sir Jeffrey's every word.

"But you need not take my word for it," Sir Jeffrey said. "Let us hear the sworn testimony of Miss Ashcroft's faithful maid and companion."

"Miss Marguerite Stowell to the witness box," called the usher.

Maggie took the stand and was sworn in.

"Now, Miss Stowell," said Sir Jeffrey in his kindest voice, "please tell the court what happened on that awful night, more than three decades ago, when Lord Claverley assaulted you and Lady Claverley in your mistress's bridal chamber."

"Aye, sir," Maggie began. "If I live to be a thousand years, I'll not soon forget that awful night. When things at the wedding supper got a wee bit rowdy, y'know, drink and all, milady and me went to her bedchamber, where I helped her get ready for the bridal night. She dressed in a beautiful silk peignoir from Paris. I made sure there was a good fire in the grate, but the room was big as a barn and I reminded her her dressin' gown was in the wardrobe in case she got cold. She said, 'Oh, no, Maggie. I can't wear that. I must look my best for his lordship.' Then I went to my room."

"Please get to the point, Miss Stowell," the judge said, not unkindly.

"Yes, sir," Maggie said. "Fast asleep I was when I hears this scream like a banshee. Up I goes to her chamber and there is milady on the bed wearing the old dressing gown—she must have put it on after all. And there's her husband cursing her and trying to rip the garment off of her. Well, I couldn't have that, so I tried to pull him off of her. Like a wild beast he hit me with his fist and knocked me to the floor. Milady jumped off of the bed and came to help me up. It was then he charged us like a bull, tripped on the mat, and took a tumble, knocking hisself as cold as death. Well, we left him were he lay and ran out into a night as cold as sin and across the fields to her father's house."

"And what happened the next day?" Sir Jeffrey asked.

"Lord Claverley came to the vicarage hat in hand acting as if butter wouldn't melt in his mouth. He talked milady into going back to him, but later when she found out that he was gambling away her fortune in London and had a who . . . a mistress, she left him for good. When he wouldn't give her a 'nullment she goes to America."

Maggie was dismissed and Sir Lionel said, "This is all very interesting, Sir Jeffrey, but what has it to do with who should have the ring? In essence your argument is that, as Lord Claverley's heir, Lady Claverley should have inherited the ring. Is that right?"

"In essence, yes, Your Honor," Sir Jeffrey said, "but it was necessary to establish why Lady Claverley fled to America and was thus unable to inherit."

"And necessary to influence the jury," the judge said sardonically. He took out his watch. "Due to Sir Jeffrey's histrionics, we will not be able to conclude these proceedings today. Thus we will adjourn and reconvene at two o'clock tomorrow afternoon."

Ken looked at his own watch. "It's not even three o'clock," he said.

"I guess judges keeps bankers' hours," Jack said.

The next morning Ken was summoned to Sir Jeffrey's office. "I was impressed with your performance yesterday, Sir Jeffrey," Ken said as he took his seat in front of the barrister's desk.

Sir Jeffrey acknowledged the compliment with a glum nod. "I think I overplayed my hand. We're in trouble. If I'd known the judge was going to cut the session short, I wouldn't have taken so long. Had we been able to wrap things up yesterday, I believe we would have won. As it is, the jury have had a night to reflect and the opposition a night to plan. The former housekeeper at Claverley Hall, a Mrs. Blackmore, has surfaced and is providing the opposition with information I'd rather they didn't know. They'll hit us with both barrels today."

Ken looked puzzled. "How did you find out about this Mrs. Blackmore?"

Sir Jeffrey dismissed the question with a grin and a wave of his hand. "Like you newspapermen, I don't reveal my sources either, but my spies are everywhere. I could tell you what each opposing barrister had for breakfast. My sources tell me that they had a meeting earlier this morning, the barristers, that is. They will no doubt make a coordinated attack on me in their summations. Yesterday, I put your mother on a pedestal. Today they'll knock her off it. Be prepared. In an affidavit, Mrs. Blackmore contends that the reason your mother fled to America was because she joined the Mormon Church. If the opposition uses this I'd like to be prepared. Tell me about your church."

For the next hour, Ken gave Sir Jeffrey a short history of The Church of Jesus Christ of Latter-day Saints, mentioning Charles Dickens's assessment of the Church members he had met aboard the *Amazon* and Sir Richard Burton's view of the Mormons in his book *The City of the Saints*. Ken also enlightened Sir Jeffrey on the current problems the Church was having with the United States federal government.

When Ken had finished, Sir Jeffrey pondered the information for several minutes and then yelled, "Nuttall!" The clerk scurried into the office. "Find me a copy of *The Uncommercial Traveller*," Sir Jeffrey said, "and *The City of the Saints,* by Burton."

Later in the courtroom, Ken again sat beside Jack in the balcony as Mr. Squibbs used his summation time to lead the assault on Sir Jeffrey. "Yesterday, Your Honor," Squibbs said, "Sir Jeffrey mounted an impassioned plea on behalf of his client—a plea designed to obscure his extremely slim case. As you pointed out so well, Your Honor, in essence his contention is simply that his client, being Lord Claverley's heir, should have inherited the ring. Sir Jeffrey contends that she did not inherit because she was forced to flee the country. But why after her husband's death did she not return to England and inherit? Why? I shall tell you why. She knew the consequences of deserting her husband and her responsibilities as mistress of Claverley Hall. And what were those consequences? In the year of our Lord eighteen hundred and fifty-one, a wife's desertion was a felony. The reason she did not return to inherit was fear of punishment, fear of punishment and no other reason."

Sir Jeffrey leapt to his feet. "Objection, Your Honor."

"Sit down, Sir Jeffrey," the judge ordered. "You'll have your chance later."

Mr. Squibbs smiled. "I repeat," he said, "Lady Claverley abdicated her responsibilities, thus allowing creditors to liquidate her husband's estate. In good faith my client's late father purchased the said estate, lock, stock, and barrel, and thus became the owner of all Lord Claverley owned on the day of his death. The object known as Saladin's ring was on his person at the point of death; hence it should have redounded to my client's late father and hence to my client. We rest our case."

Mr. Squibbs sat down with a satisfied smile on his face. He knew that he had scored points with the jury and sat back in anticipation of his co-conspirators' continued assault on Sir Jeffrey. The government's lawyer, Sir Wilfred Pilley, Q.C., was up next. Ken wondered if his friendship with Sir Jeffrey would soften his attack.

"Her Majesty's government's position remains the same, Your Honor," he said. "King John had no right to award the ring to the archbishop. It should have remained with the Crown Jewels and should now be returned there. Additionally, I feel obligated to correct a flagrant misrepresentation perpetrated yesterday by my honorable colleague, Sir Jeffrey Lyttle. In his presentation he made it appear, both in the image he displayed and in his verbal description, that Miss Ashcroft at the time of her marriage to Lord Claverley was a young, naïve girl. In actuality she was a well-educated spinster of twenty-seven years—not a naïve girl but a woman who knew exactly what she was doing. We rest our case."

Sir Lionel nodded at Sir Wilfred and then addressed the jury. "Members of the jury, Miss Ashcroft's age is a matter of record and we have no reason to doubt that she was seven and twenty when she fled England. However, the counsel for Her Majesty's government has failed to offer proof that she was not naïve or that she did not lead a sheltered life. Please consider this when you make your decision."

"Kinda hurtful t'hear your mother talked about more like an object than a person," Jack said.

Ken agreed. "I'll be glad when this whole thing's over. A wise religious leader once told his people to stay clear of court cases. Now I understand more fully what he meant. I wish I'd listened to him and my parents."

"Mr. Bradford Rampling will now present his summation," Sir Lionel said.

Mr. Rampling unfolded his long legs from beneath the table and stood. He stroked his pointed chin and swept his eyes across the twelve men who would decide the ownership of Saladin's ring. "Gentlemen," he began, "yesterday, Sir Jeffrey attempted to lead you down the garden path. As my colleagues have demonstrated, the former Miss Ashcroft, which name she used even though married, was a mature woman who feloniously deserted her husband rather than accepting her responsibilities as mistress of Claverley Hall. But that is not the whole story. Not by a long shot. In a sworn statement, Mrs. Enid Blackmore, the former housekeeper of Claverley Hall, who is too infirm to attend these proceedings, testifies that the claimant not only broke the law in deserting her husband, but that she also stole money from her husband's strongbox, money she used in purchasing a ticket for America so that she could participate in the heathenish practices of the Mormons in the valley of the Great Salt Lake." A gasp arose from the audience. "I need not elaborate on the practices of this sect as the newspapers are filled with stories of the outrage they are causing among the right-thinking citizens of the American republic.

My point here is to make it perfectly clear that rather than the paragon of virtue drawn yesterday by Sir Jeffrey, Miss Ashcroft was a woman of low moral character—"

Ken leapt to his feet, ready to jump from the balcony and strangle Langton's lawyer. Jack pulled him back into his seat. "Steady on, son," Jack said. "Let Sir Jeffrey handle it."

Karen, as outraged as Ken, scowled at Langton and his lawyer.

Ken smoldered as Sir Jeffrey, now on his feet and pointing an accusing finger at Langton's lawyer, said, "I must object, Your Honor, in the strongest terms."

"Sustained," the judge ordered. "Mr. Rampling, please moderate your presentation. You have no right to malign the former Miss Ashcroft, nor for that matter, the Mormon people, despite what the newspapers might say. Facts, man, facts are what we want, not hearsay."

"My apologies, Your Honor," Rampling said in a tone far from penitent. "I need say no more. I think my colleagues and I have sufficiently shown that Sir Jeffrey's representation of Miss Ashcroft was a fiction and that, in fact, at the time she fled to America, she was mature, a felon, and, to put it mildly, a nonconformist in religion.

"Before I conclude, let me state that Mr. Langton has instructed me to withdraw his claim in favor of Miss Gage's bid. Therefore, I end my summation by stating to the jury that in our estimation, Mr. Squibbs has demonstrated beyond doubt that Miss Gage is the rightful heir to Saladin's ring. Thank you."

Ken glanced down at Karen. Rampling's endorsement of her bid had not changed her contempt for the barrister or his client. She continued to scowl at them. Then she glanced up at Ken, her face full of empathy. She nodded at him as much as to say, "I'll show them!" Pursing her lips, she leaned down and took a document from her handbag. Ken observed her action with curiosity as she waved Mr. Nuttall to her side and handed him the document.

"Are you ready for your summation, Sir Jeffrey?" the judge asked.

"One moment, Your Honor," said Sir Jeffrey, who had observed the exchange between Karen and his clerk. Mr. Nuttall handed the document to Sir Jeffrey, who scanned it and then slowly rose.

He swept the jury with his eyes, shook his head, and heaved an outraged sigh. "Gentlemen of the jury," he began, "I am shocked and saddened at the tactics of the opposing counsel. First, they imply that a woman in her twenties cannot be naïve or unworldly. Then they label Miss Ashcroft a felon for fleeing from her brutal husband. Admittedly, she did technically break the law. What they did not say is that the unjust law, which virtually made slaves of married women, was repealed by parliament years ago, thus giving some measure of rights to married women. The fact that Miss Ashcroft used money from her husband's strongbox to buy a ticket to freedom is mute evidence that Lord Claverley had legally stolen her inheritance and had left her destitute.

"What shocks me the most about the presentations of the opposing counsel, however, is Mr. Rampling's unbridled religious intolerance. Here we are in London, the capital of one of the greatest empires the world has ever known, an empire comprising two-fifths of the world's land and a quarter of the world's population, an empire with people of all religious beliefs. If our colonial leaders shared Mr. Rampling's blatant intolerance, the empire would collapse like a house of cards. Fortunately, our leaders are not such bigots. Rather, they work hand in hand with Muhammadans in Egypt, Hindus in India, and Buddhists in Burma.

"If Mr. Rampling took the time to study the Mormon people as Sir Richard Burton and Mr. Charles Dickens did, he would come away with a favorable opinion of them, as did these two renowned writers. He would find that the Latter-day Saints are more sinned against than sinning.

"In point of fact, the main reason my client left her husband was that she shared the Mormon adherence to strict rectitude in moral matters and could not tolerate his adultery, a practice to which this society turns a blind eye and which many Christian wives are supposed to accept without complaint.

"I could go on, but the time is late and I have in my hand a document that will establish incontrovertibly that my client must be awarded the ring. Before I introduce it into evidence, let me first say this: In his presentation, Mr. Squibbs averred that Mr. Gage had purchased the Claverley estate 'lock, stock, and barrel.' As this document will prove, that was not the case. This document is an itemized list of all that Mr. Gage purchased, and Saladin's ring is conspicuous by its absence. Mr. Gage, therefore, purchased a finite number of items and did not purchase the estate lock, stock, and barrel as Mr. Squibbs has contended *ad nauseam*. Mr. Gage got what he paid for as listed herein. The ring, therefore, must go to my client and thus right a three-decade wrong. Thank you."

Sir Jeffrey was no sooner seated than Rampling was on his feet. "I protest the introduction of this new evidence," he said. "We have no way of knowing that it's not a forgery."

Sir Lionel heaved a sigh and waved his hand. It was obvious he wanted the case to be over. "Bring the document here," he said tiredly. The usher did so and Sir Lionel scrutinized it. "How did you come by this list, Sir Jeffrey?"

Ken fervently hoped that Sir Jeffrey would not say, "I never reveal my sources."

The barrister rose and glanced over at Karen. She nodded. He then turned back to the judge. "From Miss Gage, Your Honor."

The audience gasped and Langton's head snapped toward Karen, hate in his eyes. It seemed all he could do restrain himself from physically attacking her. Karen stared straight ahead and up at the judge, who said, "Is that true, Miss Gage?"

She stood. "It is, Your Honor."

"My dear young lady," Sir Lionel said, "do you realize that this could lose you the ring?"

"Yes, Your Honor."

"Then why did you do it?"

Karen glanced up at Ken and then turned her eyes to the judge. "It would be a miscarriage of justice if Mrs. Sanderson were not awarded the ring, Your Honor. She deserves it more than I or anyone else."

"A very admirable thing to do, Miss Gage," Sir Lionel said, "admirable indeed. I commend you." He then addressed the jury. "Gentlemen, do you need to retire to deliberate?"

"No, Your Honor," the foreman said. "I have polled the jury and they are unanimous in awarding the ring to the American claimant."

The audience could not restrain itself, and it took several minutes for the usher to silence it.

When the hubbub had subsided, Sir Lionel addressed the jury. "Thank you, gentlemen," he said. "The piece of jewelry known as Saladin's ring is hereby awarded to Sir Jeffrey Lyttle in trust for his client."

Again, the place was bedlam. As he looked on from the balcony, Ken saw Langton grab Karen's shoulder, spin her around and, his face full of hate, bark something at her. Langton then turned on his heel and bulldozed his way through the crowd. Soames, however, signaled the two policemen at the door and it appeared to Ken that they again took Langton into custody.

❧ CHAPTER 26 ❧

Despite the fact that his family had just won a fabulous award, Ken's only thought was for Karen. He tried to make his way to her but was hemmed in by the exited crowd. Impatiently, he awaited his turn. On finally reaching the corridor leading to the stairs, he was pulled aside by Sir Jeffrey's clerk.

"Mr. Sanderson, Sir Jeffrey wishes to see you in the judge's chambers right away," Mr. Nuttall said. "Very urgent."

"I can't go now," Ken said. "I want to thank Miss Gage for what she did."

"She's tied up with reporters right now, and I think she will be for a while."

Ken took a deep breath and exhaled. "How long do you think this meeting will take?

"I don't know, but Sir Jeffrey says it's very important—has something to do with you winning the ring. Would you like me to convey your appreciation to Miss Gage?"

Ken hesitated. "Yes. Please do. By the way, were you close enough to hear what Langton said to Miss Gage after the court adjourned?"

Nuttall rolled his eyes. "I was. He said the lady would regret her treachery and something about him not paying her legal fees. A piece of work is Mr. Langton—let me show you how to get to the judge's chambers without having to fight the crowd."

Ken and Mr. Nuttall arrived at the foyer to the judge's chambers to find the jeweler, Mr. Solomon Levi, sitting on a bench outside the closed door. The old man slid over and motioned for Ken to join him.

"I'll take your message to Miss Gage," the clerk said, leaving them.

The old man smiled at Ken. "You're the young man from the balcony," he said.

"Yes, Ken Sanderson, the former Miss Ashcroft's son." They shook hands. "And you're Mr. Levi, the master jeweler."

The jeweler nodded. "Congratulations on your family winning the ruby ring, Mr. Sanderson. It's as fine a piece of jewelry as I've ever seen. But it's only cold metal and stone. Even though I've been enamored of jewelry all my life, I firmly believe that people are much more important than things. As the Bible says, a virtuous woman is far above rubies."

Ken was startled by the man's last words and wondered where the conversation was going, but he remained politely silent.

The old man's eyes took on a dreamy aspect as he recalled the past. "When I was a young man like you, I won the heart of Miriam Winetraub, a beautiful young woman, not unlike Miss Gage. I wanted to give her something to seal our love, but I was just starting out in my profession and couldn't afford anything too expensive. So, with the little money I had and using my fledgling skills, I produced this."

He withdrew a ring from his pocket and handed it to Ken.

"It's exquisite," Ken said, holding up to the light a silver ring set with a single pearl. He attempted to hand it back, but the older man motioned him to hold onto it.

"Twenty years ago when Miriam was on her deathbed, she took that ring from her finger and gave it back to me. Since we were not blessed with children, she told me to give it to a young woman of integrity, a person whom we would have been proud to call our daughter. In the courtroom today I saw that young woman. Please give the ring to Miss Gage. Perhaps you could use it as a token of your love when you ask for her hand."

Nonplussed, Ken could only stare at the ring for a long moment. Finally, he said, "I don't know what to say, Mr. Levi. If I take your beautiful ring I'd be doing so under false pretenses. As much as I'd like to ask for Miss Gage's hand, there are obstacles in my way. For one, I inadvertently let her down, and I'm not sure how she feels about me."

The old man's lips curled in a smile. "Miss Gage would not have done what she did in court today if she hadn't forgiven you."

Ken accepted this logic, but said, "Another thing is that she's not of my faith and I have promised to marry only a member of my church."

The old man's eyebrows lifted. "Is she averse to converting?"

"Well, she has been studying my church, but something's holding her back. Also, I have the feeling that she might be in love with my cousin."

Mr. Levi shook his head and sighed. "I'm an old man, Mr. Sanderson, but I have not forgotten how a woman looks at a man with the eyes of love. From my vantage point in the courtroom, I noticed her several glances up at you. Believe me, son, you have captured her heart, and all obstacles will dissolve as the dew before the rising sun. Take the ring with Miriam's blessing and mine." He paused, lost in thought, and then he added, "Some Jews don't believe in the hereafter, but I do. It will please my Miriam to know I've fulfilled her wish so well."

Ken studied the pearl ring and said, "Thank you, Mr. Levi. I will make sure Miss Gage receives your lovely ring."

Ken's heart glowed and for a few minutes neither of them spoke.

Mr. Levi's chuckle broke the silence. "The Sadducees in the Bible didn't believe in the hereafter," he said with a grin. "That's why they were *sad, you see!*"

The door to the judge's chamber suddenly opened and Sir Jeffrey stepped into the foyer, interrupting the two men's laughter.

"Sorry for keeping you gentlemen," Sir Jeffrey said. "We got into a discussion about how best to stop Stephen Langton from continually flouting the law. Please come in."

Ken and Mr. Levi entered the room to find Sir Lionel Bradbury sitting behind his desk and Sir Wilfred Pilley sitting in front of it. "Welcome, gentlemen," Sir Lionel said. "Please be seated."

Ken acknowledged the judge with a nod, and his tight smile that said he had much better things to do than meet with these stuffy old men. Nevertheless, he took one of the empty chairs and waited.

"I've already congratulated Sir Jeffrey on winning the ring for your mother," the judge said to Ken. "Holding back the purchase document of Gage Hall to the last moment was brilliant."

"Brilliant, nothing!" Sir Wilfred exclaimed, turning to stare at Sir Jeffrey. "Admit it, Jeffrey. Miss Gage pulled your fat out of the fire."

Sir Jeffrey, a hint of a smile on his lips, retorted, "I never discuss strategy with opposing counsel."

"All right, you two," the judge said, "keep your sparring for the courtroom." Addressing Ken he added, "Congratulations to you also, Mr. Sanderson. Your trip to England has been rewarding."

Karen's lovely face came into Ken's mind. "It has, sir," he said with conviction. "And I trust that it will soon be even more rewarding."

The judge nodded. "On behalf of Her Majesty's government, Sir Wilfred has something to discuss with you."

"Let me add my congratulations, Mr. Sanderson," the Crown counsel said. "Now to business. Acquiring Saladin's ring is still the desire of Her Majesty's government, and we are prepared to make you an offer."

"Excuse me, Sir Wilfred," Ken said. "I'm afraid you'll have to send your offer to my mother. She and my father forbade me to get involved."

Sir Wilfred turned to Sir Jeffrey with raised eyebrows. The latter nodded and said, "That is true, Mr. Sanderson, regarding the trial. However, included in the sealed papers you brought me from your mother is this document." He handed Ken a sheet of paper. "As you see, it authorizes you to handle the disposition of the ring should your mother win it. Your parents have given you the power to dispose of it in any way you see fit. Please listen to the government offer."

Ken acknowledged this information with a nod to Sir Jeffrey. An enhanced feeling of self-worth at his parents' faith in him warmed his soul.

"Thank you, Sir Jeffrey," Sir Wilfred said. "First, the bad news. The government has assessed a fifty percent inheritance tax on this national treasure." Ken's mouth fell open, his feeling of well-being quickly dissipating. Noticing the shock on Ken's face, Sir Wilfred paused slightly before pressing on. "Using Mr. Levi's evaluation, that would amount to twenty-five thousand pounds, leaving you with an equal amount. Taking away Sir Jeffrey's fee of twenty percent or ten thousand dollars, it leaves you with fifteen thousand pounds. So the good news is that you will be returning to America with a bank draft of seventy-five thousand American dollars. No mean amount."

During Sir Wilfred's presentation Ken became increasingly disheartened as the vast sum diminished. He now turned an accusing eye on Sir Jeffrey.

The barrister shrugged. "Death and taxes, son. There's no getting away from them."

While Ken pondered how to respond to the offer, Sir Wilfred added, "We've invited Mr. Levi here to explain to you how he arrived at the evaluation. Of course, you are free to get a second appraisal."

Ken glanced at Mr. Levi and back at Sir Wilfred. "I'll accept Mr. Levi's appraisal," Ken said. "But what if I refuse the government's offer, sir?"

"That is certainly your right, my boy," Sir Wilfred said. "But the ring will remain in escrow until you raise the tax. Do you have access to twenty-five thousand pounds, or thirty-five if Sir Jeffrey wants his fee right away?"

Ken recalled his father's words that no family money would be used in pursuing the ring. He felt as if a noose were tightening around his neck. "No," he whispered. As he further pondered the offer, he recalled his promise to Maggie that should his mother's claim be successful, he would talk to his mother about paying Karen's legal fees. Since Langton had reneged on paying these fees and since his parents had put the money from the ring at his disposal, he felt honor bound to pay them. The fortune shrank some more.

Perhaps I can do a little horse trading, he thought. Locking eyes with Sir Wilfred, he said, "I will accept the government's offer, sir, if you agree to pay Miss Gage's legal fees."

Sir Wilfred smiled. "After what she did for you in court, you owe her a great debt. However, there is no way I could justify the expenditure on the government's books. I'm sincerely sorry, but I must reject your request."

Ken didn't know where to go from there. Sir Jeffrey rescued him.

"Never mind, Mr. Sanderson," the barrister said. "I'll take care of Miss Gage's fees out of my own pocket, and I can assure you I'll be paying Squibbs much less than he would have billed Miss Gage."

Ken pondered the offer for a moment before saying, "No, Sir Jeffrey, that wouldn't be fair."

"Of course it would," Sir Jeffrey insisted. "Miss Gage . . . ah . . . aided in my winning the case."

"Aided!" Sir Wilfred exclaimed. "Admit it, Jeffrey, she won the case for you." Turning to Ken, he added, "Let him pay Miss Gage's expenses, my boy. It's the least he can do." When Ken didn't respond immediately, Sir Wilfred pressed, "Then it's agreed? You accept the government's offer?"

Ken reluctantly nodded.

"Good," Sir Wilfred said. "I'll have a bank draft to Sir Jeffrey's chambers posthaste."

Ken and Sir Jeffrey left the office together. "I'm sorry, Mr. Sanderson," the barrister said. "I'm sure you must feel that you've fallen among thieves, but you've come out of this as well as could be expected."

"I suppose," Ken said. "By the way, congratulations on winning the case. You said you would and you did."

Sir Jeffrey stopped and turned to Ken. "Are you being facetious? As Sir Wilfred quite rightly pointed out, Miss Gage pulled my fat out of the fire and won it for me. Paying her fees will be a pleasure. Latch on to that young woman, son. Her price is far above rubies."

Ken smiled. "That's the second time today I've heard that quotation. By the way, Langton's week to sign the mortgage papers has long passed. Do you know what happened?"

"I do," he said with satisfaction. "Soames was able to keep Langton from signing it. However, when I inquired about possibly buying the mortgage on behalf of St. Swithins, I was told that it has already been purchased."

Ken's mouth fell open. "By whom?" he asked.

Sir Jeffrey shook his head. "The bank wouldn't tell me. Of course, my sources will find out sooner or later. In the meantime, we'll just have to hope that the purchaser is on our side."

Ken and Sir Jeffrey met Mr. Nuttall on the stairs. "Miss Gage conveys her thanks for your words of appreciation, Mr. Sanderson," the clerk said, "and asked me to tell you she is going to see a Mr. Kimball, then catching the steam train to Somerset."

It was with mixed feelings that Ken exited the Old Bailey into the overcast skies of a warm afternoon. He was happy that his family had won the ring and that his church would be benefited thereby. He was also pleased with Mr. Levi's opinion about Karen's feelings. On the other hand, he was displeased that the value of the award had shrunk from a quarter of a million dollars to seventy-five thousand, and he had a feeling of apprehension over why Karen had gone to see Jonathan. *Well, I'll soon find out,* he thought, as he headed for the mission home.

"Ken," Jonathan said, looking up from his paper-laden desk, a broad smile on his face. "You just missed Miss Gage. Congratulations on winning the ring. This is certainly your lucky day. Miss Gage has asked for you to baptize her!"

Ken's heart pounded as he stared at his cousin. "She has?" He fell into a chair. "I can hardly believe it. What . . . how?"

Jonathan grinned. "It all started with a highly enthusiastic letter I got from her a few days ago. In it she confessed that something she had done in her past had been holding her back from applying for baptism. For weeks she had prayed about it without success. Then one morning she woke up and knew that God had forgiven her. She immediately wrote me a letter asking for baptism."

Ken thought about the letter at the post office in Ainsley Village. "What could she possibly have done that held her back?" he asked. "Did she say?"

Jonathan shook his head. "Not to me, but I'm sure she would have mentioned it to President Lewis, who interviewed her for baptism. I'm sure she'll share it with you eventually. In the meantime, be assured it was not something that will disqualify her for baptism. We've tentatively set the baptismal date for the thirtieth."

"The thirtieth," Ken said. "That's only a week away."

Jonathan nodded. "Yes. She's gone home to prepare and although she didn't say it, I think she'd like you to follow." He pulled out his watch. "In fact, she's on the train to Somerset as we speak."

Ken leapt up and shook hands with Jonathan. "Well, cousin, you know where I'm off to," he said. He stopped at the door and said, "By the way, do you know where it says that a virtuous woman is far above rubies?"

"I think it's in Proverbs."

"Thanks, Jonathan. I'll see you on the thirtieth if not before."

Ken was soon at his lodgings. After throwing a few things into his valise, he left the house and hurried to the train station. However, he had missed the last train to the southwest and had to content himself with buying a ticket for the first train in the morning. He was no sooner back at his lodgings than the butler approached him.

"Mr. Sanderson," Mr. Bramley said, "a missive came for you while you were out. Hand delivered."

Ken took the envelope and noted Sir Wilfred Pilley's letterhead. *Oh, no. Every time I try to see Karen, something comes up. Maybe I shouldn't open it until I'm on the train tomorrow.* Curiosity, however, got the better of him and he opened it. To his dismay it was a summons to appear as a witness in the case of "Regina versus Mr. Stephen Langton," which would start the next day at ten o'clock. He wondered who Regina was, then assumed it must refer to the government as represented by the reigning head of state, Queen Victoria. He threw the summons on the dressing table. Not long afterward the butler was at the door with another note, this one from Sir Jeffrey asking Ken to be at his office the next morning at eight.

Ken threw the note on the dresser beside the summons, lay down on the bed, and stared at the ceiling. *At least this time I didn't promise Karen I'd visit her. I guess I've no choice but to get Langton's retrial over with before going to Somerset.*

His mind caressed the thought that she had asked him to baptize her and warmth spread through him. Picking up his Bible, he thumbed through it until he found the book of Proverbs and began reading.

❧ CHAPTER 27 ❧

The next day he was on time for his meeting. Besides Sir Jeffrey, Sir Wilfred Pilley and Chief Inspector Soames were also there.

"Well, here we are again," Sir Wilfred said. "I'm sorry about the short notice, Mr. Sanderson, but we felt it necessary to quickly impanel a jury before Langton or Rampling could get to any of the members. Except for calling Miss Treadwell to the stand this time, we'll follow the same strategy we used last time. I'm satisfied our strategy would have worked had Langton not tampered with the jury."

"Have you found evidence of jury tampering?" Ken asked.

Sir Wilfred shook his head. "No, but we will. We have the two dissenting jurors under surveillance."

"Why is Miss Treadwell being called as a witness this time?" Ken asked. "Does she have new evidence?"

The three men of the law exchanged satisfied glances.

"You could say that, Mr. Sanderson," Sir Jeffrey said.

Over the next hour the four men discussed ways of making sure that Stephen Langton paid for his crimes. Ken was happy to learn that Sir Lionel Bradbury would be on the bench this time instead of Sir Cedric Ellsworth. At the conclusion of the meeting, they all headed over to the Old Bailey.

Through the morning and into the afternoon session this trial was a repeat of the first one. However, Bradford Rampling was wise enough not to badger Nell when he cross-examined her.

Throughout the trial Ken kept scanning the faces of the new jury members and liked what he saw. It was late in the afternoon by the time Rampling called his client to testify. Once Langton had told his story, Sir Wilfred began his cross-examination.

"What were the weather conditions on your way across to Luss with Miss Treadwell?" Sir Wilfred asked.

Langton replied in a surly voice, "Very poor visibility. Almost 'clagged in' as they say in Scotland."

"Were you planning on returning to the lodge after you delivered Miss Treadwell?"

"Yes."

"Then because of the weather it was imperative that you get to Luss as quickly as possible so that you could get back before it was completely 'clagged in'?"

"Yes."

Sir Wilfred paused and gazed at the jury to make sure they were all paying attention. Turning back to the accused, he said, "Mr. Langton, why then, may I ask, did you disengage the engine of your launch for several minutes in deep water betwixt Inchmoan and The Narrows?"

Langton's face went pale. "I . . . I did no such thing," he stammered.

Sir Wilfred glared sternly at the accused. "I beg to differ, sir. Let me remind you that you are under oath to tell the truth. Are you sure you won't change your testimony, or should I call Miss Treadwell to the box?" Langton sat in stony silence. "Mr. Langton, did you or did you not leave the controls for several minutes in deep water, lean over the side, resume your position behind the wheel, and continue on to Luss?"

"Answer the question, Mr. Langton," the judge ordered.

Langton still refused to answer and was removed from the witness box. Miss Treadwell replaced him and confirmed that Langton had in fact left the wheel briefly.

"Miss Treadwell," Sir Wilfred asked, "did you see what Mr. Langton was doing when he was leaning over the side of the launch?"

"No sir," she said. "I was sitting in a corner out of the wind and had nodded off. I woke up when the engine slowed down and looked to see what was happening. Mr. Langton was taking something from a cupboard, but he held it close to his body and from where I sat I couldn't see what it was. He then went to the side of the boat and leaned over. When he went back to the wheel he didn't have nothing in his hands."

"Thank you, Miss Treadwell," Sir Wilfred said. Turning to the judge, he added, "Your Honor, I submit that despite Mr. Langton's testimony that he was in a hurry to get to Luss and back, he slowed the launch because he needed to get rid of an incriminating piece of evidence—the bailer. We have already established that this item disappeared from Mr. Sanderson's hired boat, and that Mr. Langton is the only one who could have taken it. Furthermore, we submit that Mr. Langton also threw overboard the dagger, the instrument with which he made the hole in the boat—"

Rampling was on his feet. "Your Honor, I object—"

"Sustained," said the judge. "Sir Wilfred, it has not yet been proven that Mr. Langton did puncture the boat."

The prosecutor acknowledged the judge with a nod. "If the court please," Sir Wilfred said, "I submit that Mr. Langton did in fact puncture the hired boat and remove the bailer in a premeditated plan to drown Mr. Sanderson. Furthermore, I submit that Mr. Langton chose the spot he did to get rid of the bailer because it was deep water—some parts of Loch Lomond are over six hundred feet deep—so it could not be recovered. The reason he did not just throw the bailer overboard was that it may have floated and been discovered. Mr. Langton had to sink the object by filling it with water, thus the necessity of stopping the boat and taking several seconds leaning over the gunwale." Turning to the opposing counsel, he said, "Your witness."

"Miss Treadwell," Langton's lawyer said, "during the time you were aboard Mr. Langton's launch, did you at any time see him with a bailer in his hands?"

"No, sir. He kept his body atween me and the object. But he certainly had something in his hands and got rid of it over the side."

"But you didn't actually see a bailer?"

"I wouldn't know one from Adam," she said. "I's not a boat person, don't y'know?"

Amid titters from the audience, Rampling said that he had no further questions.

In his closing argument, Sir Wilfred insisted that the evidence clearly pointed to Langton as the one who had made the hole in the boat and removed the bailer. As evidence of the accused's culpability, he cited Langton's refusal to answer the question about why he had slowed the boat in deep water. He then repeated verbatim what he said in the first trial about Langton's motivation in attempting to drown Ken.

His final words, delivered with greater force this time, were also verbatim from the first trial: "Stephen Langton did in fact attempt to commit the murder by drowning of Mr. Kenny Sanderson by boring a hole in his boat and removing the bailer. Furthermore, by not warning Lady Darnley that he had rendered the boat unsafe, he in effect is guilty of an attempt to murder her also. You, gentlemen, have no alternative but to find Mr. Stephen Langton guilty as charged. The prosecution rests. Thank you."

Rampling's summation was almost identical to that of the first trial. He did not even attempt to explain away Langton's refusal to answer why he had stopped the boat. As before, the jury elected to have time to deliberate. The judge recessed the court until such time as the jury reached a verdict.

Ken impatiently survived the hours until the court was called back into session just after six o'clock.

"On the charge of conspiracy to cause grievous bodily harm," Sir Lionel asked, "how do you find?"

"Guilty as charged," the foreman said.

Ken gave a relieved sigh. *One down and two to go,* he thought.

"On the first count of attempted murder," Sir Lionel asked, "how do you find?"

"Guilty as charged, Your Honor," the foreman said.

Stephen Langton was also found guilty on the second count of attempted murder.

After the jury delivered its verdict, Sir Lionel turned his eyes on Langton and said, "This is not the first time you have been before me, Mr. Langton, but I hope it will be the last. For many years you have shown a blatant disregard for the law, recklessly misusing your wealth and position. I trust that incarceration will teach you that this conduct will no longer be tolerated. I hereby sentence you to ten years in Newgate Prison." The judge rapped with his gavel and adjourned the court.

Ken trembled with elation as he arose from his seat and glanced over at Langton. The latter, his face drained of color, glowered at Ken. The menacing look in Langton's eyes convinced Ken that although Ken had won that day, the fight was not over. It was evident that Langton would not rest until he had had his revenge. In his bones Ken felt that a man with all Langton's money would not languish in prison for a decade.

Later, in the hallway of the Old Bailey, Ken ran into Nell and her husband.

"Well done, Mr. Sanderson," Lord Darnley said after introductions. "Good to see that scoundrel behind bars. Thank you for taking care of my wife in Scotland. She assures me that in the future she will be more circumspect in her relationships."

Ken shook his head. "Actually, sir, it was she who took care of me. Had she not chosen to go with me, Langton's plan to drown me may well have been successful."

The old man gazed on his young wife with unabashed admiration. "She is a marvel," he said. "I'll leave you two to say your good-byes whilst I go find our carriage." To his wife he added, "Don't be long, dear. We must see Sir Jeffrey before we leave London."

"I like him," Ken said when Lord Darnley had left.

Nell nodded and smiled with chagrin. "He is a dear. And I truly will be more circumspect in the future." She paused and looked thoughtful. "Now that you have Saladin's ring, I assume you'll be returning to America soon. Do you think we'll ever meet again?"

Ken shrugged. "Who knows. Life is so unpredictable. Who would have guessed that I'd go to Scotland and meet you? Who knows what life has in store for us."

She lowered her eyes. "I hope we do meet again." Suddenly she lifted her head and her face lit up. "Does Salt Lake City have a theatre?"

Ken nodded. "Yes, several very good ones—and not only in the city. About three years ago I attended the opening of a new opera house in American Fork, south of Salt Lake City. It's very up-to-date with a moveable floor that can be raised flush with the stage floor to give extra room for dances and such."

She clapped her hands joyfully. "Brilliant! I have often dreamed of an American tour. If that dream comes true, Utah will definitely be on my itinerary. You and your wife can come and see me perform again."

"My wife?"

"Miss Gage, of course. She'd be daft to let you get away. Have you told her about our afternoon on the island?"

Ken nodded. "In a letter. Unfortunately, right now we're not . . . as close as I'd like us to be. But through my cousin she's asked for me to baptize her into my church, so I believe she has forgiven me. Did you tell Lord Darnley?"

Nell nodded. "Yes. I told him all. He was cross with me for going to Scotland with Langton, but I knew he'd forgive me and he has." She grinned. "Although I feel foolish having gone off with Langton, I want you to know I will always treasure our adventure, yours and mine. It was much more exciting than the boring London social scene." She looked past him and saw her husband waving her to him. "I must go. Cheerio for now, my friend. Till we meet again."

Ken fondly watched her go. Once she and her husband had gone, his thoughts turned to Karen. *Finally, I'm free to go to Somerset.* He smiled. *I'm sure Karen has forgiven me, but if she hasn't, like Henry I'll camp under her window until she does!*

❈ CHAPTER 28 ❈

"Mr. Ken," Maggie said at the door to her cottage. "Miss Karen hoped you'd come. Sorry I am for givin' you the rough side of my tongue when you was here last. I wish I'd know'd you went all the way to Scotland for her. Perhaps as men go you're the exception after all."

"Thanks, Maggie," he said. "I know you were only thinking of Miss Gage. By the way, I saw Jack at Langton's second trial."

Her face tightened. "*Well,* and how was he?"

"He seemed fine. But on the afternoon of the ring trial he seemed a little out of sorts. Did you two have a falling out?"

"Aye," Maggie said and abruptly changed the subject. "Miss Karen's taken the trap and is up at the hall. She's prob'ly in her garden—her special place. She got a wire from the bank saying she didn't have to remove from the hall after all. Somebody's bought the mortgage and is letting her stay."

"So I understand. I can't wait to see her."

Maggie nodded. "Off you go, then. Good luck."

Ken found Karen sitting on a stone bench in the garden, staring up at the towers of Gage Hall. Unlike the grounds in general, this spot appeared to be lovingly cultivated. A profusion of flowers surrounded her, reminding Ken of his mother's flower garden in Utah. His footsteps on the gravel drew her eyes from the building.

"Your special place," he said. "I hope I'm not intruding."

"Ken," she said, her eyes widening. "No, you're not intruding. Thank you for coming." She picked up a folded newspaper off the bench and slid over to give him room. He sat beside her. "I'm glad you didn't go home to America as some supposed."

He smiled. "Now, why would I do that? I haven't got what I came to England for."

She raised her eyebrows. "I haven't seen you since you won Saladin's ring. Isn't that why you really came to England—for the ruby ring?"

He shook his head. Taking her hand, he looked into her soft green eyes and declared, "Karen, I came to England for you!"

She looked at him askance. "How could that be? Before you came here, you didn't even know me!"

He smiled. "True, but Heavenly Father knew you, and He sent me here for you."

She nodded thoughtfully. "A few months ago I would have laughed at such a notion, but now that I've learned the true gospel, I can believe it. Have you talked with Elder Kimball since the trial?"

"Yes. And I couldn't be more pleased at your decision to join the Church. May I ask what held you back?"

She lowered her eyes and didn't respond for a moment. Raising her eyes, she sheepishly said, "Do you remember my telling you about the man to whom I was betrothed?" Ken nodded. "Well, I . . . I was responsible for his death, and it has weighed on my mind for the past two years."

Ken stared at her in disbelief. "I can hardly believe it," he said.

Karen heaved a sigh. "Unfortunately, it's true. When he told me that he was breaking our engagement, I drove him from Gage Hall into an awful storm. He'd asked if he could wait out the storm or have Maggie drive him to the village in the trap, but I refused both requests. By the time he got to the village on foot, he was soaked through. There he hired a trap and driver to take him to Glastonbury, where he put up at an inn. The soaking caused him a chill, which turned to pneumonia. He died all alone at the inn. When I heard about it, you can imagine my guilt. Had I been more charitable, I would have allowed him to wait out the storm indoors or at the very least given him a brolly."

"So that's why you had Maggie give me the umbrella," Ken said.

Karen nodded. "Even though you only had to go as far as Ainsley, I wasn't taking any chances." She paused and concern clouded her face. "Following my study of the restored gospel, I struggled with whether or not I was worthy of baptism. I felt that I had broken the sixth commandment, albeit inadvertently. After much prayer, however, I awoke one morning and knew without doubt that God had forgiven me. I was so excited I immediately wrote to Elder Kimball and applied for baptism. As you probably know, I've chosen Friday next as my baptism day."

A surge of warmth flowed through Ken and his eyes moistened. An overpowering sense of satisfaction filled his soul in the knowledge that he'd had a role in Karen's accepting the gospel. The fact that he was now truly free to ask for Karen's hand added to his joy.

"So that's what put the rose back in your cheeks?" he asked.

She gazed at him quizzically. "Sorry?"

Ken smiled. "When I came to see you last time, Maggie said you were excited about something. She supposed that you had fallen in love and were writing your paramour."

Karen laughed. "Maggie misunderstood, of course; but knowing that I had been forgiven and knowing that the true Church had been restored to the earth is very much like falling in love—very emotional. Will you do me the honor of baptizing me?"

"Yes, I will baptize you, and the honor will be all mine. I really don't know how we go about setting it all up—we'll leave that to Jonathan—June thirtieth will be a red-letter day." He gazed at her with love and wonder. "Although I've prayed fervently for your conversion, I can hardly believe it's happened. Never in my life have I been more astonished at the power of the Holy Ghost to testify of the truth of the restored gospel. One of my greatest fears—and Jonathan's too—was that you would cease studying the gospel because of my . . . my seeming untrustworthiness."

She smiled at his reaction. "No, Ken. Our various ups and downs have not influenced my study of the gospel, not really."

He gazed at her, full of admiration, and echoed Lord Darnley's words about Nell, "You truly are a marvel."

Karen blushed. "Thank you. But you really do give me too much credit. Now, tell me the full story of why you went to Scotland."

His brow furrowed. "Was my letter not detailed enough?"

Now her brow furrowed. "Letter?"

"You didn't receive my letter?

She pursed her lips and tilted her head slightly. "No."

"Then how did you know that I'd gone off to Scotland?"

She opened the newspaper in her lap and pointed to a headline: "Stephen Langton on Trial for Attempted Murder."

Ken glanced at the date. "June sixteenth," he said. "So you knew about Scotland when you were at the ring trial."

She nodded. "Yes. I knew you'd gone to Scotland in search of a friend and that you testified under oath that you 'would go to the ends of the earth' for this friend. The reporter speculated that it was I. Was he right?"

Ken nodded. "Of course."

"As soon as I read that, I knew how deeply you cared about my well-being. Earlier, when you didn't come to Kensington as you promised, I had begun to doubt you. I thought perhaps you cared only for Saladin's ring."

"A virtuous woman is far above rubies," he said. "Proverbs chapter 31 verse 10."

"A scriptural paraphrase," she said, smiling and raising her eyebrows. "I'm impressed."

He smiled. "And I meant what I said about going to the ends of the earth for you. What else does the article say?"

"It's mostly about the trial. Please tell me all about your Scottish adventure."

Again he recited his story. When finished, he added, "And, no, nothing . . . nothing of a personal nature occurred between Nell Keene and me—in case you were wondering."

Karen looked at him innocently. "I was wondering no such thing."

"Sorry. It's just that every time I tell my story, people ask me about what went on between Nell and me on the island. Believe it or not, we discussed religion. Despite her outward brashness, she has a tender heart and sound morals. She was very much impressed that I would go off to Scotland to rescue you."

"And I am very much impressed as well—and ashamed that I doubted you even for a moment. Will you forgive me?"

"Nothing to forgive. You did have me worried, though. When I got to Kensington two days after the incident at the Savoy and your aunt's neighbor said you'd rushed off at noon in a black carriage, I was sure Langton had kidnapped you both. The neighbor was surprised that your aunt hadn't told her she was leaving."

Karen nodded as her mind went back to that bleak time. "The day before that was one of the worst in my life. When I heard a knock at the door, I thought it was you coming a day early. I rushed to greet you, but it was a man from the bank with a foreclosure notice on the hall demanding that I vacate immediately. Aunt Vi was outraged and accompanied him back to the bank. She returned saying that Stephen Langton had bought the mortgage, and since I was behind in payments he had forced the bank to foreclose. When you didn't come the next morning, I was doubly devastated. Having complete faith that you would come, I waited until the very last minute before leaving for Somerset in a coach Aunt Vi hired. I couldn't imagine what had happened to you. Auntie in her cynical way suggested that perhaps we were both wrong about you. In my state of mind, her words planted a seed of doubt in my heart. Realizing how distraught I was, Auntie insisted that she go to Somerset with me. She determined to take Bo and Peep with her and not to ask Mrs. Sharples, her neighbor, to look after them. Mrs. Sharples would have insisted on knowing why we were going to Somerset, and Auntie didn't want to tell her."

Ken took her hands in his. "I'm so sorry for my part in causing your distress. I love you, Karen, and I want you to be happy. On my way back to London after talking with Maggie the last time I was here, I gave my actions a long, hard look and decided that I had treated you shamefully. I shouldn't have let anything stop me from visiting you in Kensington as I'd promised. Tell me something, Karen. Why did you continue to copy the Ashcroft records even though you had doubts about me?"

Karen looked at him as if the reason were self-evident. "I promised to help you. Just because you had seemingly let me down, it didn't abrogate my promise or lessen my feelings for you. Love is not tit for tat." She blushed modestly. "Are you familiar with Shakespeare's 'Sonnet 116'?"

Ken shrugged. "Perhaps. Jog my memory."

"It's the Bard's definition of true love," she said. Closing her eyes, Karen paused for a moment before reciting:

Let me not to the marriage of true minds
Admit impediments; love is not love
Which alters when it alteration finds,
Or bends with the remover to remove.

O, no! it is an ever-fixed mark
That looks on tempests, and is never shaken;
It is the star to every wand'ring bark,
Whose worth's unknown, although his highth be taken.

Love's not Time's fool, though rosy lips and cheeks
Within his bending sickle's compass come,
Love alters not with his brief hours and weeks,
But bears it out even to the edge of doom.

If this be error and upon me proved,
I never writ, nor no man ever loved.

Ken could not suppress the moisture in his eyes. "The Bard is right, of course," he said. "I've noticed that too many couples make their life together a contest—I did this for you, so you must do that for me. It shouldn't be that way." After a pause he added, "Thanks."

"For what?"

"For copying the records, for making it possible for my mother to win the ring, for asking me to baptize you, for looking beyond all my faults, for . . . for your integrity. Considering what I've put you through, I'm amazed that you never gave up on me."

She lowered her eyes and shook her head in a self-depreciating manner but didn't respond.

Taking the pearl ring from his pocket, he got down on one knee and said, "Karen, I admit our romance has had a bumpy road, but life is full of bumpy roads. I know that together we can avoid most of those bumps. At least we won't let them overwhelm us. I love you with all my heart and promise to spend the rest of my life and on into eternity devoted to you." He paused and then said reflectively, "I can't imagine life without you. Please say that my hope of sharing eternity with you is not in vain; please say you'll marry me."

Visibly touched by his words, she sighed, turned her face away from him, and gazed on Gage Hall for a long moment. Then, her eyes brimming over, she turned and faced him. "Ken, I do love you and I always will, but . . . but I cannot marry you . . . not yet."

Ken's heart sank. He couldn't believe his ears. "But . . . but why not? You love me and I love you. Soon we'll be united in our faith. You told me in Wells Cathedral that rearing children was a woman's most important calling in life. I agree. Why won't you marry me?"

A plaintive sigh escaped her lips. "It would be against my principles. You see, I once vowed that I'd never take advantage of a man for his money—"

His mouth fell open and his brow creased. "Take advantage? But I have no money to speak of!"

She regarded him quizzically. "But Saladin's ring. Isn't it worth a fortune?"

Ken laughed. "Not quite as large a fortune after taxes and lawyer's fees," he said wryly. "But that aside, after expenses, all the money is going to the Church. My parents and I agreed on that even before I left America. I really have little money of my own. So you see, you wouldn't be marrying me for my money."

She bit her lip. "It's not just that. I have no dowry and am deeply in debt. I know that dowries are going out of fashion, but saddling a bridegroom with debt is a poor way to start a marriage." With eyes full of love, he gazed on her as she rambled on. "But I have a plan," she continued. "First, I will sell Gage Hall—I hope to get enough to pay off the mortgage and have some left over to settle some of my other debts. Second, I will find employment, perhaps as a governess, and commence paying off the rest. I thought I would go to live with Aunt Vi and seek employment in London. Once my debts are all paid, I will save money for passage to America and train fare to Utah. Then if you still want me—"

Ken took in her in his arms and kissed her quickly on the forehead. She crimsoned and was lost for words, giving him a chance to speak.

"I appreciate your principles, Karen, and all the thought you've put into your plan, but it could take years. I'm madly in love with you and want us to be together now. I don't want a dowry and even if you were in debt—"

"If I were?" she said incredulously. "Believe me, I *am* in debt and when I get Mr. Squibbs's bill for services rendered I'll be even more so."

"Not so," Ken said, shaking his head. "You won't be getting a bill from Mr. Squibbs. Sir Jeffrey Lyttle agreed to pay it."

She looked at him quizzically. "Why?"

He smiled. "It's a long story. As for your other debts, well, we can face them together."

She hesitated, giving him a little hope that she'd change her mind. But then her lips came together in a firm line and she shook her head. "No, Ken. As much as I appreciate Sir Jeffrey's generosity and yours, I'm resolute. I will not marry until I'm free of debt."

Ken could see that there was no use arguing with her. "Will you at least wear this ring as a token of our love?" he said, holding it out to her.

"It's beautiful," she said, taking it from him. Tears began to overflow her eyes and she dabbed them with her handkerchief. For a moment neither of them spoke. "I'll tell you what," she finally said. "With your permission I will take this token of your love and wear it on a chain around my neck. But I won't put it on my finger until I'm free of debt. Would that be acceptable?"

"I suppose," he said dolefully. "Are you sure I can't change your mind? Are you sure you won't accept my heartfelt proposal now?"

Karen was touched—and tempted—but she slowly shook her head as she wrapped the ring in her handkerchief. Laying her hand on his arm, she said, "Didn't you once say that your parents had to wait for years before they could marry?"

He nodded sadly. "True, but my father has more patience than I."

She squeezed his arm. "Please be assured that I am not rejecting your proposal. How could I reject a man who would go to the ends of the earth for me? I long for the moment when I can wear this lovely ring." Brightening, she said, "In the meantime, let's prepare for my baptism. I'd like to be baptized in the River Barle like your mother, perhaps at the Tarr Steps. How does that sound?"

"If that's what you want, you shall have it," he said.

❧ CHAPTER 29 ❧

The next morning Ken had just finished dressing when he heard a knock at the cottage door. It was Maggie.

"Good morning, Maggie," he said. "Come in. You didn't need to get me. I could have walked over to the hall."

"It's not that, Mr. Ken," Maggie began, then stopped.

"Please sit down. You look worried. What is it?"

Maggie sat on a kitchen chair, and Ken sat across from her. He was so filled with joy over Karen's upcoming baptism that he was sure that whatever Maggie's problem was, he could help her.

Uncharacteristically, Maggie hesitated before saying, "It's . . . well, it's a matter I should talk to Miss Karen about, but she's so excited about her baptism and all, I just couldn't spoil things for her. It's . . . it's about money. Miss Karen give me this list of things to do and buy and I don't know how we'll pay for it all."

Ken smiled, relieved that it was only about money. "May I see the list?" Ken studied it. He then glanced up and handed it back to her. "Can't you handle this the way you usually do?"

"Not really, Mr. Ken. There's a snag. Ordinarily, the tradesmen—green grocer, butcher, and all—would wait till after harvest to settle up. But if I gives them this big order, they'll want something on account, like."

Ken nodded. "I see. All right. Go ahead and hire the staff and buy all the things on the list." He handed her several bills. "Will that be enough?"

Maggie nodded enthusiastically. "More than enough. Are you sure you'll not be short?"

Ken shook his head. "No. I'll be fine."

"Well, I'll away. A widow lady and her grown children moved into the village a while back, an' I hope to engage them to help at the hall."

"Before you go, Maggie, may I ask about you and Jack? Karen and I were hoping . . ."

"It's a closed book, Mr. Ken," Maggie said with finality. "He won't give up his pint, and I won't keep company with a man what drinks."

"I see. All right, then, Maggie, I'll say no more."

Maggie was able to secure the services of Widow Sprott and her teenage children Mary, Chloe, and Will, and the next two days were filled with activity. On the first day, Karen moved back to the hall. While she, Aunt Vi, Maggie, and her new helpers unpacked, Ken rode over to Glastonbury in the trap to send telegraph messages about the baptism, timed for the following Friday afternoon.

"So, I'll wire Jonathan and Lady Brideswell," Ken had said to Karen before leaving for the telegraph office. "Do you think I should invite Jack anyway?"

Karen thought before answering. "Perhaps not. It would be awkward for Maggie if she truly doesn't want him here. It's unfortunate that alcohol is keeping them apart. They seemed so happy together."

Ken nodded. "Is there anyone else we should invite?"

Karen grinned. "What about your friend Lady Darnley and her husband? You said that she was interested in religion. Perhaps my baptism would be a way of introducing them to the Church."

He smiled and looked askance at her. "Not even a member yet and you're doing missionary work. Are you serious?" She nodded and he could see that she was. "All right. But I doubt they'll come."

When he returned to Gage Hall, Karen met him. "Maggie and her helpers have done wonders in preparing rooms for the guests and food for the picnic and post-baptism dinner," she said. "I've never seen Maggie in such a tizzy. I suppose hard work is helping to ease the pain in her heart."

Ken nodded sympathetically and asked, "Picnic?"

"Yes. We thought we'd have a picnic after the baptism and then a formal supper in the evening."

"Sounds great. By the way, there was this telegraph message for you in Glastonbury. I told the man that I was going here, so he let me take it."

Karen opened the telegram, and as she read it her face lit up. "It's from Sir Jeffrey Lyttle," she said excitedly. "He wants to come look at Gage Hall with the intent of making an offer of purchase." She stared wide-eyed at Ken. "How did he know I was thinking of selling?"

He grinned. "I might have mentioned something to him. He's connected with St. Swithins Foundling Association and they're looking to buy a country place. Gage Hall would be ideal."

For a moment she was lost in thought. Then her face lit up again. "Why don't we invite Sir Jeffrey down for Friday and he can attend my baptism?"

Ken smiled at her enthusiasm. "Okay, my love. I'll head back to Glastonbury and wire him."

* * *

Friday dawned bright and beautiful. As Ken, who continued to lodge at the cottage, strolled across the dew-dampened fields toward Gage Hall, he could hardly contain his elation. Today the sun seemed brighter, the foliage greener, and the birds' songs sweeter. Never had Karen looked so beautiful as she greeted him at the front door. "Let me get my shawl," she said excitedly, "and we'll go to the bench in the garden. I'd like to

share with you a passage from Mosiah chapter 18 in the Book
of Mormon." Soon they were seated side by side with the
Book of Mormon open between them. "Please read verses 8
through 10."

Ken read: "'And it came to pass that he said unto them:
Behold, here are the waters of Mormon (for thus were they
called) and now, as ye are desirous to come into the fold of
God, and to be called his people, and are willing to bear one
another's burdens, that they may be light; Yea, and are willing
to mourn with those that mourn; yea, and comfort those that
stand in need of comfort, and to stand as witnesses of God at
all times and in all things, and in all places that ye may be in,
even until death, that ye may be redeemed of God, and be
numbered with those of the first resurrection, that ye may
have eternal life—Now I say unto you, if this be the desire of
your hearts, what have you against being baptized in the name
of the Lord, as a witness before him that ye have entered into a
covenant with him, that ye will serve him and keep his
commandments, that he may pour out his Spirit more abun-
dantly upon you?'"

He stopped reading and gazed into her joy-filled countenance.

"This is the desire of my heart," she said. "I can hardly wait
for you to take me into the waters of the Barle."

"Me too," he said. "No greater honor has ever come to me."

"Not even winning the priceless Saladin's ring?"

"No, especially not that. What little excitement there was
in winning the ring pales before the joy I feel at this moment."

They embraced and held each other tight. The sound of
carriage wheels on gravel pulled them from their reverie. Hand
in hand they left the garden.

"What a magnificent coach!" Karen exclaimed.

"It's Lady Brideswell's," Ken said. "I can't believe she
decided to come." As they drew near to the coach, the door
opened and down stepped Gren Sanderson. "Father!" Ken

cried, dragging Karen with him as he ran to greet his father. By the time they reached the carriage, Ken's surprise heightened as his mother and Jonathan also climbed down.

After much embracing, Ken said to his parents, "I can't believe you're really here."

"Your father knew how much I wanted to return to England," Elisabeth said, "so he insisted we make the voyage and surprise you. We were at Lady Brideswell's when your telegraph message came. Unfortunately, her health is indifferent at present, so she wasn't able to accompany us; but she insisted we use her carriage." Turning to Karen she added, "We're thrilled to be here for your baptism, Miss Gage. It will take me back to when I was baptized in the same river. Have you picked out a spot—"

"Miss Elisabeth!" Maggie cried, running toward her former mistress. The two women fell into each other's arms and tears rolled down their flushed faces.

Ken looked on and reflected on the nature of true friendship. Almost five thousand miles and thirty years had not dimmed the love these two women had for each other. Their friendship, kept alive by correspondence, was as deep today as it had been when Elisabeth bravely left her home to gather with the Saints in the valley of the Great Salt Lake.

Ken thought of his bond with Jonathan and his friends in Utah and determined not to take them for granted as he often had. The words of Samuel Johnson came into his mind: "A man, sir, should keep his friendship in constant repair."

"You were asking if we had picked a spot for the baptism," Karen said to Elisabeth later as the six of them stood chatting in the gravel drive. "We have: the Tarr Steps. Ken and I picnicked there the day after we met." Then, including all in a wave of her hand, she said, "Please come into the house. Who's for elevenses?"

"If elevenses means food," Jonathan said, "I'm for it!"

Karen smiled. "Yes, it means food, Elder Kimball."

They were halfway to the house when another carriage came up the lane. They stopped and waited for it.

"It's Sir Jeffrey . . . and Jack," Ken said.

"How wonderful!" Karen exclaimed, clapping her gloved hands.

"I must be away inside," Maggie said quickly and scurried off.

After introductions, the barrister and the artist joined the procession to the house. Ken stayed back to give the carriage drivers instructions on where to park the vehicles. He invited the drivers to go to the kitchen for refreshments and arranged for Will Sprott to collect the baggage. When Ken joined the others in the dining room, Maggie and the hired girls were passing around lemonade, jam tarts, and currant cakes.

Jack was sitting off to one side and Ken joined him. "Are you well, Jack?" Ken asked.

"Tolerable," Jack said. "An' I'd be even more so if Maggie'd give me a look."

Ken shrugged. "Give her time, Jack. I think you surprised her in coming. Of course, I'm glad you did."

After refreshments, Ken, his parents, Karen, and Aunt Vi climbed into the Brideswell carriage. They waited while Maggie supervised the Sprott youth in loading the boot with hampers of food. Jonathan, Jack, and Sir Jeffrey were already in the latter's carriage.

"I hope Maggie chooses to ride with Jack," Karen whispered to Ken. But she was disappointed. As soon as the food was loaded, Maggie squeezed into the Brideswell carriage, and off they went to the River Barle. After an enjoyable ride through the sun-drenched countryside, the occupants of the two carriages assembled on the riverbank and listened to Jonathan give a brief discourse on the purpose of baptism. Then, lining the ancient clapper bridge, they witnessed Ken lead Karen by the hand into the flowing water.

Never in his life had Ken felt more buoyed with the Spirit. He literally shivered with joy and could feel Karen tremble as he placed his hand on her back to maneuver her into position. After a short prayer, he lowered her into the water and completely immersed her. With eager hands he assisted her out of the water, embraced her tenderly, and swept her up into his arms. Gently placing her on the grassy bank, he stood aside as Elisabeth, tears rolling down her cheeks, wrapped Karen in a blanket and embraced her. "It takes me back," she said as she led Karen to the Brideswell carriage, where, behind drawn blinds, Maggie assisted her mistress in changing to dry clothing.

Ken's heart skipped a beat when Karen, her face glowing and her red-blond hair worn forward on her shoulder in a single braid, emerged from the carriage. She radiated a beauty far beyond the physical. Taking her hand, he led her to a stool set up on the bridge. Then he, his father, and Jonathan gently laid their hands on her head, and Jonathan spoke the words confirming her a member of The Church of Jesus Christ of Latter-day Saints and bestowing upon her the gift of the Holy Ghost.

After the confirmation, the whole party indulged in the delicious picnic lunch Maggie and her helpers had prepared.

When the party returned to Gage Hall in the late afternoon, Ken was delighted to see another elegant carriage parked in the graveled drive. A stylized golden *D* graced the door of the vehicle. "It must be Lord and Lady Darnley," Ken said to Karen and his mother as they walked toward the house. "They've come after all. They must be inside."

"My hair," Karen lamented. "I don't want to meet Lady Darnley like this."

"You've never looked more beautiful," Ken said. "But if you want to slip upstairs, I'll play the host until you're ready."

"I'll go with you, dear," Elisabeth said to Karen.

Ken's heart almost burst with pleasure as he witnessed the two women he loved most in life go off arm in arm.

After giving Lord Darnley's driver instructions, Ken sought out Nell and her husband. He found them in the parlor.

"We apologize for missing the service, Mr. Sanderson," Lord Darnley said. "We were delayed in Salisbury when the carriage broke a spring. It seemed to take forever for the smith to make the repair."

"I'm so glad you arrived safely," Ken said. "Miss Gage is upstairs changing. She'll be down directly."

"I can't wait to meet her," Nell said. "We have a lot to talk about."

"That sounds ominous," Ken said with a smile. "Perhaps I should keep you two apart."

"Not likely," Nell said. "I must let her know the kind of man you are."

Ken smiled. "Will you be staying the night?"

Lord Darnley shook his head. "No, thanks just the same. We plan to spend the night in Bath and take the waters for a day or so. After that we're off to spend a week at Weston-super-Mare." He gazed at his wife fondly and added, "After the Scottish incident, we plan to spend more time together."

Ken smiled. "You'll enjoy the seaside. Miss Gage and I did. Please come with me and I'll introduce you to the other guests. I believe they're in the drawing room."

A half hour later, Karen and Elisabeth joined the others. Karen, her hair swept up, was dressed in the blue frock she had worn at the Saladin Ring trial. Not long after Ken introduced Karen to Nell, the two women were lost in conversation.

Meanwhile, the old butler took Sir Jeffrey on a tour of inspection of Gage Hall, while Ken helped Will Sprott sort out the baggage, which included three flat packages wrapped in brown paper and tied with string.

"Miss Gage'd like t'see you, sir," Chloe Sprott said to Ken. "She's in the small parlor."

"Thank you, Chloe," Ken replied.

Karen, a worried look on her face, looked up as Ken entered the room. "Ah, Ken, I need your help," she said as he sat beside her on a sofa. "I'm trying to sort out the seating arrangement for the dinner party. I've decided to have it in the small dining room; it's much more intimate. But I'm not sure in what order to seat everyone. According to protocol, guests are seated according to rank. But how do I seat you and your parents? And what am I to do with Mr. Tolley? I can't very well leave him out, but . . ." Her unfinished sentence ended in a perplexed sigh.

Ken smiled and took her hand. "When I first met Sir Jeffrey, he called me an egalitarian American. He was being facetious, of course, but I took it as a compliment. I truly *do* believe that all men are created equal. So my advice is to forget about rank and seat us any way that seems convenient. I'm sure no one—"

"Ah, there you are, Miss Gage," Sir Jeffrey said, poking his head into the room. "Sorry for interrupting. Would it be possible to have a private word with you and your aunt?"

Karen glanced at Ken. "Go ahead, Karen," he said. "I'll check with Maggie about how supper is coming."

* * *

At six o'clock the guests assembled in the dining room. Aunt Vi, flanked by Ken's parents, was seated at one end of the table and Sir Jeffrey, flanked by Ken and Karen, at the other end. Lord and Lady Darnley, Jonathan, and Jack filled in the remaining seats. As Ken glanced around the table, he smiled inwardly to see Jack, the erstwhile pavement chalker, seated beside Lord Darnley, a nobleman. Although Jack looked a little uncomfortable, Lord Darnley seemed at ease. In fact, Karen's concern about seating by rank proved to be unfounded. The ten people at the table got along famously, enjoying each other's company as they dined on roast beef, Yorkshire pudding, and all the trimmings. To Ken's delight the meal ended with trifle, his favorite dessert—or pudding—as they called dessert in England, he reminded himself.

As the meal drew to a close, Sir Jeffrey leaned over to Karen and whispered, "Would it be permissible for me to announce the result of our meeting, Miss Gage?"

Karen hesitated and glanced across the table at Ken. "I was keeping it as a surprise for Mr. Sanderson," she said, "but perhaps it wouldn't hurt for you to announce it. Yes, go right ahead. Shall I introduce you?" Sir Jeffrey nodded as he clinked a water glass with a knife to get everyone's attention.

"My dear friends, old and new," Karen said, "Sir Jeffrey would like to address us."

The barrister rose and cleared his throat. He gazed around the room, nodding with satisfaction. "On behalf of the board of St. Swithins Foundling Home Association," he said, "I am pleased to make two announcements. First, a short time ago St. Swithins received a very generous donation, which contained the proviso that we should strongly consider purchasing Gage Hall with the proceeds."

Out of the corner of his eye, Ken noticed the appreciative glance Nell flashed at her husband, who sat across the table from her.

"Second," Sir Jeffrey continued, "Miss Gage and her Aunt Violet have agreed to terms for St. Swithins to purchase this estate."

I wonder why Aunt Vi was engaged in the negotiations, Ken thought.

"After the purchase is completed," Sir Jeffrey continued, "we will begin renovating the facilities to the end of turning it into an orphanage, a home for those foundlings who are at present growing up in the polluted city. I would like to thank the Misses Gage for their generous terms. If I ever have a daughter, I'd want her to be just like Miss Karen.

"When Lady Brideswell first approached me for information on the Saladin Ring case, I had no idea the chain of events it would set in motion. As I witnessed Miss Gage's baptism today, I must say it softened my callous barrister's heart and the words of King Agrippa came to mind: 'Almost thou persuadest me to be a'—" He stopped and smiled—"to be a Mormon. Before I sit down, I would like to present Mr. and Mrs. Sanderson with a gift. Mr. Tolley, if you please."

Jack got up and fetched the three flat packages Ken had noted earlier. He removed the brown paper from one of them, revealing the picture of Ken's mother used in the courtroom, and handed it to Sir Jeffrey.

"Mr. and Mrs. Sanderson," Sir Jeffrey said, "please accept this as a token of the high esteem I have for your son and, I trust, your daughter-to-be."

Ken and Karen exchanged sheepish smiles.

Ken's mother rose. Face flushed, she gazed on the pastel portrait with wonder. For a long moment no words came. Then she said through a smile, "I don't believe I was ever that young or that angelic." Amid the resulting laughter she added, "Thank you, Sir Jeffrey. My husband and I will treasure it."

Sir Jeffrey sat down and Ken took the floor.

He took a deep breath to calm himself. "My dear friends," he began, "I wish to thank you from the bottom of my heart for blessing us with your presence today. For Miss Gage and me it will be a day never to be forgotten. To have you all here, and especially my parents, to celebrate her entrance into the Church is joy beyond measure. Thank you from the bottom of our hearts. Please feel free to express your feelings if you wish."

Jack was quick to take the offer. "If anyone'd said a few months since, Jack Tolley would be flush and hobnobbin' in such company," he said, "I'd a said they was daft. But here I am. Thanks to young Ken. So, not t'be outdone by Sir Jeffrey, here's a present for him." Once again Jack removed the covering from a picture. This time it was of Karen in the very same dress she was wearing. Amid exclamations of praise for Jack's work, he continued, "In the balcony o' the Old Bailey, young Ken asked me to make this portrait." Turning to Ken he added. "I hope it pleases you, lad."

Ken gazed on the painting, then at Karen, and finally at Jack. "It pleases me more than I can say, Jack. You've not only captured Miss Gage's outward beauty, but somehow you've seen into her soul. Thank you with all my heart."

Jack accepted the compliment with a nod. "Finally," he said, "if y'can put up with me for another minute, there's one more picture. This one's o' the woman I love." All eyes went to Maggie, who was standing beside a doorway with the other staff. "I started it in the kitchen o' this very house the first time I laid eyes on Miss Maggie Stowell. She's a rare one, is Maggie. Not one t' be jarred from her ways." He turned the picture around and pointed to a sheet of paper attached to the back. "Maggie, this here's my pledge to refrain from ardent spirits. Now, luv, will you do me the honor of walking out wi'me again?"

Maggie's mouth fell open. "Why Jack, I'm lost for words. I'm so weak in the knees you could knock me over with a feather." Chloe Sprott took the picture from Jack and gave it to Maggie. She gazed at it and turned it around. After reading Jack's pledge to refrain from alcoholic beverages, she said, "I'm not sure if I should hang it front side out or back side out. I love the image, but your pledge means the world to me. Thanks for both, Jack. I know it took a lot for you to give up your pint."

" 'Tis a small price t' pay for a woman like you, Maggie," he said.

Maggie nodded and blushed. "Aye, Jack, I will walk out with you again. Proudly I will."

A round of applause accompanied her words.

After Maggie's speech, no one spoke for a minute. Then Lord Darnley stood. "Although I don't know you well," he said, "and I must admit it took Lady Darnley some persuading to get me here, I've enjoyed my time with you and wish to thank you for your hospitality. My wife and I must take our leave soon as we would like to be on our way to Bath before the light is gone. Before going, though, I want Mr. Tolley to know how much I admire his work and that I would like to commission him to do a portrait of my wife. We should be home to Darnley Hall in about a fortnight,

Mr. Tolley, and would like for you to call on us at your convenience. Again, thank you all for a most enjoyable time."

Ken glanced around to see who might speak next. His eyes settled on Karen. She smiled and nodded as if to say, "Yes, I guess it's my turn."

Rising, she directed her gaze at her aunt. "Aunt Violet, I want you to know how much I love and appreciate you for your many kindnesses over the years, not the least of which was your recent rescuing me by purchasing the mortgage on Gage Hall." She paused to let this revelation sink in. "I will forever be in her debt—a debt I don't mind carrying. Let me also thank Sir Jeffrey and the anonymous donor for making it possible for these corridors to ring with the laughter of children and for this old house to be restored to its former glory." She smiled. "If I didn't know better, I'd think there was some truth in the old tale that a curse has blighted this house for many years. Well, that curse will soon be lifted."

She paused, withdrew her handkerchief from her sleeve, opened it, and took out the pearl ring Ken had given her. His eyes went wide and his heart pounded as she slipped it on her finger.

"And now for a very important announcement," she continued. "I can wait no longer to share my joy with all of you and especially with the man I love." She paused and looked across the table at Ken. "Yes, Ken, I will marry you, whenever and wherever you desire. I love you with all my heart!"

Karen's announcement brought the dinner party to a triumphant conclusion.

* * *

Hand in hand, Ken and Karen walked with the Darnleys to their carriage. "Thank you so much for everything," Ken said as he shook hands with Lord Darnley, "and I do mean *everything*."

Lord Darnley smiled and gazed fondly on his wife. "Be assured that anything I've done originated with my wife. Thank you again for a wonderful day."

Karen and Nell embraced before the latter climbed into the carriage.

"Why the strong emphasis on *everything?*" Karen asked as she and Ken walked arm in arm back to the hall.

Ken smiled. "Lord Darnley was the anonymous donor," he said.

"He was?"

He nodded. "I'm sure of it. I noticed the look Nell gave him when Sir Jeffrey mentioned the donation."

Karen shook her head in wonder. "I guess your trip to Scotland wasn't such a wild-goose chase after all!"

They entered the house and, wishing to be alone for a while, slipped into the parlor.

"Now I have a question for you, dear," Ken said as they sat together on a sofa. "Where did Aunt Vi get the money to buy the mortgage?"

Karen smiled. "You'd never know she was well-off, would you? She certainly had me fooled. It appears that when my grandmother died, she left the fortune she had inherited from my grandfather—who made his money in Newcastle coal— equally to my father and Aunt Vi. My father, much to Aunt Vi's disgust, spent his money on this estate. Aunt Vi put her money out to investment and lived frugally."

"But since she had all that money, why did she allow you to flounder in debt all these years?"

"For my own good. She wanted me to learn the futility of keeping this white elephant. She wanted me to sell it and remove to Kensington. Of course, my selling it was one thing, but being foreclosed on was another. When she accompanied the man who delivered the foreclosure notice back to the bank, she made it clear that if Stephen Langton faulted on signing the final papers, she would assume the mortgage. As you know, he did default and she purchased the mortgage. Which brings me to another thing. Aunt Vi has given me the mortgage as a present. All the money from the sale of Gage Hall will be mine!

That's why I accepted your proposal. Once I pay off my debts, I will still have a substantial dowry."

Ken was lost for words.

The departure of the Darnleys had broken up the party. Citing a morning meeting in London, Sir Jeffrey also prepared to leave, offering Jonathan a ride back to London. Ken and Karen saw them off. While Sir Jeffrey went in search of his driver, Ken and Karen said good-bye to Jonathan.

"When Sir Jeffrey announced his connection with St. Swithins and the generous gift of the anonymous donor," Jonathan said, "it reminded me of King Benjamin's words in the Book of Mormon that when we are in the service of our fellow beings we are only in the service of God. It has been a great blessing to me to be in God's service over these past years, and today marks the high point of that experience. To see you enter the baptismal waters today, Miss Gage, has given me supreme joy. Knowing that you will soon be marrying my favorite cousin only adds to that joy."

Karen smiled. "Thank you, Elder Kimball," she said. "I will ever appreciate your teaching me the gospel."

"Good-bye, cousin," Ken said, shaking Jonathan's hand. "Thanks for teaching me the gospel too."

The young couple stood waving as the carriage pulled away. "Sir Jeffrey asked me to remind you that there's a bank draft for twenty thousand pounds waiting for you in his safe." Karen grinned. "He said that prospective bridegrooms are often forgetful."

"Twenty thousand?" Ken said. "Are you sure he didn't say fifteen thousand?"

"No. I'm sure it was twenty."

Ken nodded and smiled. "What a friend he's turned out to be. He's not only paid your legal fees, but has waived half of mine." Ken shook his head in astonishment before saying, "When Jonathan taught the principle of tithing, he read a scripture about God opening the windows of heaven and pouring out a blessing that there wouldn't be room enough to receive it. Now I know what it means."

Later, sitting together in the parlor, Ken took Karen's left hand in his and said, "I could hardly believe it when you slipped the ring on at supper."

Karen smiled. Her faced glowed as she held her hand up and gazed on the token. With tears leaking from her eyes, she said, "To me it is the most exquisite ring in the world. Much more beautiful and valuable than any gaudy ruby ring. You couldn't have chosen a better one."

Ken smiled sheepishly. "Actually, I didn't choose it," he said, and went on to explain the origin of the ring.

"Mr. Levi must love his Miriam very much," she said. "And I must write to thank him for choosing me." She dabbed her eyes with her handkerchief before asking, "When and where shall we marry?"

Ken smiled. "My impetuous nature says tomorrow, but I want you forever. Do you mind waiting until we can be sealed for eternity in a temple ceremony in Utah?"

She smiled and stroked his cheek. "I wouldn't want it any other way."

"Good. Unfortunately, the temple in Salt Lake City is still under construction—and has been for the last thirty-three years—but we could be married in the endowment house in Salt Lake City, or perhaps in the Logan Temple, north of the city, or the one at St. George, south of Salt Lake."

Karen smiled. "I will marry you whenever and wherever you wish."

"There you are," Maggie said as she and Aunt Vi entered the parlor. "Somehow I knew you two would get together by and by."

"And you, Auntie?" Karen asked.

The little woman frowned and lowered her head. Then she raised her eyes and with a twinkle in them and a hint of a smile on her thin lips, she said, "I imagine I knew it too. Bo would never sit on the head of a person who wasn't good enough to be a member of the family!"

They all laughed. Then Maggie asked, "Will you be tyin' the knot here or across the pond?"

"In America," Karen said. "For some reason Ken wants me for more than just this life." Maggie and Aunt Vi gazed at Karen quizzically. Karen smiled. "I'll explain it to you later," she said.

Ken's parents soon joined the four of them. They all chatted happily until Aunt Vi said that it was time for her to cover Bo and Peep's cage for the night. Maggie left with her. After they had gone, Gren said, "Mother and I plan to spend the next two weeks touring the southwest in Lady Brideswell's carriage. Would you like to join us?" Ken and Karen nodded enthusiastically. "Afterward, we have time for a few days in London before we catch the boat in Liverpool. Would you like to come home to Utah with us? I've already talked with Jonathan and he thinks he can join us."

Ken glanced at Karen and she nodded her acceptance. "That would be wonderful," Ken said. "I'll telegraph Jonathan to book passage for us."

For the next half hour, the four of them made plans for the trip home to America. Then Ken and Karen slipped away for a stroll, ending up on the bench in Karen's special garden where Ken had proposed. The rosy glow of sunset was beginning to fade, and bats were about their evening's work.

"I had a lovely talk with Nell," Karen said. "I found her absolutely charming, and I want you to know that she's no longer your friend."

Ken's eyebrows arched. "She's not?"

Karen smiled. "No. She's now *our* friend. She mentioned that you discussed a Robert Burns poem with her when you were on the island. Do you have one for me?"

"As a matter of fact, I do," Ken said with a grin. "A most appropriate one. It's the companion piece to the one I discussed with Nell. It's called 'To a Louse.'"

"Oh, you!" Karen said, laughing and jabbing his arm. "Surely, you have a more romantic one than that."

He took her in his arms and kissed her cheek. "I do—one that exactly expresses my feelings for you. It's called 'A Red, Red Rose':

O My love is like a red, red rose
That's newly sprung in June:
O My love is like the melody
That's sweetly played in tune!

As fair art thou, my bonnie lass,
So deep in love am I:
And I will love thee still, my dear,
Till a' the seas gang dry:

Till a' the seas gang dry, my dear
And the rocks melt wi' the sun;
I will love thee still, my dear
While the sands o' life shall run.

He paused. "The last stanza doesn't really apply because it talks of the narrator leaving his love for a time, and I have no intentions of letting you out of my sight. But here it is anyway:

And fare thee weel, my only love,
And fare thee weel a while!
And I will come again, my love,
Tho' it were ten thousand mile.

Ken turned to see moisture glistening in Karen's eyes. She dabbed at them with her handkerchief.

"My reciting wasn't that bad, was it?" he asked playfully.

She shook her head. "No, Ken, it was beautiful. But during the last verse I had this awful premonition that someday we will be parted for a season." She paused and shook her head, impatient with herself. "Oh, I'm just being silly. You, Mr. Kenny Sanderson, are not getting out of my sight either."

He put his arms around her and together they gazed at the towers of Gage Hall in the fading light. "Are you sad to be giving up your home?" he asked.

"Under other circumstances," she said, "I'd be devastated. But with you and the gospel in my life, giving up the hall is a small thing. It thrills me no end to know that this old house will be given a new face and touch many lives for good. And I'm doubly pleased that the money from the sale has given me the means of a proper dowry, old-fashioned as that may be. There's irony in the fact that I was reluctant to accept your proposal because it would appear that I was marrying you for your money, but it is now I who have the money to help us start our life together."

He nodded thoughtfully. "There's irony all around. Originally, I coveted Saladin's ring and fantasized about returning to Utah a rich man. By promising to donate the money to the Church, I gave up that fantasy in order to get my parents' blessing. But now with you by my side I *will* be returning home a rich man—richer in more ways than I could ever have imagined. Soon we will be sealed together in the temple and share the riches of eternity."

As Ken took Karen in his arms, their lips came together and they shared the ecstasy of a first kiss. The pleasure of the kiss went far beyond the physical, and Ken knew that the joy of it was a small foretaste of the eternal joy they would someday share. His mind went back to the night he learned through inspiration that there was some greater reason for him to go to England than to obtain Saladin's ring. Now, as he held Karen in his arms he knew without doubt that their love was the fulfillment of that inspiration.

❧ EPILOGUE ❧

Jack Tolley opened the door of his London flat, shook the rain from his greatcoat, hung it on a rack, and sought out his wife. He found her in the kitchen. Coming up behind her, he kissed her on the neck.

"You're late, luv," she said, turning to face him. "Supper's warming in the oven. I hope it's not dried out."

Jack sat heavily on a kitchen chair. "They 'ad me do a sketch at the last minute for tomorra's paper. You'll never guess who."

Maggie turned from the coal stove and stared at him. "Who?"

"Stephen Langton!"

Her mouth fell open. "You don't say! Why would they be wanting his picture?"

"Escaped he has. They think he bribed a guard or two. They say he's prob'ly out o' the country by now."

"I wonder where he'd go?"

"The colonies, most like. It's a big empire. With all his money he could change his name, buy a new life, and nobody'd be the wiser."

"I hope he stays away from America," she said as she put two laden plates on the already laid table and took her place across from him. "I have news myself. A fat letter came from over the water. Karen's in the family way again. Number three. Do you remember Jonathan Kimball?"

"The missionary chap?"

"Aye. His missus is also expecting a wee one, her second—both due at the same time. And that's not all. Karen says she got a letter from Sir Jeffrey and pictures of Gage Hall lookin' like new. He's quit barristerin' and removed to Somerset. And that's still not all. You'll hardly credit it, but he's took himself a wife, a beautiful widow woman wi' six children."

Jack laughed out loud. "Sir Jeffrey married wi' six nippers? It boggles the brain. Hard to believe, that is."

"It's the truth. It's all in Karen's letter. She says the woman brought a newborn to St. Swithins sayin' her soldier husband got hisself killed somewhere's defendin' the empire and she couldn't afford one more mouth to feed on a widow's pension. The man in charge at St. Swithins said he couldn't take the babe 'cause they only took orphans. It seems the woman was at the end o' her tether and says if they only took orphans she'd oblige by jumpin' off London Bridge and letting them have all six. Well, Sir Jeffrey happened to come by and tried to reason with her. To make a long story short, he was took with her and they ended up getting wed."

Jack smiled and shook his head. "Quit the law to raise a brood o' nippers. Who'd o' believed it? Speakin' o' quitting, I think it's time I give up sketchin' pictures for the *Press*. My days is numbered anyhow now the photographer boys is getting so good. Afore long, nobody'll want to see drawings when they can see the real thing."

Maggie gazed across the table and smiled. "I'm with you, Jack. It's time you quit."

Jack stared at his wife with surprise. "No argument?"

Maggie shook her head. "No argument. With all those commissions you've got from Lord Darnley's posh friends, we've bags o'brass. And that brings me to another piece o' news. Nell Keene dropped by this afternoon. We had a grand chat. Now that it's been a year since Lord Darnley passed on, she's puttin' away her widow's weeds and planning a tour to

America. One o' her stops'll be Salt Lake City." She paused and a self-satisfied smile lit up her face. "She's offered me work. What d'you think o' that?"

Jack's eyebrows lifted. "Maggie, yer just full o' su'prises t'night. What kind o' work?"

"Wardrobe lady—just for the tour. The woman what's doin' it now's got some wee uns and can't leave London. 'Course I wouldn't go to America wi'out you. That's why I agreed so quick t'your retirin'. Should I tell Nell I'll take it?"

Jack smiled. "Aye, lass. And maybe she'll find work for me too, drawin' up playbills and the like."

For several minutes they ate in silence. Then Maggie said, "Who'd have thought the two young women I did for would end up happily married in America? You never know the twists and turns o' life."

Jack looked up from his plate and nodded. "Right, y'are, Maggie. Who'd o' thought an old, one-legged ex-sailor would go from chalking on flagstones an' livin' han' t' mouth t' livin' in a flat off Picadilly Circus wi' a darlin' wife what makes the best steak and kidney pie in the empire?"

"Better'n St. George an' the Dragon?"

"Aye, lass. They don't have a patch on you." He paused before adding, "Elisabeth and young Karen was lucky girls t' have you t'do for 'em."

"I was the lucky one," Maggie said reflectively. "Strange, though, they both ended up Mormons. I wonder if we should look into it, the Mormon Church, I mean?"

Jack smiled mischievously. "We might as well, luv. Sounds like we're goin' t' Utah, and you've already got me out o' the pub. Y'may as well take me all the way!"

❧ AUTHOR'S NOTES ❧

Inheritance is the second novel in the *Passage of Promise* series. Unlike the previous one, *Elisabeth*, which included some historical characters, all of the characters in *Inheritance* are fictional. As always, I've tried to make sure that the historical facts are as accurate as possible. The information on Saladin, the twelfth-century sultan of Egypt, is historical. However, the passing of a ruby ring from Saladin to King Richard to King John and so forth is fictional.

I have tried to approximate the speech of nineteenth-century British people as best I could while still keeping the text as readable as possible. One grammatical difference between English and American grammar is that the English treat collective nouns as plural, whereas Americans treat them as singular. For example, in America one would say, "The government *is* raising taxes," whereas in England it would be, "The government *are* raising taxes." Even though it may be irritating for my North American readers, I have observed this distinction in the speech of my English characters. Also, in keeping with nineteenth-century usage, I've chosen to use *Moslem* rather than the modern form *Muslim*.

The two humorous stories about the English theatre, "The Great Bottle Conjurer" and the one about the "cannibal savages," are historical, although I've taken some literary license with them. I found the first one online at www.theatrehistory.com and the second in the delightful *Links in the Chain of Life,* the autobiography of Baroness Orczy, the celebrated author of the *Scarlet Pimpernel.*

❧ ABOUT THE AUTHOR ❧

Tom Roulstone was born in Donegal, Ireland, and lived for a time in Glasgow, Scotland. With his parents and two brothers he immigrated to Canada, landing at Halifax on his thirteenth birthday. He joined The Church of Jesus Christ of Latter-day Saints in Toronto when he was eighteen and served a mission in western Canada. He has a BA in history from Brigham Young University and an MA in history from Utah State University.

After teaching college history for almost a quarter of a century, Tom took early retirement in 2000 to pursue a writing career. *Inheritance* is his fourth LDS novel. He and his late wife Betsy have six children and seven grandchildren. On December 29, 2005, Tom married Serenity Borrowman in the Salt Lake Temple. They have recently moved into a home overlooking Long Lake on Vancouver Island, British Columbia.

If you would like to be updated on Tom's newest releases or correspond with him, please send an e-mail to info@covenant-lds.com. You may also write to him in care of Covenant Communications, P.O. Box 416, American Fork, UT 84003-0416.